THE BEAUTY OF OUR WEAPONS

M. DARUSHA WEHM

The Beauty of Our Weapons
an Andersson Dexter novel
by M. Darusha Wehm

Copyright 2012 M. Darusha Wehm

Published by *in potentia* press

ISBN 978-0-9737467-7-8

http://darusha.ca/weapons

Cover by JT Lindroos
http://jtlindroos.carbonmade.com

Also by M. Darusha Wehm

Beautiful Red

The Andersson Dexter novels:

Self Made
Act of Will
The Beauty of Our Weapons

PROLOGUE

JEFFIE WYATT WAS not in the mood to go to work. He was one of the lucky ones — he actually liked his job. Usually, he was perfectly happy to find a comfy spot on the couch in his tiny apartment, settle in and unfocus his eyes. His implanted connection to the everywherenet allowed him online access anywhere, everywhere, without any additional hardware. He just thought about what he wanted to do and he saw the screen overlaid on his vision.

Jeffie's implants weren't unusual. He didn't know anyone without the implants — you couldn't get any job without them and he wasn't sure how you'd even be able to find your way around. He'd only ever seen a paper map in a museum, and to be honest it was a reproduction of a map in a virtual museum. But it was still the closest he'd ever come to seeing one.

Jeffie went online and logged into M City, and felt his virtual body materializing outside the door to his unimaginatively-named shop, "Discount Personalized Sexbots." Jeffie designed individually tailored bot avatars for virtual sex which were, frankly, cheap in all meanings of the word. But enough people liked them that he made enough money to be able to afford a private apartment, which meant that this was his full time job. This was unusual, and Jeffie was mostly quite thankful for his good fortune.

But this morning, he just didn't have any excitement for the sexbot business. He didn't want to deal with the clients, didn't want to talk up the various options available on the models, didn't want to code the product. He just wanted to sleep and try to forget.

He'd known for weeks that his relationship with Vonnie wasn't going anywhere good, but he still wasn't ready for the drama that happened the previous night. Two hours of screaming was a record even for him and he had terrible luck with breakups. His head still hurt in the morning and work didn't feel like a great distraction. But when you're self-employed the boss is a real ball breaker and there are no sick days, so Jeffie flopped on the couch and logged into M City.

What he saw when he rezzed into the virtual street where his shop was located was actually enough to make him forget about Vonnie completely. Too bad it was a million times worse than just a bad breakup.

• • •

"Why did this have to happen to me?" Jeffie whined. René Biagini patted his friend on the hand and flicked a finger up to the waiter for another glass of synth-wine.

"Can you tell me exactly what was done?" Biagini asked, setting his system to record the conversation. He didn't really think he'd be able to find whoever vandalized his friend's store, but he'd promised to try so he ought to put a little effort in. "Do you have a recording of the instantiation?"

Jeffie nodded. "I record every work day. Prevents a lot of disputes over price quotes."

"Good," René said. "Send me the vid." The wine arrived and René felt a download drop into his system. "You drink this," he said, handing Jeffie a large glass of red, "while I look at it, okay?"

Jeffie sniffled and nodded, sipping the wine. The vid showed a blurry image of Jeffie's storefront as it materialized in front of his vision. René had visited it more than a few times, and expected to see the familiar yellow and orange sign over the green portal door. Instead, there was a disturbing electrical buzzing sound and the door was distorted and pixellated. It did not look safe to enter, but Jeffie must have gone in anyway as the vid's point of view moved through the portal and into what should have been the small shop.

From his previous visits, René recalled that Jeffie would have two or three of his models out and available to interact with walk-in clientele. There was even a small cubicle where clients could try before they'd buy. In the vid, the walls of the cubicle appeared to be slashed and the two models — it looked like Mintra and Oolo to René — were cut into pieces and lying on the floor. There was no blood or gore, but René couldn't shake the disturbing feeling that he was looking at a murder scene. He understood now why Jeffie was so upset.

"I'm sorry," he said, and reached out for his friend's hand again. "That's just horrible."

Jeffie nodded. "I checked all the code," he said putting down the half-empty wine glass. "It's all still there and the links are fine. I don't know how anyone cracked into my private disk space, but I've reset all my passwords and tokens. I can fix the door in a few hours and I'm pretty sure I can repair the boys and girls, too." He looked at René. "It's just the sense of violation, you know?"

"Of course," René said. "Not to mention the lost business."

Jeffie shrugged. "If I'm closed for a couple of days I can manage. But I just don't feel safe anymore. If I lost the shop, I don't know what I'd do. I wouldn't be able to pay my rent, and I've been without a regular job for a year. I'd never get anything over level two now. I'd have to start over from scratch."

Jeffie looked like he was going to start crying again, so René patted his friend on the shoulder. "Don't think like that," he said. "If whoever it was wanted to destroy your shop, they could have done a lot worse. It was probably just kids or some fucked-up stim-head. You'll get over it, Jeffie. It was just pixels and code after all."

"This time it's just pixels and code," Jeffie said, "next time it could be my whole livelihood."

"There won't be a next time," René said, but he didn't know how he could promise that. He ordered two more glasses of wine, and turned on the Biagini charm. If he couldn't fix Jeffie's problems, the least he could do was help his friend forget them.

ONE

THE SUN BEAT down on their bronze bodies, as Annabelle and Dex floated on the turquoise water. "Look at that mountain," Annabelle said, turning on her side and pointing into the sky. A huge rock spire pierced the blue sky, its jagged edge looking sharp as a knife, groves of coconut trees fringing the base. Dex followed Annabelle's extended finger and smiled. "Check this out," he said, grinning. He flipped over on to his stomach, then dove headfirst down into the cool salty water.

He was naked, as was Annabelle, and they didn't have any other gear with them either. They didn't need anything, since they had no need to breathe here, in this shared dream world they'd bought the week before. Neither of them were spontaneous shoppers, but they'd been unable to stop talking about the dream holiday package they'd seen offered at Marci's Memory Mart and finally decided to splurge.

Dex swam downward effortlessly, looking back once to see Annabelle matching his pace. He swam a few strokes, then stopped and pointed over to his left. Annabelle swam up beside him and turned her head quizzically toward him. Through some mechanism Dex didn't understand, he heard her say, "What? I don't see anything."

The water in which they swam was crystal clear, but distance made objects more obscure. "Just look," Dex replied somehow.

"Look for the white parts." Annabelle focussed and made a gasping noise when she realized what she was looking at.

"It's a whale," she said, agog.

"Actually, it's two whales," Dex said, grinning. "A humpback and her baby." Annabelle looked closer and saw the two giants, slowly gliding down in front of them. Their head knobs were clearly visible, along with white streaks along their jaws and flukes. They arced their bodies, unbelievably slowly and gracefully and almost effortlessly swam down into the depths, passing below Dex and Annabelle as they floated metres under the surface. They hung there in the warm water watching the mother and child for what seemed like an hour before the giants swam away.

"That was amazing," Annabelle said, swimming a little closer to Dex and wrapping her arms and legs around him as they met. "But I think it's time to get back to the real world."

"You're probably right," Dex said and he held Annabelle closer. "See ya soon, kiddo," he said and woke up.

• • •

Dex was finally starting to get used to the quality of the sunlight in Nice — it had a bright yellow tint, compared to the greasy grey glow that had squirted through his windows back in Namerica. In comparison, it had been more an absence of darkness than anything Dex would call real illumination. And here the sunlight was actually hot, the climate appreciably changing from winter to summer and back again. This afternoon, still a cool spring day, the light that came through his window was strong enough to wake him on its own, before his system got to the task. At least, it seemed to Dex that the Mediterranean sun was what pulled him away from his dream of the Pacific and into the bed he was sharing with Annabelle.

He rolled over and looked her face, unlined and beautiful, pale in the morning sunlight, scrunched into her pillow. Her gold hair fanned out on the pillow, framing her face. He smiled, savouring the seconds he'd have to watch her sleep before her own enhanced mind woke her according to the instructions she'd have programmed the day before. He carefully moved his body slightly away from hers, knowing that it still took her a moment or two to remember that she wasn't alone. He heard her take a deep inward breath and smiled as her eyes fluttered open. She focussed and saw him, flinching back into her side of the bed only slightly, then breaking into a smile.

"Good morning, Mister Fish," she said, moving her body slightly closer to Dex and allowing him to pull her toward him.

"Good morning yourself," he said, lightly kissing the top of her head. "That was a pretty nice little holiday we had there, wasn't it?"

Annabelle smiled. "I can't believe that there is anywhere on Earth that is really so beautiful," she said. "And those whales..."

"I had no idea, either," Dex said. "I wonder what it would have been like to really see that, with real eyes..." He felt Annabelle stiffen slightly, then relax into his arms again. There was a time, not long before, when he would have apologized for being insensitive, for reminding his lover and best friend that her preference for living in a simulation of the world was as opposite to Dex's own desire for physical presence as possible. But since he had moved from Namerica to Europa and into a tiny independent apartment only a short train ride from Annabelle's top-tier employee housing, they had begun to accept each other's differences a little more. Which was why Dex found himself luxuriating in Annabelle's expensive sheets at half past two in the afternoon.

The Beauty of Our Weapons

Annabelle lay in his arms for a moment longer, then stretched and swung her legs over the side of the bed. She stood and walked to the small lav off the bedroom. Dex silently watched her go, wanting to follow her, to soap her body in the minute of hot water she was entitled to and then wand her hair as the blower dried them off. He wanted to be next to her, touching her silken skin, smelling the sweet fragrance of her. He never wanted to leave. But he knew that he was lucky to get the time with her he did and knew when to leave her alone, when to give her space to herself. And he was smart enough to know that the little time with her he got in the physical world was so much better than not getting to be with her at all. So he lay in the bed, enjoying the softness of her linens, waiting for her to be done with the shower.

Dex heard the water stop and the blower kick in and took that as his cue to get up. He would get cleaned up back at his own apartment, using his own water ration rather than making Annabelle share or pay for an extra shot. He walked over to the wall separating the bedroom from the lav and opened up Annabelle's double size autoclave. He pulled out yesterday's clothes, now clean, and got dressed. Now that he no longer worked for one of the firms, he no longer was issued a uniform that he'd wear most of time. Not exactly the king of sartorial splendour, Dex's casual wardrobe had never been particularly stellar. When he'd arrived in Nice, Annabelle had decided that Dex ought to look at least as good in the physical world as his avatar did in Marionette City, the global virtual world where they spent most of their time, so she'd forced him to go shopping.

Dex was never going to pay the kind of money that was required to replicate his virtual outfit of a charcoal pinstriped suit and dark grey fedora, but he did allow Annabelle to buy him a couple of very nice dark shirts of some kind of shiny soft material that went reasonably well with the black striped trousers he favoured. He slipped the shirt on and marvelled, not for the first time, in Annabelle's good taste. In clothes, at least. He still wondered every day what she saw in him.

"What's on tap for you today?" Annabelle called from the lav when the blower stopped.

"I'll head home when you go to work," Dex said, heating up a cup of the tea Annabelle was currently fond of in her stainless-look zapper. "I'll probably go into the office later. I need to go over the Light of the Simulacrum case again."

"Did something else happen over there?"

"Not that I know of," Dex said. "But I'm just getting started. That menace from the M City squad only sent the files over yesterday."

"What's wrong with Mack Larsen?" Annabelle chided. "Last I heard he was trying to get you to go work over on his squad."

"That's part of the problem," Dex said. "If Larsen wants detectives on his squad, well... fine. Maybe there should be a D division just for M City cases, I don't know. But it doesn't have to be me. I'm happy where I am."

"I know," Annabelle said, "but that doesn't mean you have to be nasty to Larsen."

"The man just rubs me the wrong way," Dex said. "It's obvious he wants to be a detective himself and this is just his way of trying to go about it."

"Well," Annabelle said, changing the subject before Dex got into a proper snit, "my offer still stands, if you want me to help out." Annabelle walked out of the lav, dressed in her uniform. Dex wondered how she managed to make the tan and cream one-piece look like something that would cost a week's wages at a boutique on the waterfront.

"I'll take some copies of the code," Dex said, "and if I can't get anywhere the old fashioned way, you can have a go at it."

"Those poor people," Annabelle said, sipping her tea. "I can't understand why anyone would want to destroy a religious space. I mean, it's just a place for people to gather. Ruining the building doesn't stop anyone from meeting. It's just stupid."

"We don't even know if whoever did it even knew it was a church," Dex said. "It could just be some budding cracker practicing."

"Oh, please," Annabelle said. "No one needs to prove their chops by ruining someone else's work. Not to mention that it's a hell of a lot easier to wreck something than it is to make something. That's the same in M City as it is out here." She waved her now empty mug toward the small window. Annabelle's eyes took on a faraway look and Dex knew that she was online, checking something on her personal system.

After a short moment, she refocussed on Dex and smiled. "Gotta go, old man," she said. "I have an early meeting this morning and it's going to be a killer. The plans for the new Eastern tracks are getting out of hand. You'd think by now they'd realize that spending a million euros today to save four million over a couple of years was obvious. But it's still a fight every time." She sighed. Dex started chuckling. "What's so funny, smart guy?" Annabelle asked. "Just because you've gotten out of the corporate machine doesn't make you so special, pal."

"It's not that," Dex said. "I just love how you have your own personal sense of time."

"What are you talking about?" Annabelle asked.

"You said 'early meeting this morning'," Dex said. "It's almost three o'clock in the afternoon."

Annabelle scowled, but couldn't conceal a slight smile. "You are so linear, Andersson Dexter," she said. "Clock time

— as if that means anything. If it's the beginning of my work-day, it's morning. How hard is that to understand?"

"Oh, I understand it just fine," Dex said, following Annabelle to the door of her apartment. "I just think it's funny, is all."

"Well, I think you're funny," Annabelle countered, as she swiped her left hand over the outside jamb of her door. Dex heard a sharp *snick* as the lock drove home. "Come on," she said, taking Dex's hand in hers. "Let's try not to argue for the minute and a half it takes to walk to the train, shall we?"

• • •

When Dex got back to his apartment, he was still smiling. He loved the nights when he stayed over at Annabelle's. He checked himself; they were the mornings, really — now he was doing it, too. When he'd first arrived in Nice, he had been sure that it would never get to this stage. After everything that had happened, he was amazed at Annabelle's progress. When he'd moved to Nice, Dex had decided that she was worth any sacrifice, and he put an effort into spending all their time together in Marionette City, even though to him the virtual world felt like a shallow facsimile of real life. It still amazed him, on days like this, that they'd ever come this far.

They kept odd hours, hence the three pm 'mornings,' but all cities were twenty-four hour propositions, so they had no trouble keeping normal lives even though they lived on a Namerican time schedule in Europa. Annabelle was a pro-grammer for Omnitrack, which ran cross-continent high speed maglev trains, and even though she and her teammates lived in Nice, the firm's head office was in Toronto, so she and her co-workers were all on a Namerican schedule.

Dex, on the other hand, had managed to leave the work-ing life that the vast majority of people shared, where not only income but health care, housing and security were all tied to employment. People's employment contracts dictated where and in what conditions they lived and what kind of legal protection they could enjoy. If an employer was unconcerned about a particular issue, people had nowhere to turn for protection or security. Nowhere except to people like Dex.

TWO

DEX WALKED UP to the building where he kept a small office. The Maynard Arms was a three storey walkup that had the appearance of being an office building in a small city, circa mid-twentieth century. Most of the occupants were freelancers like himself, but the vast majority of the visitors were for the bar on the top floor. It was, like many structures in M City, much larger inside than it appeared to be from the outside, and was usually full to capacity with fashionable-looking avatars, dancing, chatting and generally enjoying themselves. At least, that was how Dex imagined the place to be. He had never darkened the establishment's door.

He didn't need to walk to work, of course. He could more easily have linked straight in to his office, finding himself sitting comfortably behind the large wood-grain desk. He could even have his avatar materialize with his feet up and his hat pulled down over his eyes. But Dex liked to walk, both in the physical world and in Marionette City. So he hoofed it to the building, and up the two flights of stairs to the door with *Andersson Dexter, Investigator* stencilled on the frosted glass.

His office was not really in the building, even in the sense that any of the offices in the Maynard Arms were in the building. His space in the Arms — which was actually just a link and a redirect in the shape of the frosted glass door — was part of an in-kind payment from a former client. Dex had a tiny slice of the client's disk space and rez allotment for his door but the office space in behind was actually hosted on a public node that Dex paid for himself.

The Maynard Arms owner would have happily supplied Dex with the space for the office, too, but Dex wanted to be able to have complete control over his own area and no amount of gratitude would persuade someone with a space as big as a whole building to let a tenant have root access. Since the expensive part of virtual real estate was the storefront and the link address, the cost for the actual office space was marginal. And Dex had an expert programmer in Annabelle to build and maintain the space for him.

If she'd been left to her own devices, Annabelle would have built Dex a contemporary set of professional suites, complete with a reception bot and conference room. But he was clear — he wanted a simple, one room affair with a desk and a couple of chairs. He managed to almost keep it that simple, acquiescing only to a small marble statue on the corner of his desk and the large venetian-blind covered window that showed a sunny city view. He unlocked his door in the Maynard Arms with his private key and walked over to his desk.

Dex had to admit that he'd become quite fond of the view from his window and stood watching the elaborate display for several minutes. He was still waiting to notice it loop. Annabelle's talents were wasted on making the trains run on time, Dex thought to himself. But he knew she liked the work, found it challenging, and had no desire to run off and become a freelancer like he'd done. He tore his gaze from the amazingly realistic images playing on his window and turned to his desk. He sat in the overstuffed brown tweed office chair and leaned back. He planted his big black wingtips on the desktop and crossed his ankles. He had to admit that he liked this office. He liked it a lot.

Dex had never really felt comfortable in the virtual world, unlike many people who found an escape there from the dull drudgery of everyday existence. Dex was no lover of the grime and stink of the physical world, he simply found the plasticity and obvious imitation of the virtual world to be a barrier he couldn't overcome. It just wasn't real, and therefore anything that happened in the virtual world wasn't as good as experiences in the real world. He hadn't changed his mind, but he'd come to recognize that M City could offer things that were impossible in the physical world, and it was as good as any way to communicate with people. Once in a while he even found himself forgetting that in his office he was really just a simulation of himself working in a simulation of the world.

This morning, or afternoon or whatever it was — time didn't mean much in Nice and it meant a whole lot less in M City — Dex was puzzling over his current case. The client hadn't walked through the faux glass door in the Maynard Arms; this case had been assigned to him by his squad captain Zahara Zhang. Dex may have moved to Europa, but his professional life still revolved around his squad which was based in Namerica. His name had come up in the rotation among the detectives when the Reverend Martina Alford of the Light of the Simulacrum Temple asked for help.

Their congregation had been meeting in a room off a clothing boutique in M City for years, and had finally gotten enough money and disk for a building of their own. They'd had the new space for less than a year when one day Reverend Alford linked in to work and discovered the building had been destroyed.

There were still walls and rooms, and the members could still link into the space, but everything that had made it their temple was gone. The decorative walls were recovered with images from a slaughterhouse, the pews were smashed and the altar was now an incongruous hot tub. It might have been funny if it weren't for the fact that fixing it would take a fund-raising effort that could last months or years. The congregation was now trying to decide whether they should continue to meet in the vandalized space or go back to the rented room in the clothes shop. Reverend Alford didn't know what to do about the temple and finally contacted the organization Dex worked for to try and find a solution.

• • •

Dex pulled a manila folder from his top desk drawer and opened it. Those virtual actions triggered a part of his personal system to open the digital files on the LoS case, and present the information as if on paper in front of him. Dex flipped though the sheets, trying to see something new. He had images of the building from both before and after the attack and a statement from Reverend Alford. He decided to start with the statement, and watched as the paper transformed into a screen which grew to fill his entire vision.

The reverend's avatar face was centred in the video record, and Dex watched as she told her story. Dex was surprised at how adorned the spiritual leader's avatar was. He'd never been involved with any religious group, but he assumed that spiritual people would be more concerned with loftier ideas than virtual adornment. But Martina Alford wore no generic body. Her chocolate coloured skin was set off by golden hair, not blonde but metallic gold. Her eyes were sepia cat's eyes, glinting out of an attractive oval face. She wore some kind of wrap gown made of a silky cream coloured material. Dex thought she looked more like a dancer at some kind of cabaret than his idea of a preacher. But when she spoke, Dex could well understand why her congregation was one of the fastest growing religious groups operating in M City.

Dex hadn't interviewed Reverend Alford himself, but even if he had he'd still have kept a recording of the conversation. Even before he was a member of the organization he called the Cubicle Men, he routinely recorded his life, and as a detective found that reviewing the vids were an excellent way not only to review conversations, but also to think about the case. He had already watched the interview the M City squad lieutenant had had with the reverend, but he sat back and ran through it again.

"Thank you for seeing me," she began, speaking over a communications link with Mack Larsen, the leader of the Cubicle Men squad assigned to police the various activities which took place in M City.

"It's what we're here for, ma'am," Larsen said from outside the field of view of the recording.

"Yes," the reverend said, sounding less sure of herself than the declarative would indicate. "Well, where should I start?"

"Why don't you begin with when you arrived at the building site?"

"Okay," she said. "I linked in to the temple three days ago, and found it completely trashed." She had provided still images and a panorama vid of the site, which Dex pulled up alongside the vid of her speaking.

"Did you experience anything unusual with the link?" Larsen asked.

"No," the reverend thought for a moment before continuing, "I don't think so. I had no idea that anything was wrong until I rezzed into the space. At first I thought that I'd somehow gotten a wrong link, because I hardly recognized the place. It was like I'd linked into some kind of, I don't know, bordello or something."

The Beauty of Our Weapons

Dex paused the playback and studied the images the reverend had captured. She had provided images from before the damage, showing a squat, square yellow building with a blue roof which curved upward at the edges. Inside were rows of wood-look pews with a plush red cushion along each seat. Stained glass windows along each wall gave the interior space a soft glow, and showed scenes that Dex assumed were from whatever mythos to which the religion ascribed. He had to admit to himself that it was attractive, comfortable and welcoming. Now, though, the atmosphere of the place was completely changed.

Externally, the building was covered in a new texture which made it a garish swirl of red and black. The distinctive roof shape was gone, in its place was a dull flat top, ringed by a neon-lit balcony. On top of the pattern was a series of photorealistic images of nude people. There was nothing overly pornographic about the images, though, so Dex guessed that the vandal's goal wasn't exactly to deface the building, but rather to make it look like it was something else. There were plenty of spaces in certain neighbourhoods of M City decorated in a similar style. He looked at the images from the interior space and could not even recognize it as the same place. It seemed that even the shape of the room had changed.

Dex ran his hands over his closely cropped skull, thinking that it was no wonder that the reverend and her congregation were distraught over the devastation. He wondered how he would feel if he walked into his own small office and found it transformed into a disco or a restaurant. It was an invasion of privacy, a desecration of space. He looked at the pictures, and couldn't understand what the motivation of someone could be to do such a thing. Once you got past the whorehouse look of the exterior, there didn't seem to be any kind of pattern to the destruction — some aspects were disturbing, like the images of slaughtered animals on the walls, but other aspects were almost comical. Dex had a hard time believing that someone trying to terrorize the congregation would turn an altar into a whirlpool spa.

He closed the image files and restarted the vid of Reverend Alford. Her voice was strong and clear, even though the emotion of the situation was clearly visible on her face and in her tone. She described walking through the temple, noting the changes that had been made. After she finished describing the scene, Larsen asked her some background questions. Dex opened a case file and began marking down reminders to himself.

"Tell me a little bit about your religion, Reverend," Larsen asked.

"The Light of the Simulacrum is a fairly new faith," Alford said, clearly having gone though this speech before. "We believe that existence as we can perceive it is an illusion, that true reality is hidden behind our daily lives. This is not a new concept, of course. Many traditions sought to uncover the true nature of reality through various means. Unlike many of those faiths, like the Buddhists or the New Revelators, for example, we believe that the path to communion with the divine is through the illusion, rather than past it."

"I'm not sure I follow you," Larsen said.

Alford smiled, her face taking on a palpable glow as she did. "Where others try to see beyond the illusion, to deny the validity of the mirage in favour of searching for a more real existence, we embrace the fantasy. We believe that the divine has made the world a dream for us to play in, and it is through the full exploration of this dream that we come closer to a relationship with that divine force."

"Go on," Larsen said.

"The creation of Marionette City — a vast, shared virtual community, a giant representation of a world — is the moment that opened the doors to the Great Simulacrum."

"Excuse me," Larsen said, and Dex thought he could hear a trace of embarrassment in the man's voice. "What does that word mean?"

"I'm sorry," the reverend said. "It's such a common term for us; I often forget that not many other people use it. A simulacrum refers to an image or reproduction of something. It is the technical term for what M City is, and it is also the term we use to refer to the entire illusory reality that humans can perceive."

"Okay," Larsen said, not sounding that sure of himself. "Go on."

Alford continued. "M City is, of course, the perfect vehicle for Similes — that's what we call ourselves — to practice our faith. As a shared hallucination within the greater illusion which is the world, it is the ultimate representation of reality. In fact, we believe that the very existence of M City is a sign from the divine."

"So," Larsen said, doing an excellent job of keeping any incredulity out of his voice, "you believe that M City is God?"

"No," Alford said, smiling indulgently. "M City isn't God. But, while we don't generally use that term, you could say that M City is the path through which we seek to find God. Which is why it's so hard for us that our meeting place in this, the holiest of possible spaces for us, has been desecrated."

THREE

DEX WAS READING over his notes on the LoS case when the ancient black Bakelite telephone on his desk sounded. The ring startled him and he swung his feet down to the floor as he leaned toward the instrument. He lifted the receiver off the cradle to end the pealing noise, but didn't bother to put the object up to his ear. The phone was another of Annabelle's touches and Dex found it amusing enough that he didn't turn it off. However, all the thing did was replace the soft ping of Dex's own personal messaging system and he answered the voice call by silently subvocalizing, "This is Dex, go."

"Biagini," the rough voice at the other end of the call said, "how's your evening going?"

"It's barely afternoon by my watch, René," Dex said. "I've hardly started my day. How are things on your patch?"

"Oh, you know," the other man said, a lilt to his voice, "a policeman's work is never done, right, my friend?"

"I don't know anything about that," Dex said, laughing at his friend's choice of words, "but I'm not sitting here twiddling my thumbs, if that's what you mean."

"I do not know how they do things back in Namerica, what with this twiddling you speak of," René said, "but you must be entitled to a break from the salt mines at some time, am I correct?"

"Indeed you are, sir," Dex said. "You wouldn't happen to be heading to Le Rétro, would you?"

"The great detective at work," René said, laughing. "Shall I see you in thirty minutes?"

"Only if I don't see you first, Biagini," Dex answered and ended the call.

• • •

Dex linked out of his office and found himself sitting in his small apartment in the dark. The sun had gone down and he hadn't bothered to set his system to turn on the lights automatically. He got the illumination going and stood up, then rotated his neck, working the kinks out. He'd been on-line for a couple of hours and hadn't stopped to move or get a drink of water. His mouth was dry and filmed with a nasty taste. He drew a glass of water and drank it down while pacing his small space.

He checked his appearance out in the small mirror in the lav and determined that it would have to do. His hair was cropped close to his skull, setting off his dark skin and eyes, which he thought looked a little tired but passable. He'd showered after getting home from Annabelle's that afternoon and while a few hours in the chair hadn't done anything too great for his shirt, the silky material failed to hold any wrinkles and still looked presentable enough. Certainly, he didn't need to get dressed up just to meet René Biagini at their local watering hole.

Dex left his apartment and spiralled down the eighteen floors to the lobby of the complex. He walked through the courtyard and even though it was early evening he was surprised to see none of his neighbours in the small green space. There were usually some people around at all times of day or night and there were still some people out on the street. Dex walked down the road for a couple of blocks, then caught a local train to the Pietonne.

He walked into the open air bar at Le Rétro and saw his friend at a small table near the back. Dex walked over to the man, who stood and came around the table. They embraced quickly and sat across from each other. "So what is going on across the pond, my friend?" Biagini asked after they had each ordered drinks from the automatic menu scrolling across the tabletop.

"You probably know more than I do, René," Dex said. "I don't pay that much attention to what's going on on the streets now that they aren't my streets, you know?"

"Understandable," Biagini said. "So why not just make it official and move over here professionally? There's always room on the squad for a detective, Dex."

A fashionable-looking human server arrived with their drinks, synth-wine for Biagini and rum and water for Dex. Biagini winked at the pale, long-haired server, who smiled in return. "You know each other?" Dex asked when the server had gone.

"Not yet," the other man said with a sly smile.

"You are such a cad," Dex said, lifting his glass in a toast to the other man.

"Just making the most of my meagre time on this planet," Biagini said, taking a sip of his drink. "And don't change the subject."

"What is it with you people?" Dex said. "Everyone seems to want to poach me away from Captain Zhang these days."

"You're a popular man," Biagini said, "for no small reason, either." He turned on his thousand watt grin and Dex rolled his eyes.

"I'm not going to fall for your flattery, Biagini," Dex said and his friend laughed.

"So who is my rival?" Biagini asked.

"Larsen, that lieutenant from the M City squad."

"Hmmm," Biagini said. "They don't have detectives on that patch, do they?"

"No," Dex said. "And I'm not about to be the first, either."

"Fair enough," Biagini said, "but why not come over to my house? You do live here, after all."

"I'm sure you're a great captain," Dex said, "and there's nothing wrong with the Nice squad, but I've got a home with Zizou's team. I like it there and I don't want to move. Moving house, quitting the workaday world and going full-time free-lance has been tough enough. I need a little stability, René. At least for a while."

"Fine, fine," Biagini said, smiling. "I just want you to know that there is always a spot for you on my squad. I'd be happy to have you on the team, Dex. You're a good man."

"Thanks, René. It means a lot to me to hear you say that. I'm just not ready to make the move yet."

"I know. I just want to keep asking in case you change your mind someday. I don't want to miss out."

Dex laughed. "I don't think you miss out on much, René."

"I try not to, my friend, I try not to." They sat for a moment, sipping their drinks. René flipped through the menu and ordered a small bowl of salad.

"It's real food here, isn't it?" Dex asked.

"Fresh from the hydroponic garden on the roof," Biagini said.

"Celebrating something?" Dex asked, looking at the price out of the corner of his eye, his eyebrows raising.

"Nothing special," Biagini said. "I'm just in the mood for something wonderful. You know that sufficiently advanced food is indistinguishable from magic."

Dex laughed. "You are a very strange man, René Biagini."

"Thank you very much," he answered, smiling.

The server arrived again with René's salad and another pair of drinks. Dex eyeballed the unordered rum and water placed before him and said, "I'm still on the clock, you know."

"Last one, then," Biagini said before lifting a forkful of greens into his mouth. He chewed slowly with his eyes closed and sighed loudly after swallowing. "*Magnifique*," he said, smiling broadly.

"Say what?" Dex asked.

"It's French," René said. "I'm taking a class."

"Whatever for?" Dex asked, laughing. "Who cares about a dead language?"

"It's energizing for the mind," Biagini said, haughtily. He took another bite of the salad, then sipped his wine.

"I met a woman once who spoke French," Dex said, finishing off his first rum.

"Really?" Biagini asked.

"Yup," Dex said. "Had an accent and everything. Apparently her parents were quite strange and brought her up with it as a first language. Caused her no end of problems as a child, I imagine."

"Indeed," Biagini said. "So what's on the go for you these days?"

"Someone desecrated a church in Felipe Gates."

"Where?" Biagini asked, a tiny bit of green shooting from his mouth.

"A neighbourhood in M City," Dex explained. "Mostly clubhouses and libraries around there. I can see why you'd never have heard of it," he chided his friend.

"Well, I certainly would not be likely to be in an area full of religious zealots," Biagini said with a scowl. "That's not my style at all."

"Mine neither," Dex said, laughing. "But they still don't deserve to have their space crapped on."

"Someone defecated on this church?" Biagini asked, his eyes wide.

"No, not literally," Dex said. "They just tore up the place some, changed all the textures and a bunch of the objects."

"Sounds like a common or garden variety act of vandalism to me," Biagini said. "A friend of mine had his shop fucked with just last week. They broke the locks, destroyed the door and wrecked the inside. It took him days to fix it."

"Shit," Dex said.

Biagini nodded. "And these aren't isolated incidents. Overall, the numbers say vandalism in M City is on the rise all over."

"Really?" Dex enquired.

"Um, let me see..." Biagini took on the thousand metre stare people get when they are accessing online information. "Up eleven percent in the last quarter overall and thirty-eight percent in the high risk areas."

Dex whistled. "That's a big jump," he said. "Any idea what's behind it?"

Biagini shrugged. "You friend Larsen has a whole unit working on some kind of extortion ring making the rounds in M City, but my friend Jeffie didn't get any threats or anything, so what would be the point?"

"Extortion?"

"Sure, the old protection money racket," Biagini said. "It's probably a couple of script kiddies who watched too many old mob vids trying the shakedown route, not some major organized crime ring. But who knows."

"You don't think it was extortion on your friend, though?"

"Naw," Biagini said. "Jeffie thought it was probably a jealous ex-lover, but he's just a narcissist. Really, who knows why people are assholes?" he said philosophically and went back to his dwindling pile of greens.

• • •

The city nightlife was already in full swing when Dex said farewell to René, after a promise to meet again the next week. It was a nice night, warm without being hot, and Dex decided to take the long walk back to his apartment. When he arrived, he saw a group of his neighbours in the courtyard of his building. A few people were just enjoying the small decorative garden, but the majority were engaged in Yuprazhnyëi, a popular exercise regime that reminded Dex of trying to tie yourself in knots while fighting invisible sloths. People seemed to like it, though and he often saw groups in the yard or on the squares in town making the synchronized moves.

He spiralled up the lift to his floor and back to his apartment. He unlocked the door with a wave of his hand, the embedded identity chip under his skin electronically handshaking with his apartment's system. Once inside, he drew a large glass of water and pulled out a food brick from the economy size box in his small cupboard. He peeled off the wrapper and took a big bite of the glutinous lump. Chewing, he walked the two steps to his small pull down table and sat in the one chair in the tiny room.

His apartment was very small — containing only a bed, the chair and a small storage cubicle in the main room. A zapper and recyclatron were inset into one wall, next to the small lav. On the opposite wall, a four decimetre shelf could be pulled down to fashion a table or desk area. When it was down, there was barely enough room for the large, comfortable chair which dominated the space. It was ideal for one person, but became immediately cramped with another body in the space. It was one of the reasons that Dex stayed over at Annabelle's much more often than she visited him.

The Beauty of Our Weapons

With his water and late lunch, Dex sat at his small table and leaned back into his chair. He lost focus and let the overlay of his system's viewer impose itself over his vision. He could still see his apartment in the background of the icons and images of the interface. He paged over to his account on the Cubicle Men's system and checked to see what was new in the past twenty-four hours. He scanned the news board and checked his private messages. His personal system automatically set a reminder for the weekly squad meeting in a couple of days and he checked to see if anything had miraculously been added to the Light of the Simulacrum file by another officer. As he'd expected, the file hadn't been touched, except for a log entry showing that it had been accessed by Lieutenant Larsen.

Dex sighed as he paged out of the organization's system and linked in to his office in M City. There was no particular reason why he should be virtually present there in order to work, other than it was a location where it was becoming known that he could be found by the few clients who came to him specifically. However, Dex discovered that he liked the interface that Annabelle had created for him in the office and it appealed to his anachronistic aesthetic sense. As he gazed out his artificial window at a constructed image, he wondered if Annabelle's embrace of all things virtual was rubbing off on him.

• • •

His desk was cluttered with files — there were papers, pictures, and vids which represented themselves as three-dimensional holos covering the horizontal surface — and Dex was seemingly randomly picking through them. He wasn't even really seeing the files any longer; it was more like some kind of meditational activity to keep his virtual body moving while his mind turned over the facts of the LoS case. He was so completely lost in thought that at first he didn't hear the light knocking on his glass door. It was only when the sultry voice outside called, "Mr. Dexter, are you in?" that Dex realized that he possibly had a client.

She opened the door and Dex had to fight to ensure that his avatar didn't betray the reaction his body had in the physical world. She was tall, almost filling the doorway vertically, wearing a pale green tailored skirt suit, which was calculated to show off her voluptuous body extremely well. Her lips were bright red, a shade darker than the pillbox hat perched atop the not quite black chignon of hair. Dex's gaze was drawn to those lips, as they drew into a smile that filled him with a complex soup of emotions.

"Mr. Dexter," she said, taking a step into his small office. "We meet again."

FOUR

"Ms. BISH," DEX said, as he struggled to get his feet off his desk, tidy up the mess, stand and smooth his tie without falling over. "It's been a long time." He reached across the desk to take her gloved hand in his. The handshake felt more like a caress than he'd hoped it would and he forced himself not to jerk his hand out of her grasp.

"Too long, Mr. Dexter," she purred, her smile piercing Dex's resolve.

"Indeed," he said, unconvincingly. He gestured at the hard wooden chair on her side of the desk. "Please, have a seat." She settled on the chair lightly, the fabric of her skirt riding up on creamy thighs which Dex failed to avoid noticing.

Forcing his eyes to meet hers, Dex leaned back in his chair. "To what do I owe the pleasure of your visit?" he asked.

Stella Bish crossed her legs slowly and Dex reminded himself that the dame was as calculating as any computer program, even though he was well aware that she was a flesh and blood woman. "Business, Mr. Dexter," she replied. "I assume by the lettering on your door that you are still engaged in investigations of a, shall we say, less than corporate nature?"

"I'm available for discreet enquiries," Dex said.

Her lips curled into a not entirely unattractive smirk. "I seem to recall that your idea of discretion includes barging into a crowded café and accusing people of murder in front of their friends and colleagues," Bish countered.

Dex felt his face flush in the physical world, but his avatar played it cool and merely shrugged. "I do what I need to in order to get results, Ms. Bish," he said. "I'm sure you can appreciate that."

"Indeed, Mr. Dexter," she answered. "Results are exactly why I chose to come to you directly rather than share my little situation with strangers."

"We are not exactly bosom friends, Ms. Bish," Dex said, smirking himself.

"Mr. Dexter," Bish said, her voice sounding shocked, "it pains me to hear you say such a thing. I think we have more in common than you'd like to admit. After all, I understand that we share excellent taste in accommodations, do we not?"

Dex did not know what to say to that. He shouldn't have been surprised that a woman like Stella Bish, who ran the empire which brokered the best freelance programmers and designers in M City and had business fingers in more pies than he could count, would know the names of all the tenants in the buildings she owned. Because Stella Bish wasn't just a high-powered mogul who had made Dex's life very difficult in the past; she was also his landlord.

• • •

"I haven't noticed you in the common areas of Liberté," Dex said, after he got over his surprise.

"I still live in Guadalajara," Bish said. "I'm hoping that the community at Liberté will be successful enough to build a sister complex in my own hometown."

"And how is that going?" Dex asked. Bish smiled and said nothing, so Dex answered his own question. "I suspect well enough. The buildings are getting full and there are always people around doing things. I'm sure your goals, financial and otherwise, are being met well enough."

"I couldn't do it without people like you," Bish said.

"True enough," Dex said. "And speaking of which, what brings you to people like me? You have a situation, you said. Could you be a little more specific?"

"Of course," Bish said, her manner instantly becoming all business. "I'm not sure exactly how to describe it, so I'll just begin at the beginning."

"That's usually a good place to start," Dex said, making sure that he would have enough clear disk space to record the conversation. "Go ahead."

"Well," Bish said, "it started a couple of weeks ago. I was linking in to a meeting in Market Street and when I rezzed in I found myself nowhere near where I was trying to go."

"Oh," Dex prompted, wondering how that was even possible. Links to locations in M City were hardcoded to force an avatar to emerge in a particular location. There was no other way to enter the virtual world than by a link — from what he understood from Annabelle, links were like the doors into the world, doors which were fixed by the programming of the virtual world itself. You couldn't change or break an existing link. At least, that was how Dex thought it worked.

"Yes, it was very disturbing," Bish continued. "I think I was in some unused corner of the space — I don't know if you've ever been in an empty part of M City, but I have visited a few unrezzed locations as the preliminary to a large construction project. They have always been represented as just a grey three-D grid. But this wasn't even as well formed as those spaces."

"How so?" Dex asked.

"I found myself sort of floating in a space I can only describe as a void," she said. "I had no sense of how large it was, no idea if I was alone or merely blind. It was very distressing and I am most thankful that I was able to link back out of there immediately."

Bish looked visibly shaken by the memory and Dex was surprised to discover that her discomfort did not amuse him in the least. He opened the lower right corner drawer in his desk and withdrew a bottle of whisky with about a third missing from it. He found a pair of short tumblers in the back of the drawer and poured two generous measures of the brown liquid. He passed one glass over to Bish and said, "This will provide any of the usual stims, just pick from the list."

He watched as Bish paused, presumably checking the menu of neurostimulants available. The stims would effect her brain directly, the dosage regulated by her avatar's action of drinking from the glass. Something in the list would surely be to her taste and calming her down would make the interview go easier. Dex, on the other hand, drank his whisky for the simulated taste of it only, never having grown to enjoy the strange sensation of direct electric stimulation of his central nervous system calculated, monitored and constantly adjusted by his implants.

She took a long sip of her drink and closed her eyes. A moment later, she took a deep breath and said, "Thank you," toasting Dex with her glass. "After that happened, I immediately called my best technician to check my system. We ran a series of diagnostics — it took days to clear the list and I was completely incapacitated the whole time."

"Why is that?" Dex asked.

"Lila wouldn't let me enter M City until the full diagnostic had run."

"Lila?"

"Lila Avalon," Bish explained. "Probably the best M City interface jockey in any world. At least since Reuben Cobalt."

Dex looked up at Bish sharply, the name of the man whose murder had first introduced them ringing in his ears.

"I can't say that the similarities hadn't escaped me," Bish said, bitterness in her voice. "I never did hear about how that case resolved. The grapevine made it sound like you identified the culprit, but I could never find anyone who knew who it was."

"I doubt you ever will," Dex said. "But I can assure you that the person responsible for Reuben Cobalt's death is very unlikely to be behind what happened to you."

"Perhaps," Bish said, "but it did make me think of you nonetheless."

"What did Ms. Avalon find?" Dex asked, changing the subject.

"Nothing," Bish said. "She could find nothing wrong in my system, nothing wrong with the location in M City I was trying to reach, nothing at all. She ran several sets of scans, some of which were surprisingly painful, I might add, to no avail at all. I fear that she eventually came to believe that I was hallucinating the entire experience and she cleared me to travel interdimensionally again."

She took a sip of her drink and cleared her throat. "As I'm sure you can appreciate, I was apprehensive the first time I tried to link into M City after this. I was terrified that I would be stuck in some no man's land with no way to link out again. At least I can say that it hasn't happened again."

"I'm pleased to hear that," Dex said. "But that begs the question — why come to see me now?"

"It's because of all the other little things," Bish said.

"Oh," he prompted.

"I am not making this up, Mr. Dexter," Bish said, darkly.

"I did not suggest that you were," he said. "Please, just tell me what's been happening."

Bish sighed and drained her drink. "At first I was sure I was just imagining it myself," she began. "You know, that I was so confused by what had happened, or that I'd just forgotten what the details of some places were like. Or maybe the creators had changed them since I was gone. I was offline for nearly a week for the tests, it was possible. But, as you know, I spend time offline regularly and this hadn't ever happened before, so that seemed unlikely." Dex waited, hoping that she would start making sense at some point soon.

"The first thing I noticed was in my office," she continued. "Like you, I keep a virtual office in M City. Though there is very little similarity between my space and yours, I must admit," she smiled slightly and Dex made sure to keep his avatar's expression neutral.

"What about your office?" he prompted.

"There's this pattern in the floor," she said. "It's barely noticeable and I'm sure I've never even really looked at it before. But I was convinced that it was different. I couldn't even tell you what was different about it, but it just seemed wrong."

Dex nodded and said, "Anything else?"

"Yes," Bish said. "A lot of other things, very much like that. Subtle changes to the places I frequent, so subtle that it is hard to explain what the difference is."

"Anything more immediate," Dex asked, "like the experience with the broken link?"

"No," Bish said, "that only ever happened the one time. I was starting to think that I really was just imagining it all." She picked up her glass and examined it. Dex lifted the bottle toward her, offering her a refill, but she shook her head and put the glass back down on the desk in front of her. "But yesterday I knew that I wasn't imagining anything and that I might be in real danger."

"Go on," Dex said, leaning forward a little.

"I'd been offline for a while," Bish said, "you know, one of my little holidays from virtuality." Dex knew that Bish, like he himself, strongly preferred the physical world to life in M City, which was part of the reason why she had built the housing community in Nice where he now lived. "When I reconnected my system to the 'net, I couldn't get in."

Dex frowned. "Were you trying to run a multi?" he asked, referring to the practice some people had of creating entirely separate identities for use online. The conglomerate of firms which maintained the everywherenet, the global business and personal communications system which was also the backbone of M City, had a policy of deleting multi accounts without prejudice. They claimed that the possibility of fraud was the issue, though most believed that it was a concern for additional bandwidth usage that prompted the ban. Regardless, running a multi was one of the online activities that was closest to illegal and Dex knew that in most circles he was being offensive by even asking the question.

Bish did not bat an eye at the question, however. "No," she answered simply, "I don't have a multi account. It was just me; my regular login, my regular account."

"So what happened?" Dex asked.

"Nothing," Bish said. "And that was the problem."

Dex thought for a moment. "Well," he said. "You're here now. What happened?"

"That's the real problem," Bish said. "I have no idea what happened. Yesterday I couldn't access anything — no M City, no messages, no boards. It was as if my connection was just gone. I couldn't even contact anyone. I was starting to panic — my business was in real jeopardy. I was starting to try to see if I could find anyone in Guadalajara who might be able to help me when all of a sudden everything just started working again. And it's been fine ever since. But I can't go on with these things happening all the time. So here I am. After your experience with the Reuben Cobalt incident, I thought of you first."

"I'm desperate Mr. Dexter," Bish said and Dex could hear true fear under the usual seductive tones of the woman's voice. "Please help me. I have nowhere else to turn."

FIVE

STELLA BISH AGREED to Dex's fee schedule without any nego-
tiation and transferred a substantial retainer to Dex's escrow
account on the Cubicle Men's system. The organization
would take a small percentage for overhead, but Dex would
easily keep enough to cover his expenses for a few months.
He'd briefly thought about suggesting some kind of barter for
his rent, but it seemed too complicated, especially with Bish's
fragile emotional state.

She'd left his office after extracting a promise to provide
her with regular updates and had managed to leave behind a
lingering scent of perfume. Dex inhaled the woman's fragrance and pondered her effect on him. He knew that her
seductive qualities were calculated as part of her business per-
sona and he was in many ways actually repelled by her personally. She had been more of an impediment than a help in
his previous dealings with her and he knew that she had no
qualms about using anyone and everyone she came across to
her advantage. That being said, they shared uncommon pro-
clivities and Dex felt himself drawn to her through a strange
sense of kinship. He also had to admit to himself that he
failed to be unmoved by her very real plea for help. Dex was,
he knew, a sucker for a beautiful woman in distress.

He linked out of the office and stretched. The moon was
bright in the sky and Dex had his apartment system untint

the small window. He generally saw little natural light and the moonlight was better than no light. In fact, Dex quite enjoyed its soft white glow. He used the lav and poured a large glass of water. He drank it down while pinging Annabelle. Being on the same schedule made sharing time together easy and they usually spent an hour or two at their favourite watering hole in M City. On rare occasions, Dex had coaxed her to join him at Le Rétro, but most days after work they met at Monte's. After the previous days at her apartment, Dex knew to suggest the M City location.

He linked in first and found himself materializing in the middle of the small ginmill, facing the wood and brass bar. Instead of finding a table first, Dex walked up to the bar and spoke to the non-human bartender. "Evening, Jim," Dex said, causing the bot to pay attention to him.

"What'll it be?" the smart program asked.

"The usual," Dex replied, knowing that the bar's system kept a record of his every order and would know that he requested stim-free rum and ginger beer nine times out of ten.

"You wanna pack of smokes with that?" the bot asked as it mixed Dex's virtual drink.

"Sure," Dex answered and palmed the red and gold pack that Jim placed in front of him. He took the drink and felt the icy cool humidity of the condensation on the glass. The intensity of the sensations he experienced with his newly upgraded interface still unnerved him, but he was getting much better at managing the difference between what his physical body felt and what his body seemed to experience online. He took a sip of the drink, enjoying the taste and feeling of spicy-sweet liquid roll over his tongue and walked over to a small booth in the shadows.

He sat and checked the time on his head up display. He was early by a few minutes and Annabelle was generally very punctual. He picked up the package of cigarettes and ran a thumbnail under the cellophane, opening the pack. He tossed the wrappings into the middle of the table and watched as they disappeared in what looked like a shower of sparkles. He lit one and felt the tingling sensation of smoke drawn deep into his lungs. He blew out a plume of blue smoke and through the haze saw Annabelle walking toward him.

She was, in many ways, as different from Stella Bish as a woman could be, but Dex had to admit that both of them were beautiful. Of course, most avatars in M City were beautiful, but unlike many people Annabelle and Bish both wore avatars which looked somewhat similar to their physical bodies. Dex knew that Annabelle had used physical cosmetic adjustment to get there and he guessed that Bish had probably done the same. He couldn't be bothered with putting any great effort into his physical form; the complex nutrient mix in the food bricks he ate sculpted his body into a thin, muscular shape, as well as ensuring a healthy and long life. Beyond that, he didn't really care about his looks. But he was happy to admire others who did put in the effort.

Annabelle wore a simple pair of slim trousers, the same colour as her hair which she had changed to a dark auburn. Above the ochre pants she wore a clingy cream tee shirt decorated with the image of one of the old paintings she favoured. She'd tried to educate Dex on abstract art, but he could never get past the seeming randomness of the colours and patterns. As Annabelle got closer, though, he thought he recognized the design on her chest. "What's that?" he asked as she approached. "Kandinsky?"

She smiled and leaned over for a kiss. "I think you might just be turning into an antiquated art lover after all," she said, settling into the seat next to Dex.

"Nope," he said, "it still looks like the aftermath of an explosion in a paint store to me. I just recognize the explosion is all."

Annabelle laughed and shook her head. "You just want to be a philistine, I can tell."

"And you just want to show off your new dictionary, apparently," Dex countered. He waited while she ordered a drink from the table's automatic menu. The space between them seemed to shimmer and a pink libation appeared in front of Annabelle. Dex couldn't tell by looking, but he knew from experience that unlike his own beverage, hers was most likely a delivery system for some kind of neurostim. Dex didn't care; he'd poured a real rum and water back in his apartment to sip. To each her own poison, he figured.

They clicked virtual glasses and drank, then Dex asked, "So, how was your day?"

"Nothing special," Annabelle said. "Meetings, more meetings and a few minutes of real work. This move east is unbelievably complicated."

"I thought the eastern zone trains were run by Aronson," Dex said. "What's Omnitrack doing in their zone?"

"Beats me," Annabelle said. "Pushing into the competitor's territory is what's causing most of the problems, but the higher ups have decided this is what's happening, so damn it all, we have to make it fly. It's a pain in the ass is what it is. But enough of my woes. How was your day?"

"You would not believe who darkened my door this afternoon," Dex said.

"Who?" she asked.

"Stella Bish," Dex said, wondering what Annabelle's reaction would be. At first she seemed not to recognize the name, then her face became stormy.

"What did that..." she seemed to struggle for the right word. "Harlot... shyster... woman want with you?"

Dex laughed. "Tell me how you really feel about her," he said. He spent the next half hour telling Annabelle about the problems Bish was encountering and partway through the story, Annabelle softened.

"I don't think I'm ever going to like that woman," she said, "but I can't imagine how awful that must be. How could a person live without access..." She shivered. "What do you think is going on?"

"I was hoping you might be able to shed some light on that," Dex said.

"She said that her technician couldn't find anything wrong after the first incident," Annabelle confirmed.

"I didn't get a copy of the report," Dex said, "but that's what she told me."

"I'd like to see the report of the scans," Annabelle said. "And maybe do a scan or two of my own. This sounds a lot like what happened to that multi from a couple of years back."

"That's what I thought," Dex said, "and that was why Ms. Bish thought of me."

"But she's no multi," Annabelle said, "or at least she wasn't running an alternate a couple of years back."

"I asked her specifically about that," Dex said. "It was her bona fide login."

"That's scary shit," Annabelle said.

"That's what I thought," Dex said, sourly. "If you're scared, then I'm terrified."

"You should be," Annabelle said. "If Bish is telling the truth, then access to everything is threatened. Business, banking, communication, the whole works could be cut off."

• • •

"It's the lifeline of everything we do now," Annabelle explained. "Even those of us who work in a building with other people communicate over the 'net, access our files from the 'net — hell, you need the 'net to buy a food brick from the store."

"So, if people have found a way to prevent individual accounts from accessing the everywherenet, they could really fuck everything up for that person."

"Totally," Annabelle agreed. "You'd be locked out of your job, your money and if you don't know anyone with skills in the physical world, you don't even have any way of getting help."

"Shit," Dex said. "I'd better get Bish to send us copies of the reports of her scans as soon as possible." While he was still talking to Annabelle, he sent Bish an urgent message to that effect. "I just hope she's able to access her messages," Dex said.

"That's what confuses me about this," Annabelle said, a frown creasing her face. "If someone was able to completely lock her out of the 'net, why did they give her access back?"

"What do you mean?" Dex asked.

"Well, what's the point of locking her out and then letting her back in? If you're trying to actually stop her from getting online, why let her back on? And if you're trying to hold her access ransom, shouldn't there be some kind of demands or something? It just doesn't make sense."

"Hmm..." Dex thought. "That is kind of strange." He pondered it for a moment. "Could we be looking at this all wrong?" he asked, thinking out loud. "What if it's not some evil person out to cause havoc or scare the hell out of her. What if it's just a straight up malfunction."

"Whoa," Annabelle said. "That seems impossible." She sipped her drink and thought. "But it would explain why there's no obvious reason for it to be happening. Now I really want to see those reports. And I've got some questions of my own I'd like answered."

"I'm sure that Ms. Bish would be happy to let you poke around," Dex said. "She seemed honestly terrified."

"I would be, too," Annabelle said. "I would be, too."

• • •

They each stayed for another drink, but linked out of the bar before it got too late. After spending the previous night together, they were ready for a small break from each other's company.

The taste of Annabelle's lips was still lingering on Dex's mouth when he refocussed on his apartment. He spent a few minutes just enjoying being offline — using the lav, looking out the small window at the early morning scene in the court-yard, determining if he was hungry or thirsty. When he felt like he'd reconnected with his physical body, he logged into the Cubicle Men's system. He updated the case file on Stella Bish's case with Annabelle's observations, then paged over to his messenger.

He sent Martina Alford, the pastor at the Light of the Simulacrum Temple, a request for a brief interview. Dex admitted to himself that Mack Larsen had done a fine job, but he still always wanted to meet with clients himself. He didn't fully trust talking with avatars in M City, but he felt that he got a better sense of the people he was dealing with if he had some direct communication and a virtual meeting was better than nothing. The keys to an investigation often weren't found in what a person said as much as how it was said.

As he reviewed the file, he wondered if it were possible that the two cases were related somehow. Both involved some kind of tampering with the fabric of the virtual reality which was M City and both seemed more like pranks or random incidents rather than acts perpetrated for some particular end. But Dex knew that he had a predilection to see patterns where there were not necessarily any to be found and he tried to keep an open mind. At that back of that open mind, he wondered if it wasn't that there was a common perpetrator so much as a common cause — a deeply insidious and cata-strophic bug in the global communications backbone.

SIX

THE SUN WAS high in the sky when Dex woke up, but he had gotten used to the schedule. His apartment kept the window tinted almost opaque for the eight hours Dex was sleeping and regardless the small hit of SleepingJuice he often took before sacking out would have let him sleep through a supernova. Dex usually had his system slowly untint his windows, so that the sun's light would wake him. His small window was cracked open and Dex could smell the tang of salt water and intertidal decay on the breeze.

He swung his legs over the side of the small bed and stretched. He ran a hand over his closely cropped hair, feeling the familiar bumps of his skull. He padded over to the cupboard and got a cup of coffee going in the zapper. While it was heating, he pulled out an Econoline food brick from the large box and unwrapped it. Chewing, he took his mug over to the chair and sat. He went online and checked his messenger.

Reverend Alford had agreed to a meeting later that day and Stella Bish had sent copies of the reports from her technician. Dex didn't even open the files from Bish, knowing that he'd never understand the contents. Instead, he forwarded the whole thing to Annabelle, along with a link to the case file on the Cubicle Men's system.

Annabelle was the premier cracker on Dex's squad back in Namerica and they had worked on the Reuben Cobalt murder together. That was when their relationship had moved from a professional to a personal one, though not without a fair measure of difficulty. Annabelle had been living in Nice even then, after a transfer from her day job. Dex moved a couple of years later, not exactly following her but happy to be closer. As far as they knew, they were the only members of Zahara Zhang's squad that didn't actually live in the same physical locale, but since the squad met mainly in Marionette City and they worked with clients all over the globe it didn't seem to matter where they were physically located.

Dex was sure that Annabelle was the most talented programmer he knew and he suspected that she might be one of the brightest there was. She had worked out back door access to all kinds of parts of everywherenet that Dex hadn't even known existed and she was invaluable in any case that involved the online system. He was sure that if there was a clue in Stella Bish's scan reports, Annabelle would find it.

He'd often suggested to her that her talents were wasted working for Omnitrack, but she liked the work. "I'm doing something useful," she'd often say. "This is much more important that making a better war simulation or building vid backgrounds." Of course, that wasn't what Dex was referring to, but he knew better than to argue with her about this. She was never shy about expressing her opinions and particularly not when they concerned her own life.

Dex checked the time and saw that he had a couple of hours before he was meeting Reverend Alford. One of the great joys of leaving the life of a regular working stiff was the ability to take these natural breaks in the workday to do other things. He could have met his friend and almost-colleague René Biagini, who also made his own schedule, or he could run household errands, but Dex had other ideas.

After a quick shower and change of clothes, he picked up the inexpensive mandolin Annabelle had given him about a year previously. He had been a musician back in his youth, living the starving artist life on the fringes of society. After he gave it all up to become a productive member of society, he thought he'd never go back to music. Annabelle's gift of the mandolin had brought back memories — many painful, but others were surprisingly poignant. He began playing the plywood instrument, alone in his small room, but soon was playing a virtual mandolin in a small band that met in M City.

The five of them played a few gigs and did reasonably well for a bunch of newcomers. After talking with some of the other musicians he met at the shows, Dex began experimenting with playing his physical mandolin instead of the virtual one and piping the sound in as part of the band performance. The idea took off and now both Javier, the keyboardist and Suzi, the horn player were including physical instruments in the mix. The band, Chemical Celeste, was developing its own small following among the mixed live and virtual music scene.

• • •

Dex spent ninety minutes running through the setlist for the band's upcoming gig and at the end started working on a couple of new pieces. His system pinged to give him a ten minute warning before his meeting with the reverend and he put the instrument back in its Ultrafoam carrying case. Dex pulled up his case notes, using one eye as a viewer to his system while he puttered around the apartment. He was settling into his chair when his system pinged again, letting him know that someone was linking in to his office building. He linked directly into his office and found himself materializing behind his desk just as he heard a knock on the virtual glass door.

"Mr. Dexter," a muffled, but confident and persuasive voice sounded from the hallway. "Are you in? It's Martina Alford."

Dex rose and opened the door to his guest. "Come in, reverend," Dex said, standing aside to let the woman enter.

"Please," she said, "call me Martina."

"Of course," Dex said, offering her the hard wooden chair. "You can just call me Dex." She smiled and nodded, settling into the seat across the desk from the detective.

"So," Dex began, "I've reviewed your conversation with Lieutenant Larsen and I've gone over the image files you included. But I have a few questions for you myself, if you don't mind."

"Go ahead," Alford said. "I'll give you as much time as you need. If we don't find the person responsible for the destruction, we may never be able to rebuild."

"That's a good place to start," Dex said. "How did you manage to raise the funds for the original temple? And how did your congregation meet before it was built?"

"We began as a board — members would post conversations and we had a weekly interactive vid service. It was quite active and a core group of members began suggesting that we could acquire our own space in M City. A whole private building is quite expensive, as I'm sure you know, Mr... uh, Dex."

"Indeed," he said. "Even renting a room isn't a minor proposition."

Alford looked around at Dex's small office and nodded. "We first went that route ourselves," she said. "One of our congregants worked part time in a small M City boutique and managed to broker a deal with the owner. We met in their back room for a long time and it was such a better experience that it was probably only a year before we started talking about getting our own building. Of course, as the congregation grew, the small room in the shop was getting more and more difficult."

"I didn't think that space was a constraint here," Dex said, confused.

"It isn't exactly," Alford said. "We could serve as many avatars as wanted to participate, however there is only so much resolution bandwidth available in a smaller area. In short, everyone could see me, but I couldn't see everyone. And they couldn't interact with each other simultaneously, either. It was better than the vid feed, by a long shot, but we were aching for a fuller community experience.

"For us, the full immersion of existence in M City is an integral part of our beliefs — being able to worship together in the virtual experience is one of the best ways we can practice our faith. We'd been supporting ourselves with small voluntary donations, but the leaders and I decided to embark on a full fundraising campaign. It took some time, but between the generosity of our members and a special deal with a sympathetic developer, we were able to purchase a piece of rez space and a building large enough to accommodate not just the current congregation, but a group as large as what we hope to grow into.

"The temple was the end result of years of hard work, not just for me but for dozens of members. To see all that time, effort and money reduced to garbage..." The reverend had been matter of fact in telling her story up to this point, but now Dex heard a crack in her voice. "This has all been very difficult, Mr. Dexter," she said, pulling herself together.

"I understand," he said and wondered whether or not it would be appropriate to offer a minster of religion a shot from his desk drawer bottle. He was saved from having to make the decision when she took a deep breath and gave him a weak smile.

"Thank you for your sympathy," she said. "What else do you want to know?"

"Well, the first thing that comes to mind," Dex said, "and forgive me if this sounds overly... practical, is why don't you just reinstantiate the space from a backup? I realize that there would be expenses, but..."

The reverend shook her head. "I'm no programmer/designer," she said, "and I see that you aren't, either." Dex shook his head. "Well, one of the things that made our temple such an exceptional meeting space is that M City code is, for lack of a better word, alive."

"Excuse me?"

"The code rendering the space changes as avatars interact with it," Alford explained. "There is no realistic way to take backups of the code since it is constantly in flux. This is why we so desperately need to find the responsible party. We aren't that concerned with retribution, it's that we hope whoever it was took a snapshot of the code before it was," her voice cracked, "changed."

"I see," Dex said and made a note to ask Annabelle about this. "Well, let's see what we can do. Now, this is a difficult question," Dex began, "but I need you to think carefully and be completely honest with me."

"Of course," Alford said, frowning.

"Can you think of anyone, any individual or group, who may have some kind of grudge against your religion?" he asked. "I know that faith can be a very emotional and controversial thing and this wouldn't be the first time that a religious group is targeted by its detractors."

Dex expected a denial or argument from Alford, but the pastor was silent and thoughtful. "You aren't the first to suggest such a thing," she said, "even within our congregation, this idea has been mentioned. And it is a difficult thing for me to say. I can tell you that other than this, we've had no threatening correspondence, no protestors at our meetings or even anyone joining our discussion groups merely to argue. Of course, there are many who do not share our views and in other contexts I have encountered people who wish to debate the merits of our central tenets. But even then, our faith is not particularly controversial and those exchanges are generally pleasant enough encounters."

Dex didn't reply and Alford thought further. "Of course, I am so close to the centre of our faith that I am sure I don't have a good handle on the general opinion outsiders have of our religion. I know that I feel as if there is no great outcry against us, but I fully admit that I could easily be unaware of such a feeling."

"Fair enough," Dex said. "But this act of sabotage, if that is what it was, came as a surprise to you?"

"Definitely," Alford said, then looked at Dex quizzically. "Do you think that it is possible that this was not a deliberate attack?" she asked.

"At this stage I'm not ruling anything out," Dex said. "It's dangerous to get tunnel vision at the beginning of an investigation."

"I see," the reverend said. "I suppose you know best," she said. Dex didn't know what to say to that, so smiled gently and remained quiet.

"Do you have anything else?" Alford asked.

"I'd just like your permission to tour the site," Dex said. "And I may bring a colleague with me, if that's all right with you."

"Absolutely," the reverend said. "We will be unable to use the space in its current state, so any time you need to visit the temple, feel free to link in." She passed Dex a small card, which was the representation of a direct link to the site. He accepted the card and added it to his file.

"I'll also want a list of the names of the members of your congregation," Dex said. "I may or may not need to speak to anyone, but if you could also mark the names of the leaders that you mentioned earlier, that would be very helpful."

The reverend frowned and shifted in her seat. "That may be more of a problem," she said. "Our faith may not be controversial, but being a member of a religious group of any kind can be, as I'm sure you know, something that a person may want to keep private."

"I can guarantee discretion," Dex said. "Both for the list itself and I also will endeavour to keep my enquiries circumspect, should I need to make any."

"I'll have to discuss it with the congregation," Alford said.

"Very well," Dex said. "You know how to get in touch with me." He stood and walked around the desk to the door. The reverend walked to the door and extended a slim hand. Dex took it and they shook perfunctorily. "I'll have something for you as soon as I can."

"Thank you again," Alford said. "I'll let you know about the list one way or another soon."

"Until then," Dex said and opened the door. Alford walked into the hallway and disappeared into a slight cloud of fog.

SEVEN

DEX MANAGED TO get a bite to eat before the squad meeting in M City. Now that he lived halfway across the world from the rest of the team, he appreciated the fact that the meetings were held online. When he'd been living in Namerica, though, it struck him as ridiculous. Particularly odd was the fact that until recently he had never met most of his colleagues in the physical world. He could have easily walked past any of them on the street and never recognized them.

He linked into the squad room a few minutes early. He waved to Jay Shiraishi, the new head of the goon squad. He had big shoes to fill after the retirement of Pat Malone, who had been the lieutenant in charge of the street team for as long as Dex could remember. Malone had been an institution on the squad and Shiraishi could never truly replace the man. However, Dex thought that the younger man was rising to the challenge surprisingly well and the transition had gone smoothly.

He found himself a seat near the back of the room and smiled as he felt Annabelle slip in next to him. The whole squad knew that the two were a couple, but after the years that Annabelle had chased Dex they were pleased that he'd finally accepted what they all saw as a foregone conclusion. Annabelle wasn't just a great cracker, she was as tenacious as any detective on the squad. Once she'd set her cap on Dex, the squad's numbers team had set low odds indeed on his being able to withstand her assault.

As the room filled, Dex noticed an enormous man trying to catch his eye. He waved the giant over and the man introduced himself.

"Hi," he said. "I'm Mack Larsen. M City squad lieutenant."

"Andersson Dexter, but you can call me Dex. What brings you our way?"

"You're running the Light of the Simulacrum case, right?" Larsen asked.

"Yup," Dex said.

"Captain Zhang asked me to sit in on the meeting," he said. "After all, it's sort of a joint case between my squad and hers."

"Is it?" Dex asked. Annabelle elbowed Dex hard in the ribs and gave him a pointed look.

"You know that I feel the M City squad ought to have its own detective division," Larsen said. "Until that happens, I'm not giving up all connections to a case that came from my community, from the streets my squad patrols. The LoS are my people, detective. I'm not just going to hand over their problems and forget about them."

"Fine," Dex said. "You're free to read the case file and I always keep them updated." He smiled, then turned back to Annabelle.

Larsen nodded and smiled broadly. "I will, don't you worry about that." He turned to walk away.

"You don't like him much," Annabelle said privately to Dex as they sat.

Dex shrugged. "It's nothing personal," he said. "I just don't need half a dozen eyes peeking over my shoulder. It's not my fault he's not a detective. He doesn't need to take his career frustrations out on me."

"All right, let's get on with it." Squad captain, Zahara Zhang, called out from her lectern at the front of the room. Everyone stopped talking and focussed their attention on her.

"Everyone say hello to Mack Larsen, the lieutenant from the M City squad." Larsen stood and waved at the crowd. "The lieutenant is liaising with us on Dex's new case. We'll get to that in a moment." She turned to Larsen and said, "Thank you, Mack." He sat and Dex rolled his eyes toward Annabelle.

"Liaising?" he whispered, incredulously.

"Shut up," Annabelle whispered back.

Next, Jay Shiraishi gave a brief run down on the week's activities on the street. It sounded like the usual mess, mainly keeping the peace among the folks who lived on the fringes of society — the people who didn't get housing with their jobs, if they're even employed. The fringe seemed to be increasing, as people like Dex and Stella Bish gave up jobs with the firms, so there were now whole classes of people who didn't fall into the neat categories that the firms envisioned.

There were the streeters, people living in abandoned old buildings, scavenging for food or eking out a living by selling scraps. Above them were the artists, writers, musicians and other people who eschewed regular employment. They still had a hard scrabble, but there were a few privately owned and operated apartment buildings and enough people who supported live entertainment to keep them with roofs over their heads and food bricks in their bellies.

And now there was a growing cohort of independents, people who were earning enough of a living from businesses in M City to pay for a decent apartment. Liberté, the complex where Dex lived, was one of a handful in Europa which catered to independent contractors. More were being built all the time to house the physical bodies of people who spent more and more of their time in M City. The Cubicle

Men's street teams were also growing to meet the increasing demand and Shiraishi took his time reviewing his team's recent activities.

After he was done, the captain asked for reports from the detectives. When it was his turn, Dex briefly described the vandalism at the Light of the Simulacrum Temple, then outlined the login issue that Stella Bish had reported.

"You think there's a connection?" asked the captain, knowing how Dex's mind worked.

"It's a possibility," he conceded. "Particularly concerning is a theory," he shot a glance at Annabelle, who nodded silently, "that Bish's issue isn't third party involvement at all."

"Explain," Captain Zhang demanded.

"It's my theory, sir," Annabelle spoke up. "It's possible that what Ms. Bish experienced was due to a serious, persistent malfunction in the everywherenet itself."

The technicians in the room exploded in talk, while most of the others looked on in confusion. "If this is a result of a massive bug," Annabelle explained, "then the whole system is at risk. Everything could just stop working, the same as it did for Ms. Bish."

Now there were gasps from all around the room. "It's just a theory for now," Dex said. "But it could explain the troubles at the LoS Temple as well."

"Hmm..." the captain thought. Facing Annabelle, she said, "Look into it. It's your top priority, Lewis. Larsen, can you have your people compile a list of any anomalies they've encountered recently?"

"Sure," Larsen said. "But there's been a rash of shakedowns among the business community lately. A lot of those ended up in vandalism, broken code and even lock outs. This is probably more of the same."

"Could be," Captain Zhang said, "still, it's a good idea to keep our eyes on it. Mack, can we set up a joint case file for information or observations on online anomalies?"

"I'll get it done right away," he said, "and shoot your group the link when it's up."

"Thank you," the captain said. "And everyone else, keep your eyes peeled in M City and elsewhere online. It's too early to start worrying about it, but if there is a problem here we need to be on top of it. If you spot anything, I want as much information as possible logged. Lewis," she faced Annabelle again, "keep on top of that file."

"Sir," Annabelle agreed.

"Okay," the captain said, effectively ending discussion on that topic. "Anything else before we adjourn to the bars?" The squad was silent and after a beat Captain Zhang said, "Very good. Same time next week people. Take care."

• • •

Dex and Annabelle joined the rest of the detective and technical group at Three Card Monte's, the usual meeting place for that bunch after squad meetings. The street team had their own hangout, a nearby dive called Sally's Slipper. The captain tended to leave each group to their own devices — she understood the need to bond without an authority figure hanging around to overhear the scuttlebutt. However, Dex had learned that she was a music buff and he often saw her at music events around M City. She was remarkably diligent in making it to Chemical Celeste's gigs.

The general chat after the meeting was about Dex's cases, specifically Annabelle's theory about the bug. "I realize that this is just a possibility," Ginger Ayala was saying, her glass of chilled white wine dripping on the wood grain of Monte's bar, "but if there's something wrong with the whole 'net, shouldn't we shift this issue over to the everywherenet consortium?"

"We can't go to the firms with a half baked story about a maybe-bug in their system," John Ochoa countered. "There's no love lost between them and us and if we start butting in on their turf, they could start making things very sticky for us."

"But they are the ones responsible," Ayala argued. "And they're the only ones who can fix it if it is a problem."

"Sure," Annabelle said, "but John's right. At least for now, it's just a possibility. Unless we have some real proof, the firms aren't going to do anything but get pissed off at us for poking around in their code. And, don't forget, there's plenty of stuff we do in there that they would be very unhappy about. If we tell them about this, we'll be giving up a lot of our secrets. It's just too soon, Ginger."

The small, wiry woman grunted unhappily, but stopped pushing her point. She drained her wine glass and a refill appeared quickly. She moved away from the bar and started talking to a couple of the other crackers on the team. "She's awfully quick to pass the buck," Ochoa said.

"It would be the right thing to do," Annabelle said, "if we were sure. But I'm not ready to risk it on a hunch. Which is all it is at the moment."

"I kind of wish I hadn't said anything," Dex said, dark and stormy in one hand, cigarette in the other. "Especially with that wannabe dick Larsen there, running his mouth off."

"Captain would have kicked your ass if you'd withheld," Ochoa said.

"True," Dex said, "but I can take it. My ass is industrial-strength." The three laughed and Annabelle reached out and goosed Dex. He yelped and she and Ochoa laughed harder.

"Apparently not, tough guy," Ochoa said, between guffaws.

"Very funny," Dex said. "I should sue for harassment or something."

"Good luck, pal," Ochoa said. "I should be so lucky to get that kind of harassment." He wandered off, still laughing and Dex and Annabelle moved over to one of Monte's private booths. They moved their conversation to a private channel as well, so as not to be interrupted or the victims of eavesdropping.

"I took a look at those scans Bish sent over," Annabelle said. "And?"

"There really doesn't seem to be anything wrong with her system," Annabelle continued, a fresh drink appearing in front of her. "The technician ran all the scans I would have and a few I hadn't even thought of yet. The hardware and wetware is working correctly. The tech tested each node offline and everything was kosher. Since we don't have any hard data on what happened while Bish was experiencing her online blackout, we don't have any information on the software or network end."

"Hmm..." Dex thought. "It seems interesting that she's had several experiences like this in a relatively short time. You think there's a strong likelihood that she'll have another?"

Annabelle looked up sharply and grinned. "Of course," she said. "We could fit her out with a monitoring program and hope to get some bytes as it happens." She leaned over the table and kissed Dex hard on the mouth. "You're a genius!"

"Thanks," he said. "I was just thinking out loud."

"Well, keep thinking," Annabelle said. "I'll gin up a monitoring script, something she can run entirely locally. And you should probably give her some kind of physical world access info, too, just in case the worst happens."

"Well, she already has my address," Dex said, grinning wryly. "She is my landlord, after all."

EIGHT

"ARE YOU SURE that this script is safe?" Stella Bish sat on Dex's client chair, wearing a gold trouser suit that hugged her impossible curves as tightly as a terrified four-year old hugged his teddy bear.

"My best programmer designed it specifically for your system," Dex assured her. He wanted to add, how safe does it need to be considering what you're trying to avoid. "I'm told it's safer than walking into your average bar or restaurant in M City."

"Well," Bish said, wrinkling her nose, "I don't know how much better that makes me feel." She took the small envelope from Dex, which was the manifestation of the program Annabelle had designed to monitor her activities online.

"If there are any things you don't want us to be able to see," Dex continued, "there's a force delete function. You'd need to use it after logging out of the 'net and if the script detects anything unusual in the login or out process, the delete function is disabled."

"Why is that?" Bish asked.

"We just want to be sure that whatever is happening to you when you're online isn't going to try and hijack the script to remove traces of itself," Dex said. "It is, as always, entirely up to you whether or not you share the data with us. The information the script collects can't be passed online without a full uninstall, which you have to do offline. You're in complete control, Ms. Bish," Dex reassured her.

"That is just how I like it," Bish said, her eyes lighting on Dex in a very uncomfortable manner. "Very well," she said, placing the envelope in her small clutch purse. "I will contact you immediately if anything untoward occurs." She stood and began to walk to the door.

"One more thing," Dex said, standing.

"Yes," Bish turned, taking a step closer to Dex so that her mouth was almost brushing against his cheek. Dex ignored it, as best he could.

"If the worst happens," he said, "and you can't get online at all, you can get a message to me through these people." He gave her a contact card for Gabriel Van Moore, the Guadalajara squad captain. "I'm told that Mr. Van Moore can usually be found at Emilio's Cantina most nights."

"Let's hope it doesn't come to that," she purred, then said, "thank you. I appreciate the forethought."

"Take care Ms. Bish," Dex said, stepping back to let her out the door. "Speak with you soon."

• • •

Dex wasn't entirely certain what it was about Stella Bish that made him feel like an adolescent. He was sure that it wasn't specifically for him that she turned on the charm — he'd seen her interact with other people and it was always the same. It was just how she operated; dripping sex appeal while taking care of her business interests with surgical precision. And none of that bothered Dex. He spent enough time in the seedy parts of M City to be immune to come ons of every imaginable kind and some that were quite unimaginable. And he had nothing against her business endeavours, either. In fact, if his skills were of a different sort, he'd be quite happy to work with Bish.

But there was definitely something about her that made him blush. He wasn't attracted to her, at least he didn't think he was. He certainly wasn't on the prowl and he couldn't imagine any woman turning his eye away from Annabelle. But every time he had to interact with Stella Bish, Dex felt like he had to take a cold shower after, both to clean off and cool off. It was disconcerting.

He spent a few minutes staring out the window in his office, enjoying the seemingly random images scroll past. Then he decided that he could just as easily look at the real thing and logged off. He sat in his chair and looked out the window of his apartment. He didn't have much of a view; he mostly looked at the wall of the south tower, but if he angled himself just right he could see down into the courtyard. The sun was low in the sky and the courtyard was buzzing with activity. He craned his neck and saw that several dozen people were mingling and chatting. He went online briefly and paged over to the private board for his building. He saw that a group of his neighbours had organized a get together.

What the hell, he thought. He wasn't planning on visiting the LoS Temple until later, because he wanted Annabelle to come with him and he'd have to wait until she got off work. He could afford to take off for a couple of hours now, he figured, and changed into going out clothes. He checked himself over in the mirror and decided that there was nothing too terrifying to be seen there and grabbed his mandolin.

He recognized a few of the other people at the party, having attended a couple of these mixers in the past. He headed straight for Zeke Torres, his next door neighbour. Zeke and Dex kept dissimilar hours, so they rarely saw one another, but they got on well. Zeke was a hot shot game designer, but in his off hours he played the theremin and it was the music which drew Dex to the man.

"Hey, Dex," Torres said, embracing Dex and favouring him with a double cheek kiss. The first time Torres had greeted Dex in this manner, he'd been at a loss as to how to react. Now he was used to Zeke's desire to make every physical world encounter particularly physical and he was beginning to appreciate the contact.

"Zeke," Dex said, "how are things going? I haven't seen you much lately."

"Big deadline on Zombie Lunch Hour," Zeke said, referring to the M City multiplayer game he was currently working on. "You'd be amazed at how complex rendering splatter pattern is. Visuals are okay, but it's creating the feel of the gore rainfall that's the tough part."

"Has anyone ever mentioned that you are a deeply disturbed individual?" Dex asked.

"Only you, buddy," Torres said and laughed. He looked down a the case at Dex's feet and asked, "So you came down to play?"

"I was hoping to get a jam going," Dex admitted. "If anyone's up for it."

"Always," Torres said. "Let's see if we can round up the usual suspects." He walked over to one of the benches and climbed on to the seat. "Oi!" he shouted. "Anyone up for playing a little music? Bring your instruments over here and we'll do it up. Thanks." He climbed down and grinned at Dex. "That ought to take care of it."

• • •

Four other people eventually joined Dex and Zeke and the six of them played for a couple of hours. The sun had been down for a while when Dex begged off from another song. "Sorry gang," he apologized. "I'm on Namerican time and I have to go back to work."

"What a shame," Noemi Petersen, the flautist, said. "We were just getting into it."

"Maybe next time," Dex said, closing the lid of his case and standing. "It was fun."

He walked back to the lobby of his tower, listening to the harmonies his neighbours were making out on the courtyard. He looked over shoulder, watching them play and laugh together. He wished he was staying, but knew that he still had work to do. As he spiralled up to the eleventh floor, he thought back to his life just a year previously — living in an anonymous corporately supplied apartment, with no friends in the physical world at all and only Annabelle online. He'd been alone for so long that it never even occurred to him that there was another way for him to live.

Now he could hardly imagine that his life had been so empty. As he walked into his apartment, he shook his head, marvelling at the changes his life had taken. He used the lav, washed his face and sat down. He had a couple of hours before he would meet Annabelle at the Light of the Simulacrum Temple and he logged into the Cubicle Men's system to check the case files. He found an urgent message waiting for him and followed the link it gave him. It was the file where people were reporting the strange occurrences they encountered online. It had some entries already. In fact, as Dex quickly paged through the file, he saw that it had an awful lot of entries.

• • •

"It seems like there are three main categories," Annabelle said. She was talking to Dex on a voice only channel, still at work but looking at the case file on the Cubicle Men's system. Theoretically, since she was inside her employer's firewall, she couldn't access anything outside of the firm's internal system. Practically, there was very little security that a programmer with Annabelle's skills couldn't defeat. Indeed, every member of the Cubicle Men had a small onboard program which allowed them to get out from any corporate firewall, leaving no traces. Most of Dex and Annabelle's colleagues held positions much lower on the food chain than Annabelle's lead programmer role. Most people kept corporate jobs for the easy access to housing and other benefits and there were some advantages to having people inside the firms. But for most of the detectives, technicians and street team, their jobs with the organization were much more important than their corporate positions.

Annabelle was an exception — she liked her job and if she'd had to choose between working for Omnitrack or for the Cubicle Men, it would be a terrible choice. However, she was talented enough to manage her duties in both posts. Dex often wondered what else she was doing while she was talking to him when she was still on the clock. He was sure she could easily manage two complex tasks at the same time, while he found it tricky enough to follow a map on his visual overlay and still walk in a straight line down the street.

"I've lumped the observations into three kinds," Annabelle went on. "I'm calling them *Image Distortions*, *Procedural Errors* and *Off Target Links*. There are a lot more of the first kind, but it's possible that it's just observational bias."

"In English, please," Dex requested.

"Sorry," Annabelle laughed. "There are a lot more reports of things looking wrong. This is the zone where an extortion ring would be operating, but it includes everything from obviously vandalized property to people reporting that they were sure their pet cat was blue yesterday and now it's purple."

"So you think there is some kind of organized extortion going on?"

She shrugged. "No way of knowing from these reports. These kinds of anomalies are more common just because they are the kinds of things that people notice and report. If your house is burned down, it's hard to ignore. Even the subtle stuff is the kind of thing people talk about, even if they don't really believe that anything's wrong."

"Okay," Dex said, "I can see that. So, what kind of stuff falls into the other categories?"

"I'm calling it a Procedural Error when a person just can't log on to the system. What happened to Stella Bish, for example. Or this one case of this guy who tried to link from one part of M City to another and nothing happened. He was still online, still in M City and able to access everything from his original space, but the link didn't work. These are events where it appears, to my mind, anyway, that the commands just aren't functioning. Which is subtly different from the user's perspective, but entirely different from a back end view, from the Off Target Link events."

"Let me guess," Dex said. "That's where I try to go to Monte's but end up in someone's back yard?"

"Bingo," Annabelle said. "Again, there aren't many of these reports in the bucket, but I suspect that it's because when it happens, you just assume you punched in the code wrong. It's hard to know how many of these there really are. And this is definitely not the work of some kind of shakedown crew. There's not much percentage in a threat that's so subtle you don't know if it's even real."

"Well, it seems to me there's a hell of a lot more going on than we guessed," Dex said, "even if we are managing to get every event reported."

"Absolutely," Annabelle said. "And there's no way we're even scratching the surface." There was silence for a moment, then she came back on the call. "I don't know what this is, Dex," she said, her voice hard, "but it's bad. Very, very bad."

NINE

DEX WAS STILL thinking about the worry in Annabelle's voice as he linked in to the ruins of the Light of the Simulacrum Temple. She wasn't a particularly nervous person; indeed she usually talked Dex out of the little panics he often got himself into. So, if she was worried, then he was worried. Very worried.

Dex found himself materializing in a large room that reminded him of some of the more progressive art galleries he'd visited in M City. Annabelle had dragged him to a couple of art shows the previous year and he surprised himself by finding contemporary virtual art quite compelling. The wreckage of the temple had such a familiar feel to it that Dex scanned his memory for the most recent shows he'd gone to see. He set his system to scan the images of the temple that Reverend Alford had supplied and look for any similarities among the work of the artists Dex had recently seen. It was a long shot, but Dex knew that it was often the strangest hunch that paid off in the end.

He was walking up to the steaming hot tub which was taking up most of the chancel and looked around the walls. High up near the vaulted ceiling were a series of ultra-realistic images of animal slaughter. It was disturbing, even to Dex, and he wondered if there was some message in the choice of imagery. Walking through the space had given him the strong impression that this was the calculated work of a person or group, rather than the random mutations of a program gone wrong. He wasn't sure if that made him feel better or worse.

He was studying the images when he felt Annabelle link in to the room. "Ugh," she said, following Dex's gaze to the images on the walls. "Can you believe that people used to eat that?" she pointed at one of the pictures. "It's enough to make you want to shuffle off the mortal coil entirely."

"Huh?" Dex grunted. "What are you talking about?"

"Oh, sorry," Annabelle said. "I wanted a stretch before I came over, so I went home first. On the way I was reading this paper about the possibility of installing human consciousness to the 'net. It's a still a ways off and with the stuff we're seeing right now, I sure wouldn't be an early adopter, but it was on my mind."

"Jesus," Dex said and Annabelle shushed him.

"We're in a church," she chided.

"It's not a Jesus church," Dex said. "And don't change the subject. Human consciousness online? You mean moving lock stock and barrel to M City?"

"It wouldn't have to be M City, necessarily," Annabelle said. "Actually, there would probably have to be a whole new construct built for us to live in, much more robust, I'd think..."

"But, you do mean dumping the physical body, right?" Dex asked.

"Yeah," Annabelle said. "No more dying. Or at least not permanently."

"That's insane," Dex exclaimed.

"Why?" Annabelle asked. "If we have the ability to live online, which in many ways we're doing just fine at the moment..." She took Dex's hand, squeezed and spun him around, "why should we be held hostage by inferior hardware? The body dies, there's no way around that as far as I know. But software can live a hell of a lot longer and that's really all our minds are."

"That's pretty heavy," Dex said, pulling his hand out of Annabelle's grip. "Too much for me right now." He took a step away from her and said, "Let's just see what we can figure out here, okay?"

"Sure," Annabelle said after a moment's pause. "Whatever you want."

• • •

They walked through the interior of the building, noting the areas where changes had been made. Annabelle paid particular attention to the spots between where there was new imagery and where the original building was still in evidence, taking samples of the actual code which rendered the images. "I'm hoping I'll be able to tell if this was done by a person or a program," she said, "once I get a good analysis of the code."

"You can tell that kind of thing?" Dex asked.

"Sure," Annabelle said. "People are logical in one way, machines are logical in another. And random bugs aren't logical at all. I hope there's enough here for me to get a handle on how this particular set of Image Distortions were made."

Dex left her to it and walked through the front door to look at the exterior. From the stock files of the original building that Reverend Alford had given him, Dex knew that the door was supposed to look like a hazy portal. It was round, with a blue, starry field in it. Walking though it mimicked a sensation of shooting through space at an extremely high velocity. Now, it appeared as nothing more than a hole in the wall, as ordinary as the door to Dex's own office.

The external face of the building had been completely redone, making it seem smaller and more boxy than the original design. Dex knew enough to know that each structure in M City could have any shape and the internal dimensions need not correlate to the outside shape. Separate fees were paid for the external space including easements which contained no resolution, the interior space for imagery and the interior capacity for individual accounts to view and interact with the space. Resolution spaces — those parts which looked like a physical structure, were most expensive, the outside coordinates more so than interior space.

The temple still owned the space the building occupied inside and out, the problem was rebuilding the structure itself. It would probably have to be done again and while they surely had access to the original plans, the code would have to be re-written and more expensively, re-rezzed into M City. The main reason that only a handful of people owned virtual property of their own was the cost to instantiate the imagery. Dex wondered if the church would be able to afford the repairs.

He had to admit that the building looked pretty terrible from the outside. Even if it were just a shop, he could imagine its owners being distraught over the changes. Considering that it was a weird sect that seemed to worship virtuality... he felt pretty bad for them.

Annabelle came out of the interior and looked over the façade. "This is pretty awful," she said.

"Agreed," Dex said, then paused a moment. "I don't want to influence your analysis of the code," he began, "but does this remind you of anything?"

"Like what?" Annabelle asked, taking a step back and cocking her head.

"Never mind," Dex said. "It's a cockamamie theory and I don't want to give you any ideas. If anything comes of it I'll let you know."

"Hmm..." Annabelle grunted. "Now I'm really intrigued. But I can be patient." She took one last look at the building, then turned to Dex. "I want to get a head start on looking at this code," she said, "and I have a feeling that Zizou is going to have me pretty busy on those anomalies soon."

"I don't doubt it," Dex said and moved a step closer. "Hopefully we can find an hour or two to get away from it all again soon," he grinned at her and felt her come into his arms.

"That would be nice," she said, as she snuggled into his chest. She looked up at him and they kissed, long and slowly. "I better go," she whispered.

"Yup, you'd better," Dex growled. "I love you, kiddo."

"You, too," she answered and disappeared.

• • •

Dex linked out of M City and saw the beginnings of a sunrise peeking though his window. He stretched and decided that a walk would do him good. He left his apartment and passed the morning Yuprazhnÿei practitioners twisting themselves into pretzels. It looked uncomfortable, but they all seemed to be enjoying themselves. Takes all kinds, thought Dex.

He walked down to the waterfront and looked out at the sea. He'd lived on the coast before, but he didn't think he'd ever been to the seashore until he came to Nice. He squinted against the rising sun, which glinted off the blue ocean. It reminded him of the shared dream he had with Annabelle the other night. He wondered why they felt they had to purchase a virtual package to experience the ocean, when it was right here all along. It made him think about what Annabelle was talking about while they were at the temple.

Even if she couldn't admit it yet, Dex knew that if there was a safe way to move her entire life to the virtual world, Annabelle would take that option. She tolerated the physical world better now than she had ever before, but it was still a challenge for her to interact with people. She was strong and confident, completely in her element in M City, but it was a different story in the physical world. Dex was grateful for the few moments of her time he got with her outside the virtual world.

He wondered if he would be willing to give it all up, the physicality he still believed was the only real reality, in order to be with her. He watched a tour boat bob in the distance and hoped that it would be a long time before he had to make that decision. He stared off into the endless blue for a few more moments, then turned to head back toward downtown.

He stopped in at Le Rétro, ordering a small hot cocoa, with a shot of liqueur. He was sipping the frothy drink when he felt a hand on his shoulder. He looked up and back into the round face of René Biagini.

"What are you doing out at this ungodly time of day?" the short man asked, his glossy moustache curled up from his grin.

"Just having a little nightcap," Dex said. "Spending my clients' exorbitant fees." Biagini laughed aloud.

"Business is good, then?" he asked, slipping into the seat opposite Dex.

"I've picked up another case since last we spoke," Dex said. "More weird things happening in M City. Maybe it's sabotage, maybe it's vandalism. Maybe something else. It's hard to tell at this stage."

"Vandalism, you say?" Biagini said, frowning. "Is this turning into a real issue?"

"Maybe," Dex said. "Maybe not. You got a request from Zizou to keep an eye out?"

"If I remember rightly it was a joint request from Larsen on the M City squad and your captain Zhang," Biagini said, arching an eyebrow.

"Details," Dex said. "Are your people seeing anything interesting here?"

"Now that we're looking for it," Biagini said, "our contacts in M City are seeing things all over the place. It's not just us noticing, either."

"Oh?" Dex queried.

"I spent a little time trolling over some popular boards," Biagini said. "The things we do in a day's work, eh, my friend." A server appeared with a steaming coffee, which was placed before Biagini. He took a sip and literally smacked his lips. Before he met René Biagini, Dex had always assumed that it was just a phrase. Now he saw it enacted in reality most weeks.

"And," Dex prompted. "What are the masses talking about?"

"Mostly," Biagini said, "you don't want to know. But they are also talking about things being wrecked online. Mostly it's small stuff, but a handful of online retailers have had their storefronts busted, just like that friend of mine I was telling you about. Seems like he got off pretty easy."

"How so?"

"A couple of the worst cases forced the shopkeepers to close down for a while to get things back on track," Biagini said. "Some folks were offline for days getting their places fixed." He took another sip of coffee. "There are accusations being thrown around already."

"A protection racket?"

Biagini shook his head. "No one knows anyone who's actually been hit up for cash. It doesn't mean it's not happening, but the talk on the boards is heading in a different direction."

"Anything look interesting?"

Biagini looked at Dex and nodded slowly. "There's some strong feelings about some of those groups, you know the ones. They like to go offline for a few days a month, or they don't ever socialize in M City. There are a few outspoken nuts, who claim that the virtual world is ruining society. The consensus, in as much as there is ever a consensus on those boards, is that it's probably someone like that."

Dex thought for a moment. "It must be someone with pretty good skills," he said. "A programmer who's anti-technology? That's a bit odd."

"True," Biagini said, "but it takes all kinds."

"Indeed," Dex said, remembering the ideas shared by some of the people he'd met when he first encountered Stella Bish. "Maybe it's not as farfetched as it sounds."

"Very little is, my friend," Biagini said. "Truth is stranger, after all."

"Stranger than what?" Dex asked.

"Everything else," Biagini said, laughing.

TEN

IT WAS MORNING in Guadalajara when Dex sent the message to Stella Bish. He didn't expect to hear from her immediately and he got what he expected. He'd mentioned in his message that he'd be available in his office all day, so he settled in to review the notes he'd made and to think. There was nothing new from Annabelle in any of the case files, so Dex knew that she hadn't finished her analysis. She was as fastidious as he was about updating files, but she preferred to leave her hunches out of the official record. Dex was actually a little surprised that she'd spoken up at the squad meeting, though that was probably his fault for bringing it up. Regardless, his system would ping him when she updated the files and he wouldn't have anything from her before that.

He opened up the search results from the scan his system had done on similarities between the scene at the Light of the Simulacrum Temple and the contemporary art installations he and Annabelle had attended. Machines were not terribly great at comparing images, so there were several matches that Dex discarded immediately. He could see how the scan picked them — a similarity in colour schemes, perhaps, or the objects making similar shapes on a large scale. But the human eye immediately could tell that there was no true relationship between many of the examples the system scan had found and the LoS site.

However, there was one installation which caught his eye. It was set in a private library and the artist had retextured all the books as body parts. From a distance it looked almost normal, but up close you could see the arms, legs and navels instead of texts. What really made Dex look closely was that the place that should have held the administration counter had been replaced by a giant recliner couch. It was the kind of thing that certain nightclubs might place in dark corners, for groups of people to lie about and frolic upon.

Dex wasn't sure exactly what it was that reminded him of the LoS Temple, but he looked up the artist. Fredric Ahmad was well known in the contemporary virtual art scene, having been commissioned for a number of large scale installations by some of the best known galleries. His bio was the usual purple prose gushing about his unique creative vision, but in between the public relations hyperbole Dex learned a few things. Ahmad was a follower of the mysteriously named Open Gateway school, which focussed on public virtual spaces as their canvasses. Many of the early OG artists practiced their craft on spaces that they neither owned nor had permission to use. Ahmad didn't seem to ever have gone that route, but Dex wondered if perhaps the man wasn't expanding his own creative vision back to the roots of the artistic movement which nurtured his style.

He also wondered if he wasn't grasping at straws. Artists tend to sign their work, especially celebrity artists like Ahmad. What's the point of creating something if no one knows it's you who did it? Dex shook his head. That was the key to the whole LoS problem. If it was a personal attack on the congregation, shouldn't there be some clear statement? Some obvious graffiti decrying their beliefs as heretical or the group itself as a cult? If it were meant to send a message, where was the message?

Which brought Dex back to Annabelle's random bug theory. Dex was disinclined to ascribe to randomness what could more easily be pinned on one or two anti-social humans, but in the absence of any reason for the attacks he had little to go on. He stood and stared out his false window, watching people walking on the sidewalk below. A young man wearing a tight sparkly tee shirt and walking a small gold and blue dog caught his eye and winked at him. Dex almost returned the gesture, then remembered that everything he was watching was a simulation.

He turned his back on the interactive show, just in time to see a shadow stop on the other side of his door. Dex saw a hand come up and lightly rap on the glass of his window. His system informed him that it was Stella Bish and he said, "Come in."

She opened the door and Dex could see that she was unimpressed with something. From the way she glared at him, he guessed that whatever it was that left a bad taste in her mouth originated with him.

• • •

"What do you want?" she demanded, having refused his offer of the hard chair.

"Excuse me?" Dex asked, settling himself into the plush office chair on his side of the desk.

"Your message," she barked. "I hired you to find out what is causing these inconvenient episodes," she said, "not to have you inconvenience me more." Dex raised an eyebrow and Bish deflated slightly. She sat in the chair and put her small handbag in her lap.

"First, have you had any more of those inconvenient episodes," he asked, "excepting, of course, any that I have caused?"

She smiled slightly, but otherwise ignored Dex's sarcasm. "Everything has been normal in the last few days," she said. "I will inform you immediately if anything does occur." She lowered her eyelids and her voice. "I promise."

"Good," Dex said. "Now, the main reason I called is a bit more, shall we say, delicate."

"Oh," Bish said, warming slightly, "that sounds interesting."

"I doubt you'll think so in a few minutes," Dex said, then hurriedly carried on. "I have to ask about the little group you organized. The Offline Cleanse, I think you called it."

Bish frowned. "What about it?" she asked. "If you're looking for a local chapter meeting, we have a public board."

"I'm afraid that's not it," Dex said. "Our preliminary investigation is leading us to believe that your strange experiences online aren't unique. In fact, incidences of vandalism and other problems with the system are up several percent across the 'net. We are following several different lines of inquiry, but one that has already come up in the popular media is that it's a member of some group who is critical of virtual living."

Dex waited for the penny to drop and didn't have to wait long before Bish shot out of her seat and planted both hands on his desk. Her face a scant few centimetres from his, she said in a quiet rage, "You can't be saying what I think you're saying. That someone who is involved in my program is responsible for what is happening to me? That's ridiculous."

"Perhaps," Dex said, calmly. "But perhaps not. I thought you should be aware of what people are saying and also to keep it in the back of your mind. As the creator of the Offline Cleanse, people might be more inclined to speak to you about their more outlandish ideas. At your monthly meetings, perhaps, when you've all logged off for your time away from the 'nets, maybe someone mentions something they've heard about, or maybe there's a rumour of some programmer with a way to show the rest of us the light. It's not unheard of and I know that your group has more than its fair share of people who have the skills to pull this sort of thing off."

Bish sat back and thought. Dex knew that, emotional as she could appear, Bish was smart enough to recognize what he was saying could be the case. Finally, she nodded once. "It's not impossible," she admitted. "Though it seems unlikely that someone who follows my ideas would target me."

"Maybe," Dex said. "Or maybe they feel like your successful online business is a bit hypocritical for someone who espouses living more in the physical world." He anticipated another outburst, but instead Bish merely smiled again.

"Touché, Mr. Dexter," she said. "I don't want to believe that, of course, but it has a certain logic." She stood and took her purse off the edge of Dex's desk. "I don't think anything will come of it, but I'll keep my ears open." She turned and walked to the door. "And I will be certain to let you know if I hear anything. So, unless you have something definite to tell me, perhaps be patient enough to let me call you this time, Mr. Dexter."

She didn't wait for a response before winking out of Dex's office like a light going out.

• • •

Dex was walking through the Pietonne, twilight turning the windows of the bars, cafés and restaurants a particular gold colour he found strangely soothing. He'd spent the afternoon paging through a few of the local boards, looking for possible hangouts for people who were disenchanted with online living. He didn't expect to stumble across the vandals; real life was never that easy. He just wanted to get a feel for whether or not there was enough animosity or energy to support someone spending the time and effort to put forward a campaign like he was seeing.

He also just wanted to get out of the apartment for a while. Annabelle would still be at work for another few hours and he'd just seen René the previous day. So he walked through the commercial district, trying to find a coffee house called Antoine's.

The place wasn't very big and there weren't too many patrons even though it was one of the busiest times in this neighbourhood. Dex was reminded a bit of the bar he'd visited in Guadalajara, *Robustezas Libres*. He wondered if these people were followers of Stella Bish's Offline Cleanse program as well. Dex had rather a lot of sympathy with the idea that people take a specific amount of time to get away from the virtual world and actually do things with other people here in the physical world. He was neither a joiner nor a follower, though and he would rather spend his offline time playing his mandolin in a tiny dive or drinking the rotgut rum served up at Le Rétro than talking about how much better it is to live offline than on.

Even so, the small group at Antoine's was welcoming, most of the people being strangers to one another. A small man who had the odd affectation of wearing wire rimmed spectacles stood after about a half dozen people had gathered around the small table decorated by a holosign depicting a bushy tree. "Hi, everyone," he said in a quiet but powerful voice. "I'm Homer Valencia and I'm glad to see you all here. It's good to see a few friendly faces who came down to spend some quality time in the real world."

"Thanks for organizing this," the woman who was sitting next to Dex said. "I've been wanting to meet some people for a long time, but it's hard to do if you don't already have a scene, you know?"

"Exactly," Valencia said, smiling. "So, I don't have a particular program set out for today. I was hoping we could just let things evolve organically." Dex stole a glance around the table to see if anyone else found this guy a little much. Either he was alone in his opinion or everyone else was good at hiding their amusement. Valencia continued, "So, why don't we all just get a drink or something and we'll see where things go. You know, just communicate with each other for a while, really be present together." He smiled at the group again, then busied himself with the tabletop menu system.

Dex turned to the woman beside him who had spoken up and broke the ice. "So," he began, "you've been trying to meet people. Are you new in town?" He realized that he sounded like a has-been pick up artist, but she didn't seem to mind.

"I am, actually," she said. "I lived in Paris until about six months ago. I just wanted to get out of the big city, maybe try and find a community out here in the world. It's been tough, though."

Dex nodded. "I just moved here a year ago," he said. "Nice has a lot more happening on the street than my old hometown, but if you're on your own it can be hard to meet people. No one at your job wanted to spend time in their off hours?"

"No," she said, a small frown creasing her otherwise unlined face. "They're all M City citizens." She made air quotes around the word 'citizens' and Dex detected a trace of disgust in her voice.

"Lots of folks are," he said, diplomatically.

She snorted. "Those poor people," she said. "What do they think they're doing in there? Sitting alone in their apartments, playing at life in a simulation. It's sad, really."

"Some people would say it's just another way to communicate," Dex said.

"Please," the woman retorted. "It's no substitute for real life, it's just another way to isolate yourself. Can't they see that they're just making things worse for themselves in the long run? It's not like you can have a real relationship online, you don't even really know who you're talking to." She took a sip of her foamy drink. "They're all just going to end up alone."

Dex didn't know what to say to that, after all it wasn't as if she had any idea who he was, but she was happily chatting away. He just made some kind of noise that he hoped sounded vaguely positive.

"You know what someone ought to do?" she continued.

"What?" Dex asked.

"Blow the whole damn thing up," she said, venomously. "Then everyone would be forced back to the real world. It would do them all good."

ELEVEN

DEX NEVER LEARNED the name of the woman at the café, but that didn't bother him. She held strong opinions, all right, and maybe would even act on them given the opportunity, but after another half hour of conversation it became obvious that she didn't have the ability to do any of the things she advocated. The rest of the conversation was mostly more of the same, but Dex found it almost amusing. And it proved that even if this particular person wasn't a real threat, the ideas were out there.

On his way back to his apartment, his system pinged him with a call from Annabelle. "Can we meet tonight?" she asked. "I've looked over the reports from Larsen's case file, including some of the new entries."

"And?" Dex asked.

"It's kind of confusing," Annabelle said. "Let's get together and I'll tell you all about it."

"Sure," Dex said. "Shall we say Monte's?"

"Sounds good," Annabelle answered. "I'll link in as soon as my shift here is over. And maybe after we can go over to that hole in the wall you and René Biagini seem to like so much."

Dex grinned widely to himself and for a brief moment wondered how funny he looked walking down the street, alone, smiling like a madman. "Sounds wonderful," he said.

"Now you'd better get back to work, or millions of people might have to wait an extra thirty seconds for their train."

"Oh, shut up, you," Annabelle laughed. "See you tonight."

• • •

Dex spent a couple of hours in his apartment paging around several different boards — he'd poke around one for a while, see a post that gave a link to another board, page over there for a while and repeat. He ended up wasting the afternoon following the link trails and getting no real clues. No one was talking about perpetrating the specific kind of mayhem that he was seeing in M City, but there was plenty of disturbing talk. He flagged the more overtly antagonistic posts to the general enquiry case file, wondering if anyone anywhere was monitoring these boards.

He then started to think about the feeling he'd had at the Light of the Simulacrum Temple, how it reminded him of an art installation. He wondered if there was anyone he could talk to who knew more than him, someone in the industry. He looked through his video files, trying to find a record of one of the galleries he'd gone to with Annabelle. Eventually, he remembered that he and Annabelle had gone to see a show at the Looking Through Doors and Windows Gallery a few months previously and had met the curator briefly. He couldn't remember the woman's name, but he must have liked what he'd seen that day, because the video record was still in his files. He paged over to his viewer and loaded the file.

• • •

The space was, as most M City locations were constructed, much larger on the inside than on the outside. In this case, the small storefront opened into a single almost cavernous white room, with only a small table near the door. The curator had installed herself at the table, greeting the visitors and offering audio or text overlay didactic narratives to accompany the work. Dex had taken the audio file, not wanting to pollute his visual space with the floating text.

It was an installation of work from several new artists, who Dex's audio tutor explained were exploring post-humanist trans-spacial themes. He hadn't known what that meant at the time and didn't have any more of an idea now, but he did know that some of the pieces were very interesting. When the curator turned on the piece from the first artist, nothing seemed to happen. However, as Dex and Annabelle had walked through the space, imagery would become instantiated in the places they visited, but only once they had moved on. There were almost invisible footprints which followed their movements and strange, almost cartoonish images of speed lines or ghostly figures. The whole experience was quite odd, as if Dex and Annabelle were the tools of the artist and created the show themselves.

The next piece was more conventional, at least in that when it was instantiated, the gallery space was instantly transformed into the installation. It was a representation of space, as seen from the perspective of a craft hurtling through a solar system. As each planet or asteroid was approached, a loud warning bleeping noise would occur and a garish advert would cover the simulated viewscreen. Dex didn't like it as much and they quickly moved on to the next one.

Dex watched the rest of his video memory and smiled at the reminiscence of a very nice time out with Annabelle. He brought himself back to the task at hand and reversed the file back to the beginning and had the video focus on only the sections containing the curator. Dex and Annabelle really had very little interaction with the woman, tending to talk on a private channel with each other rather than on the public gallery feed. Dex watched her response to their reactions to the pieces, though, and saw that she, too, seemed to be more impressed with the first artwork. He could see her appraising look on all the pieces as they'd toured the gallery and he wondered about her.

He sent a message through the contact link for the gallery, hoping that the curator would get back to him. He could use a professional opinion. He closed out the video record and not for the first time was thankful for his expensive habit of recording his life.

He occasionally considered junking his old vids of his ancient musical career. He used to play in a small bar band, back before the Cubicle Men days. He fancied himself a real rebel: holding no job, making do on tips and scrounging. He used to think that those were the best days of his life, that everything else was downhill from there. Now, he knew that he had recaptured a lot of what had made those days special — the joy of the music, the sense of freedom, the connection with his friends. If he lost those old vids, he guessed that could free up enough space to possibly make a play in the hosting space for M City, which could be quite lucrative.

Unlike the everywherenet backbone, space in M City wasn't regulated by a single consortium of the firms. Rather, the memory that was needed to run it was distributed among hundreds of thousands of different nodes. Dex believed that divisions of a couple of the smaller firms were responsible for supplying a good amount of the space, but a large amount of it was actually run by individuals or independent groups. Dex had often thought that if his cash flow became tight, he could rent out some of his own onboard disk space for rendering in M City. If he were more ruthless in terms of the files he kept, he could easily host his own office, as well as up to a couple more similar spaces. It would easily double his net take home pay, but he still wasn't quite ready to give up the memories.

He might only rarely watch the vids, but he liked the way he felt knowing that they were there.

• • •

A half hour before he was scheduled to meet Annabelle, Dex ate a food brick and poured a small tumbler of Caña rum, the expensive liquor made from real sugar cane that he treated himself to when he had some spare cash. When things were really flush, he also bought real ginger beer from a woman in the south tower at Liberté who brewed her own. He wasn't that well off now, though, so it was just rum and water. Compared to the synthetic Jamaica's Best he used to drink, it was almost a shame to add another flavour anyway.

He was settled comfortably in his chair, drink close at hand, when he linked into Monte's. Annabelle was already there, her own pink concoction sweating on the table in front of her. Dex walked over to her table and she slipped out of the seat to give him a hug. He kissed her long and then sat down across from her.

"Sorry about yesterday," he said. "I didn't mean to go off on you like that about the uploading. I just wasn't ready for that conversation right then."

"It's okay," Annabelle said. "I shouldn't have sprung it on you like that. Amazingly, I still sometimes forget that you're not exactly like me." She grinned and Dex laughed.

"How you could ever forget that, I'll never know," he said. "We're like the dictionary example of opposites attracting."

"Only sometimes, honey," Annabelle said. "Sometimes we're so alike it's scary."

"Like when?" Dex asked, genuinely curious.

"Like now," Annabelle said. "You really think most people want to spend a night out with their sweetheart talking shop?"

Dex thought for a moment, then laughed. "I guess not," he said. "Maybe we are well suited after all. Okay then, let's get down to business."

"You sweet talker, you," Annabelle said. "So, the sort of good news is that I'm pretty certain that the Simulacrum Temple was done by a human operator."

"Okay," Dex said. "And that's good news because a bug would be way worse than a person, right?"

"Bingo," Annabelle said. "And also because it means we might actually be able to identify the jerk and maybe even get some compensation for the Temple."

"All right," Dex said. "So, what's the confusing part?"

"Well, I was operating under the assumption that what happened with Stella Bish, the Simulacrum people and the rest of the anomalies were all the result of a common cause."

"And they aren't," Dex guessed. Annabelle shook her head.

"There's no data for Bish's experiences, so I can't determine anything about that," she said. "But the other events that have been reported show entirely different results." She took a sip of her drink, then went on. "I got copies of code from similar scenes around M City — those Image Distortions I was telling you about." Dex nodded. "And what's confusing me is that they all shared some similarities. All except the code from the Light of the Simulacrum."

"Huh," Dex grunted. "You're right, that is confusing. Is there something special about the original objects at the Temple that might account for the differences?"

Annabelle shook her head. "It's not the original code that shows the similarities," she explained. "In the intersection between the original imagery and the distorted objects there are a few lines of code that are very similar in all the cases I looked at from the file. Everything is pretty fucked up of course and I can't quite make out what it's trying to execute.

From what I can tell it's some kind of a timer, but that's just guesswork."

"A timer," Dex repeated, mulling over the information Annabelle had given him. Annabelle nodded and Dex noticed a small smile begin to creep over her face. "So, if these events are timed," Dex mused aloud, "then it follows that they are deliberate acts. Which means that some intelligent agent is probably responsible."

"Bingo, again. Give the pretty fella a prize," Annabelle said, the smile fully blossoming. "I'd bet the farm that we have human perpetrators and at least two completely separate sets."

"Now that is why we keep you around," Dex said, grinning. "But I have to ask one thing."

"What's that?"

"The farm?" Dex questioned, raising an eyebrow. "Even if you had a farm, would you care if you lost it?"

"I might like a farm," Annabelle answered, mock indignation in her face. "Why not? I could see myself on a farm, maybe."

"Right," Dex laughed. "I can just see you, elbow deep in a mount of dirt, pulling some vegetable out of the ground."

Annabelle wrinkled her nose. "Now you're just being disgusting."

• • •

As Annabelle was finishing her drink, she looked at Dex and smiled. "Why don't we blow this joint?" she said. "I've been home for a bit, eaten something and I could stand to get out and stretch my legs a little."

"Le Rétro?" Dex asked.

"Why not?" Annabelle suggested. "It's pretty quiet at this time of night, isn't it?"

"Sure," Dex said. "The rowdies never last long at The Ret. They usually clear out by midnight local, so by now it should just be the real nighthawks."

"And the other timeshifters," Annabelle pointed out.

"Right," Dex agreed. "Sounds like a good plan to me. I'll pick you up at your place in, say, twenty minutes?"

"I'll be ready," Annabelle said and linked out of Monte's.

• • •

Dex waved his chipped hand over the reader on the gleaming stainless door of Annabelle's apartment. Almost immediately, the door slid open and Annabelle's voice sounded in his head through his onboard system while simultaneously Dex could hear her call out, "Come in." She was walking out of the lav while wanding her hair as Dex stepped into her large sitting room.

"You look great," he said, eying her oddly familiar-looking diaphanous yellow dress. "What's the occasion?"

"What do mean?" she said, giving him a dirty look. "You're saying I usually look like meatloaf?"

"Come on," Dex said, then Annabelle laughed.

"I'm just playing with you," she said. "I found this cute little shop that specializes in online/offline reproductions. I really liked this dress and figured it was about time I got a new outfit for out here. Since I'm actually going places where I can be seen in them."

"Well," Dex said. "It's a winner in my books. Let's go show it off a little." He took her arm and they walked to the local train stop. After a short ride they were easing into a booth in Le Rétro.

As Dex had predicted, the café and bar was quiet. There were about a dozen or more patrons in groups of two or three, but there were plenty of seats and the atmosphere was casual. A server came over to their table quickly and Dex ordered his usual rum and ginger.

"And for the lady?" the waiter asked.

"How's your bubbly water?" Annabelle asked.

"Wet and fizzy," the server answered, deadpan.

"I'll take it," Annabelle said and turned on a thousand watt smile for the server. She got a tired but genuine smile in return before the waiter walked back to the bar.

"This is a tough shift," Annabelle said.

"I think it's one of those jobs where being run off your feet is better than a slow day," Dex said. "The time goes by a little faster."

Annabelle nodded and the server returned with their drinks. Dex lifted his glass to Annabelle and said, "Here's to all your tedious checking and rechecking and the first real lead we've had in this thing."

Annabelle toasted Dex, but shook her head. "It's all just hard work, Dex. You know that. Every case is about plugging away at the puzzle until it has no choice but to unravel. I'm just glad I can be helpful."

Dex grinned. "Now that's a real stumper," he said, his eyes twinkling. "What kind of puzzle unravels? A knitted one? And how do you plug at knitting?"

"You know what I meant," Annabelle protested and Dex laughed.

"Of course," he said. "It's just that that was one of the worst mixed metaphors I've ever heard. And you should hear René Biagini after he's had a bottle of synth-wine."

"Maybe I should, at that," Annabelle said, though her voice sounded less sure than her words. "The three of us could go out sometime, I suppose."

"That would be a hoot," Dex said. "But it wouldn't be three — that man has new human arm jewelry every time I talk to him."

"More's a party," Annabelle said, sounding less sure about the whole idea. "Maybe next month sometime."

They stayed at the bar for a couple of hours, Dex putting away another cheap dark and stormy, Annabelle sticking to the wet and fizzy. Dex knew that she was probably using some kind of online stim — he didn't begrudge her choice of poison, he simply didn't share it. The sun was peeking up over the horizon when they settled their tab and Annabelle took Dex's arm as they walked to the train stop.

"We've got a gig at Fred's in a couple of days," Dex was saying as they waited for the train. "I was hoping I'd see you there."

"I wouldn't miss it," Annabelle said. "But, you'll be seeing plenty of me before then. If you want to, of course." She looked up at him with a sly look on her face.

"Oh, really?" Dex asked, slipping his arm around her shoulder. The train pulled into the stop and Annabelle put her arm around Dex's waist. She stepped on to the train and pulled him along with her.

"Come on," she said as the door shut behind them. "I'm just about ready for bed. Aren't you?"

TWELVE

IT WAS ALREADY late afternoon when Dex woke and he had a slight moment of panic when he rolled over and saw Annabelle's sleeping face scrunched into the pillow next to him. Then he remembered that her weekend was just starting and she could sleep as long as she liked. He slipped quietly out of the bed and made his way as softly as he could to the lav. He was hoping to let her rest as long as he could.

She woke about a half hour later and Dex smiled over the lip of the mug of coffee he'd made himself. "Morning, gorgeous," he said, as she blinked the sleep out of her eyes.

"Did I ever sleep in," she said. "Why didn't you get me up?"

"Why should I?" Dex asked. "There's nowhere you need to be and it's not like I get to watch you sleep every day." He grinned at her and she dropped her eyelids bashfully.

"I have to pick a guy with a drool fixation," she said, swinging her legs over the side of the bed. "What next? You'll want to watch me cut my nails?"

"Not now," Dex said. "I can't handle that kind of excitement this early." Annabelle laughed as she walked into the lav and Dex busied himself by making her a small pot of tea.

They were sitting on her small sofa, looking out the window and chatting when both of their systems pinged simultaneously. They shared a glance at each other, then each accessed their messengers. "Stella Bish," Dex said.

"And it looks like she's gotten into a real spot of bother this time," Annabelle said, reading the note from Captain Van Moore of the Guadalajara squad. "She's still offline now," Annabelle said. "This must be killing her business."

"It can't be good for it," Dex agreed. "Not to mention how disturbing it would be to be cut off from all communications — I don't envy her, that's for sure."

"It's kind of ironic, though, don't you think?" Annabelle said.

"What is?" Dex asked, patching a video channel through to Gabriel Van Moore.

"Bish being forced off the 'nets," Annabelle said. "After all the noise she's made about how people should spend more time offline, isn't it funny that now she's getting to spend all the time in the world out here."

"I guess," Dex said. "This isn't what she had in mind, you know."

"I know," Annabelle said. "It just kind of makes me laugh."

"I know you don't like her very much," Dex said.

"Last I heard," Annabelle countered, "you didn't, either."

"She's not my favourite person," Dex said. "But she doesn't deserve this." Annabelle nodded, then jumped in as a silent observer to the video call.

• • •

"Captain Van Moore," Dex said, as the face of the Guadalajara captain appeared on his screen. The man looked young, the unnatural youth that everyone over age fifty enjoyed, the same strange stunted maturity that he, Annabelle and just about everyone else he knew shared. Van Moore was as ordinary-looking as anyone, including the small, blonde woman sitting on his right. But Dex knew that she was no ordinary person, rather that she was physical embodiment of the online mogul, Stella Bish.

"Lieutenant Dexter," Van Moore answered. "I'm glad I was able to connect with you so quickly. Ms. Bish is, understandably, very concerned."

"Yes," Dex said, "Stella, are you all right?"

Bish looked toward the tiny lens Van Moore had set into the opposite wall and said in a small voice, "Yes, I'm fine for the moment. But I hope very much that this does not last long. I've just learned that the Sunera Group is trying to poach two of my best designers away from me — they claim to be opening a dress shop in M City, if you can believe it. This is very inconvenient timing."

"Have you been able to contact any of your technicians?" Dex asked.

Bish shook her head. "I know a few freelancers here," she said. "But no one I trust with something like this."

"I have a colleague on the call with us who may be able to help," Dex said, looking over at Annabelle in her apartment. She nodded slightly and he continued. "Annabelle Lewis. She may be able to help from here."

Bish looked at Van Moore, who said, "Lewis is possibly the best cracker and technician we have in the whole organization, Ms. Bish. You couldn't be in better hands."

Bish didn't look entirely convinced, but she also must have realized that she had little choice. "Okay," she said. "What do I have to do?"

• • •

They spent over two hours on the call, Annabelle having Bish try several times to log in to the 'nets. Finally, they resorted to an assisted remote diagnostic — Annabelle would tell Van Moore what to do and he'd tell her what happened. Dex didn't understand a tenth of what they were talking about, so he busied himself by getting Annabelle more tea and the occasional bit of a food brick. Eventually, Annabelle shook her head.

"There's nothing wrong with your system," she diagnosed. "It looks like your biometric token has somehow been revoked. I'm not even sure how that could happen."

"Very well," Bish said, "but what do I do now?"

"First," Annabelle said, "I'll get the captain to access the monitoring file we gave you. Feel free to delete anything sensitive that you don't want us to see." She explained what to do and a few minutes later she'd received a copy of the file's data.

"Now what?" Bish asked.

"I'll have to go over that very carefully and see if we can reverse whatever has happened. In the meantime, I can gin up a reasonably good copy of your account from file records and such. It will technically be a multi, but it should fool most everyone, especially since you'll control it. You'll have trouble accessing some banking and other highly secure files, but if we can't get your regular access back, in time we can break the chain on the rest of it. Obviously," Annabelle continued, "we don't want to crack into your regular accounts any more than is required, so if it can wait I'd like to try to fix the problem first."

"Fine," Bish said. "How long with it take for this new login?"

"I'll send the package to Captain Van Moore as soon as it's ready," Annabelle said. "But it will likely take a day. I'd like to go over Reuben Cobalt's old method and use that if I can, but even so it takes time to mimic a well used legitimate account."

"I think I can manage another day," Bish said. "I've managed to get word to a few aides through the captain here," she finally turned on one of her trademark smiles and beamed it at Van Moore, "and they can keep things afloat for a little while."

"I'll try to have it for you tomorrow," Annabelle said, then paged out of the call.

"Thanks for your help, captain," Dex said.

"No problem, lieutenant," the captain said. "You can send me pretty ladies anytime." He turned to Bish and favoured her with a smarmy grin.

After the call was over, Annabelle said, "Yuck. Those two deserve each other."

Dex laughed. "At least she'll probably have something to do while she waits for your magic."

"Ugh," Annabelle groaned. "Now there's a mental image I did not want."

"Well," Dex said, standing up. "I guess that puts paid to our lazy day off."

"Well, mine anyway," Annabelle said.

"Hey, if you have to work," Dex said, "I might as well work too." He leaned forward and kissed Annabelle on the cheek. "I'm going to go back to the apartment and do some detecting or something. Call me if you need anything."

"Will do," Annabelle said and Dex saw her eyes unfocus as she already began to get lost in the challenge of her work. He let himself out of the apartment.

• • •

Dex spent the afternoon — evening local time — rereading Annabelle's conclusions about the changes to the Light of the Simulacrum Temple site. The technical details were beyond him, but he thought he might be able to recognize similar work. He ran a search for technical information about the artist Fredric Ahmad's work and let his system compile the data into a summary. While it worked, he played a little mandolin and let his mind wander.

It seemed evident that there were actual people behind most of the events that were causing havoc in M City and while he couldn't be sure yet that this was true of Stella Bish's problems, he guessed that it was the case. And it also seemed clear that there were at least two people at work, maybe in conjunction with each other, but probably not. And that worried Dex.

If it were a lone nut, he could almost understand it — someone who felt left behind by what seemed like a mass migration to an online space which Dex himself found unsatisfying and false. He'd heard plenty of people state the opinion that theft or destruction of virtual property wasn't as severe as similar acts in the physical world and more especially that offences against a person online were hardly even worth complaining about. It wouldn't be tough for a certain type of person to rationalize that vandalizing property or hijacking an account here or there might be a reasonable political — or artistic — act.

What Dex didn't understand was why there would be a concerted effort to virtually wreck up the place. Or what could motivate people who didn't even necessarily know one another to commit such similar acts. He knew that he was assuming a lot of variables in this thought process, but he was just freewheeling now. He knew enough not to get too attached to any particular set of ideas, but also that theories that seemed farfetched could become useful in the long run.

He'd run through his set for the upcoming show with Chemical Celeste and played a few of his new songs too, when he finally put the instrument away and went back to his system. He looked over the Fredric Ahmad synopsis and tried to find similarities in the way he coded his installations with what had happened at the LoS site. He paged back and forth between the synopsis and Annabelle's report, his mind getting foggier with each minute. One moment, he thought he saw a pattern, then another moment it was gone.

His system pinged and Dex saw an unfamiliar name on the ID — D. Ashall. However, the ID line showed that Ashall was returning Dex's own message, so he took the call.

"Mr. Dexter, my name is Des Ashall," the voice at the other end of the call said. "I got your message from the Looking Through Doors and Windows gallery."

Dex thought for a moment, then remembered his fishing expedition to the art gallery. "You're the curator there?" Dex asked and when she said yes, he said, "The gallery has hosted shows for several emerging virtual artists, hasn't it?"

"You're familiar with the gallery?" Ashall asked.

"I saw the transhuman show," Dex said, "what was it called..."

"*Bodies in Motion*," Ashall said.

"Yes, that was it," Dex said. "I was very fond of the interactive piece with the ghostly footsteps."

"Ah yes," Ashall said, warming to the subject. "That was Kenji O'Rourke's work. *Memories of Patterns*. I find that O'Rourke is quite an interesting artist."

"Indeed," Dex said. "Have you done any work with Frederic Ahmad or any of those artists?"

"You mean the Open Gateway people?"

"Yes," Dex said.

"OG is a bit out of date these days," Ashall said.

"Can you tell me a bit more about it?" Dex asked.

"It's a kind of public art," she explained. "Very outré in its heyday. Sort of a mix of graffiti, vandalism and social commentary. Why is an investigator interested in last week's art movement?" she asked.

Dex explained briefly about the vandalism attacks going on in M City, then asked, somewhat sheepishly, "I was wondering if it's possible that it's just some art installation gone awry. Like a massive virtual graffiti piece or something?"

He heard the curator pause, as if thinking, then she said, "I don't think so, Mr. Dexter. OG is quite passé nowadays and even at its height it was never about actually destroying anything. I highly doubt that any of those artists would be involved in something like this."

"So you haven't heard anything about it in the art world," Dex asked, "no one is talking about some underground art prank or anything?"

"Hardly," Ashall laughed. "This is the first I've heard of it. I'm afraid you're looking in the wrong place, Mr. Dexter. But I commend your open mind. Most people in your line of work would never consider the creative aspects of something like this."

"Well, I appreciate your help, Ms. Ashall," Dex said and ended the call. So much for the art angle, he thought.

As a last resort, Dex asked his system to take the raw code from the LoS Temple and compare it with code from Fredric Ahmad's installations. In almost no time, the report spat out a figure: 62% similarity. At first glance, Dex thought it was promisingly high, but reading further into the report, he saw that most of the similarities were in syntax and code that was integral to many object renderings in M City. Dex guessed that you could take any two pieces of virtual property at random and they'd probably share 62% of the same code.

He was disappointed, but only a little bit. It had always been a wild card and he was now glad that he hadn't shared his idea with anyone else. The trouble was that now that he'd given up on the art angle, he was plumb out of ideas. All that was left was to infiltrate every group of café-going M City haters in the hopes of finding one person who might lead him to whoever was behind one of these attacks. And he wasn't sure that he even had enough cash for the drinks, let alone the stomach to sit through more of their boring diatribes, especially for a mission with so little hope for success that it was clearly conceived out of boredom rather than strategy.

On the other hand, he didn't have anything better to do and there was a band playing at one of the joints he'd read about on the boards the previous day. He took a quick shower, changed into a clean shirt and went downtown.

THIRTEEN

DEX HAD NEVER been into Big Bad John's before and it was easy to see why. He guessed that the place had been seedy when it was new and it sure wasn't new any more. The tables were few and rickety, the bar short and unpolished. The stage was just a somewhat uncluttered end of the barroom, set up with a mishmash of instruments. It smelled like old beer and human bodies.

The clientele were surprisingly urbane for such a down at heel locale. Dex noticed plenty of trendy looking people, all chatting with each other earnestly while sipping pints of watery looking beer. They were probably the posters on the board Dex had been reading when he saw the listing for this place, but he didn't feel like insinuating himself into one of their conversations any more. He'd had enough of that kind of talk with the woman the other day and he didn't think that he'd really learn anything new anyway. He was just killing time before the band came on, so he pushed his way through the throng of people lining the bar to get a drink.

After several more minutes than should have been strictly necessary, he got the barkeep's attention and she grunted a surly acknowledgement when he asked for a beer. He waved his chip over the nearest reader when the pale yellow pint was sloshed toward him. He took a sip, grimaced and turned around, directly running into the tall man standing behind him and spilling the majority of the pint down the other guy's front.

"Hey, buddy, I'm sorry," Dex said into the guy's neck, then looked up and froze. It was Maksym Voronin, the person who had once been Dex's closest friend. They hadn't seen or spoken to one another in decades.

• • •

Dex and Maks had been roommates back in the wild days, when they were trying to live outside the system. They were both musicians and played in a band in the local bars. There was a time when Dex thought they would make it, that together they could have a life that was more than just going in to work every day at some dead end job and wasting your off hours trying to forget about it. He thought they could make something beautiful out of the squats they lived in and the hustle they performed scrounging for food and rent money.

Then one day Maks decided that he was past it and was going to get a real job. A real job that came with a real apartment and a real life. A life that didn't include Dex any more.

Dex had a collection of vids from that time, the collection he hardly remembered ever watching but that he could never bring himself to delete. It didn't come up that often, but when he was reminded of his old life, his life with Maks, Dex had this unshakable feeling that he was somehow stuck in the memories of that time. Only since he'd moved to Nice had he begun to free himself from the feeling that he'd lost something precious and could never hope to regain the kind of happiness he'd felt in those dank tenement apartments and seedy bars.

• • •

"Andy?" Maks said, astonished, when he recognized the man standing in front of him with his mouth gaping open. "Andy Dexter? Could it really be you?"

Dex nodded dumbly, still unable to speak.

"My god," Maks said, clapping Dex on the shoulder. "How long has it been? And where have you been all this time? Christ, it's so good to see you," he babbled on, as Dex felt the world swim just little beneath his feet.

"Are you with someone?" Maks asked.

"Uh..." Dex managed, wondering why such a personal question was coming out this early.

"Here, I mean," Maks said, indicating the bar with a sweep of his hand. "You with people?"

Dex shook his head and Maks grinned. "That's good luck," he said. "Me neither. Let's go find a seat and catch up." He put his arm around Dex's shoulder and led him off to a table away from the hubbub of the rest of the bar. Dex still hadn't managed to say a real word when they sat.

"So," Maks said, after he took a pull on his cocktail. "What happened to your hair?"

The banality of the question and its casual tone were classic Maks and it pulled Dex out of his stupor. He ran a hand over his closely cropped skull and said, "I've been a cue ball for ages now. I cut it just after you left, I guess." He looked at his old friend carefully and noticed that he had changed as well. More, Dex suspected, than he himself had. Maks had lines at the corners of his eyes now and his skin seemed looser all over. And Dex thought he saw streaks of silver in Maks's gold hair. It reminded Dex a little of how his friend Pat Malone had looked after the longevity magic in the food supplements finally wore off, but Maks was no older than Dex himself, so it couldn't be that. Dex wondered if it were a new fashion.

"It looks good," Maks said. "Suits you."

"Thanks," Dex said.

"So..." Maks said, after a long pull on his drink. "What did you do after I went off to join the rat race?"

Dex took a sip of what was left of the terrible beer and said, "Well, Maks, I did what I always did. I followed you."

The other man frowned. "What do you mean?" he said. "I never saw you."

"I don't mean literally," Dex said. "I didn't know where you'd gone and I didn't go looking either. But I just followed your lead." He thought for a moment, remembering those days — the hurt, the betrayal, the loss of identity and direction. "I didn't know what to do with myself, so I just did what you did."

"I know you planned to go get a job, too," Maks said, "but you said you were going to look for something right, something you'd like."

"Yeah," Dex said, "but once you were gone I couldn't really see the point. The day after you left I sold my mandolin and just abandoned the apartment, furniture and all. I went into the city and I got a job."

"Jesus, Andy," Maks said. "Then what?"

"Then what, what?" Dex countered. "You know the drill as well as I do — one job, then another job, maybe a promotion with a better apartment, repeat until you die. That's life." Dex wasn't about to tell his old friend about his career with the Cubicle Men or his life now as a freelancer. For one thing, he didn't know anything about Maks any more. He could have made it up the ladder at one of the firms and while Dex's organization was well known to everyone, including the corporate heads, it paid to be discreet.

And, if he was really being honest with himself, he didn't want Maks to know that his life had turned out well. He found sitting there, across from the one person whose absence had been an almost tangible part of most of Dex's life, that he wanted Maks to feel bad. He wanted to twist the knife in little and try to make his friend realize how painful those days had been. He wanted a little payback.

"Oh, hell, Andy," Maks said, his face crumpling and Dex felt momentarily pleased with his ability to wound, then immediately felt awful for making his old friend distressed. "I'm so sorry," Maks said, looking across the table earnestly at Dex. "I made such a terrible mistake and I really hoped that you hadn't gone off and done the same thing." Dex was confused, but let the other man carry on.

"I only lasted a few months," Maks explained. "I thought I wanted the simplicity of a normal life, the ease of a regular paycheque and a company apartment. I thought it would be a kind of freedom, you know?" Dex just shook his head. "No more scrounging for food and cash, no more being stuck in the bad part of town. I thought we were just being kids, just deluding ourselves that things could be different. But then, after a few weeks of numbing work all day and nothing real to do outside of work, I knew I'd made a horrible mistake.

"Sure, I was well supplied with food bricks and synth wine. Sure, I could afford the fees for one of those immersion games in M City to pass the time between shifts. But what kind of a life was that? So I went back to the old neighbourhood. I went to the apartment, but you were gone. You remember Jennie, from the band?" Dex nodded. "Well, her friend Elena was there. I guess she took the place over from you. Anyway, she didn't know where you'd gone. I went over to Milo's, you know, where we used to play? No one there had seen you, either. You'd just disappeared. Jennie and I played a few sets together when I was on weekend, but it wasn't the same. Everyone knew I'd gone corporate and I just felt like a tourist. And it wasn't the same without you.

"I quit playing and stayed away for a while. Tried to get back into the regular grind, you know? But I just couldn't do it. I felt like I was dying by tiny little increments every hour, like every day I stayed there I was losing myself a little more. So one day, I just walked away. I didn't quit, or give notice, I just took the opposite train one morning. I didn't know where else to go, but Elena let me in. I stayed with her a long time, but that's another story." He took a deep breath and drained his glass.

"Looks like things have gone better for you," he said, hopefully. "You're at least out and about with people, not sitting alone in a sterile corporate apartment every night."

Dex smiled. "It's okay," Dex said. "Better now than it was, though, that's for sure."

"Oh?" Maks asked.

"I spent a lot of years like you described," Dex said. "Only I never tried to do anything about it. I was lucky — I fell into a few things which made life bearable." He thought for a moment. "No, that's not totally fair," he said. "I lucked into a great gig that I did outside my regular job for a long time," he continued. "And now I'm freelancing and it's a tougher battle to make ends meet, but it's a better life, for sure." He looked into his pint glass thoughtfully, but didn't drink. "So, how did you manage on the outside all this time?" Dex asked. "Did you go back to music?"

Maks laughed. "There's still no money in music, Andy," he said. "No, I spent some time grasping for anything I could get at the beginning. But when the baby came, I had to do better than that. So I ended up running a bar down in green sector and learning virtual design on the side."

"You sure got around," Dex said. "Hey, wait. Did you say baby?"

FOURTEEN

IT'S KIND OF complicated," Maks said. They had each ordered another round of drinks, this time Dex tried a rum and ginger, hoping for better quality than the beer.

"No shit," Dex agreed. "People like us don't have children! I didn't even think we could."

"That's what Elena and I thought, too," Maks said. "You go your whole adult life never once seeing a pregnant person or kids outside of a vid, you just assume things. I thought us lower classes were sterilized at birth or something. But it turns out that the contraceptives are in the food bricks, along with the rest of the nutrient cocktail that keeps you all young and handsome."

"How did you figure that out?" Dex asked.

"Once Elena got pregnant, which was a huge surprise, we puzzled it out eventually."

"Whoa," Dex said thoughtfully. "I don't really know what to ask about first."

"It's okay," Maks said. "I've told the story a few times.

"I was working at a real food restaurant," he began. "It was a fairly posh place and I was a waiter there. The whole joint was about this nostalgia deal, so all the staff were humans, not a bot in the place. The pay was all right, nothing to get excited about, but the real upside was that you could take home all the leftovers. Food made from organic ingredients doesn't last like the bricks do, so they would just have to chuck it. It was enough of a perk that it turned any old job into a great catch. The staff were loyal and eager to please, as long as we had the food train to ride on.

"Anyway, I had worked there for about a year when Elena started getting sick. We'd been living exclusively off the leavings from the restaurant the whole time. You know how scarce cash is when you're on your own and there was no way we were paying for food when there was free stuff around. So neither of us had had a bite of the processed meals in months. We found out after that if you stay off the bricks and special drinks for about six months, you lose the buildup of chemicals. Hardly anyone can afford to do that, of course, but we just happened to be in the right circumstance.

"So, I was fertile and she was fertile and it takes two fertile people to make a baby and that's just what happened. She was starting to get big when we finally found a doctor who figured it out. By then it was getting late to do anything about it and we had started to think that a baby might just be the thing for us. Andrea was born a few months later and everything changed for me. And for Elena."

"I can't even imagine how you did it," Dex said. "Did you put her in school? Some place like Forest Green?" Dex remembered the huge institution where he'd met Maks in his later years at the place. The kids lived and were trained there until they were seventeen years old; most never even saw their parents. Then they got an account with a hundred euros and the advice to look for a job. Almost everyone took the advice immediately, but a handful, like Dex and Maks, turned to the seedy side of town.

"It was tough," Maks admitted. "We didn't send her to school. We taught her ourselves, got friends to help. Everybody knows a lot about something and with all the people in the neighbourhood helping out, I think Andrea got a terrific education."

"How old is she now?" Dex asked.

"Just turned twenty-one," Maks said, proudly. "She's a designer in M City, now. She's a million times better than I ever was, too. A real natural. She took to M City like a fish to water."

"What kind of work does she do?" Dex asked.

"Sims, mostly," Maks said. "Interactive vids, game spaces, some sex stuff. She's doing great." He sipped his drink. "That's why I'm here," he said.

Dex frowned. "In this dive?" he asked, waving a hand to encompass the bar.

Maks laughed. "No," he said, "why I'm here in Europa. In Nice."

"Oh."

"She lives here now," Maks explained. "The person who handles her contracts has a freelancer community here. You know, decent apartments you can pay cash for, access to a med facility, that sort of thing." He leaned in close to Dex. "Can you imagine? It's amazing what a few years have done. Back in our day there was no chance of anything that good for us, no matter how much scratch we could have saved up. Now, my little girl has a place as good as anything I ever would have earned at a corp job. She sent me the cost of the flight just so I could come and see it."

"That's not small change," Dex said, remembering the one trip he took to see Annabelle.

"Nope," Maks said. "But she's that kind of a kid. Besides, once Elena died, it was just the two of us. We're pretty close."

"Elena died?" Dex asked. Maks nodded sadly.

"It was a long time ago now. Andrea was only fourteen."

"I'm sorry," Dex said, fighting the urge to reach out to his old friend. In the old days, he would have put his hand on Maks's arm, maybe even come around the table to embrace the man. Now, they weren't exactly strangers, but there was more than just time between them.

"She was too young," Maks said, only a hint of emotion showing through his resolve. "Though she was quite a bit older than me, as it turned out. That year off the food bricks did more than just get us knocked up." He smiled sadly. "She had some kind of genetic condition you just never see anymore because of the pharma. It was triggered in that year and when we got back on to the supplements it was too late."

"That's why you..." Dex stopped himself from finishing the thought, but Maks had guessed what he was going to say.

"Yeah, that's why I look old," he said. "The aging I did can't be reversed. But they tell me it's just cosmetic, so who cares, right?"

Dex grinned. "I think it looks pretty good, actually."

"You always did like an older man," Maks said archly and Dex felt his face flush. "Well, that's me in a nutshell," he said, changing the subject. "What have you been doing in the last decades? And what are you doing here, anyway?"

Maks had been so candid about his life, Dex felt like a heel for even thinking that he had to keep the truth about his own history from his old friend. He glossed over the early years working at terrible menial jobs, focussing instead on when he was recruited for the Cubicle Men. In his years living free with Elena and Andrea, Maks had dealt with many members of the street team and had only positive thing to say about the encounters.

Dex told a few funny stories from his time on the street, then said, "It's kind of surprising that we never ran into each other. I was only on the goon squad a couple of years, but I was down in green and brown sectors all the time."

Maks frowned. "Sounds like you were walking the beat when Andrea was just a little kid. I was totally wrapped up in her back then. I tell you, weeks could go by when I didn't even leave the apartment. If it didn't have to do with her, those days, I didn't know about it."

Dex went on to describe his promotion to detective and how he seemed to finally find his aptitude there. "Solving cases is kind of like picking out a really tough song," he said. "I can get totally lost in it for hours and it seems like it's an impossible task. Then there's this incredible moment when all of a sudden it starts to come together. And it's beautiful." He flushed again when he heard how he was gushing. "I guess that sounds kind of stupid, huh?"

"Not really," Maks said. "The kind of stuff you see as a detective is pretty ugly at times, I bet." Dex nodded. "But figuring it out and getting some kind of resolution for someone, that is a wonderful thing. And what more could you want to do in this world than try to turn ugliness into something a little more beautiful?"

Dex laughed. "They should get you to write our recruiting slogans," he joked.

"So, what else?" Maks said. "Is there anyone special in your life?"

Dex was getting tired of feeling his face get hot, so he ignored the sensation. "Actually, yes," he said. "We work together at the organization; she's a cracker."

"Like, she's a hot little pistol," Maks asked, grinning, "or she screws around with programs?"

Dex laughed. "Both, actually," he said. "I'm really lucky."

The Beauty of Our Weapons

Maks smiled and reached across the table to take Dex's hand. The intimate touch, after so long sitting across from each other, brought back a flood of memories and he felt his breath catch. Maks squeezed his hand and looked earnestly into his eyes. "I'm happy for you," he said. "You deserve someone wonderful. You always did. I'm just sorry it took so long for it to happen."

Dex slowly pulled his hand away and with trembling fingers, brought his drink up to his lips. He downed the glass, managing to blink away the wetness in his eyes as he did so. When he put the glass down, Maks was leaning back in his seat and looking toward the makeshift stage area.

"I'm staying with Andrea while I'm here," he non-sequitured, "and she finally kicked me out of the house so she could get some work done. I saw on a local board that these guys were playing and I figured it would be a great way to kill a few hours. I've heard them virtually a few times and they're pretty great. Have you heard them before?"

Dex shook his head. "I had no idea what I was getting into," he said, as they both sat back to listen to the band. "No idea at all."

FIFTEEN

DEX HAD STAYED until the band finished, then walked back to Liberté with Maks. Of course, his daughter lived in the same building as Dex — there were only so many places like that and when Maks described the building Dex had known that they had to be living in the same complex.

For a moment when they'd arrived at the lobby, Dex had an almost paralyzing desire to invite Maks up to his apartment. He imagined the two of them drinking his quality rum, listening to music, staying up until well past dawn just like they used to do. But he caught a glimpse of his old friend's face in the soft lobby lights, the silver in his hair glinting and the lines around his eyes and mouth etched deeply. So much time had gone by, Dex thought, and it only ever flows one way. This man standing in the lobby was merely related to the Maksym Voronin that Dex had loved in his youth. Dex himself was barely the same man as he'd been then. There was no going back.

Dex had smiled at Maks and said, "It was wonderful seeing you again. Are you going to be in Nice for a while?"

"A few more days at least," Maks said. "I'd love for you to meet Andrea."

"I'd like that," Dex said.

"And I want to meet your tame cracker," Maks said, a comical leer on his face.

"Well, that I'm not so sure about," Dex said, laughing, then thought for a moment. He really wasn't sure that he wanted Maks and Annabelle to meet. It already felt awkward to have spent the evening with Maks and he wasn't sure how to explain it to Annabelle. He flashed a weak grin at Maks and said goodnight, grabbing the upward spiral cable for his tower. He saw Maks disappear as he ascended and when he stepped out on to his floor he'd already begun to wonder if he'd imagined the whole thing.

The surrealism of the situation combined with several of the bar's terrible drinks played with Dex's mind and after he'd spent his minute in the shower, he resolved himself to worry about it only after a good night's sleep. He fell into bed and proceeded to not worry about anything for several hours.

• • •

Dex opened a bleary eye and scanned his dim apartment. He had his system untint the window fully, but even then the light that entered was weak. He checked the time and saw that he'd slept late. Shaking his head, he remembered the previous night and wondered if he'd dreamed it all. He pulled up his on-board system and opened the file that contained his recording of the previous night. It was real. He'd really met Maks again. He shook his head, saved the file and got out of bed.

A shot of Flying Fish Tonix, a large mug of coffee and a food brick later, he was feeling fine. He went online and saw that he had several messages waiting. Three from Annabelle and one from Captain Van Moore of Guadalajara. Dex sighed. He'd been offline for hours and wondered how much hell he was going to catch. The Namerican captain he could deal with, but Annabelle was a bear when she worried. And she worried about Dex an awful lot.

He steeled himself against the onslaught and punched up Van Moore's message first. It was a short one, just thanking

Dex for his help and reiterating that if Ms. Bish needed any other assistance out in the physical world, that he'd happily be able to help. Dex read between the lines just fine and guessed that Van Moore was offering plenty of assistance that had nothing whatsoever to do with Dex. He grinned. Annabelle was right — those two did deserve each other.

His smiled faded. Annabelle. He couldn't put it off much longer, so fired up the first of her messages. Nothing to fear in this one; she was simply letting him know that she'd cooked up a replacement login for Stella Bish and had sent it off to Gabriel Van Moore for installation. She added that she'd begun sifting through the records from the monitoring script that Bish had been using and that she'd have more for Dex later. 'Later' rolled around for Dex with a swipe of his eyes as he moved on to Annabelle's next message.

"I've got something pretty interesting in here," she said without preamble. "Sort of a good news bad news scenario. Let's get together and talk. And where are you, anyway? Call me."

So far so good, Dex thought, but he knew that the next message would be the heartbreaker. He took a breath and opened the sound file.

"Dex," Annabelle's worried voice sounded in his ears. "Where are you? You've been offline all day now and I'm starting to freak out a little. Call me right away, or I'm coming over there. I mean it. Call me."

Dex let out a breath he didn't realize he'd even been holding. That could have been worse. He didn't even bother to figure out what he was going to tell her, he just pinged Annabelle immediately.

"What's going on?" she demanded as soon as the connection was live.

"I'm sorry, kiddo," Dex said. "I went out to go see a band and stayed until the ugly lights came on. Then I went to sleep and of course I slept in. I'm sorry I didn't get your messages until now, but nothing's wrong, I promise."

There was silence at the other end of the connection for a moment, then Annabelle sighed. "Shit, Dex," she said, "you had me worried is all. With what happened to the Bish woman, I had these visions that you'd been locked out, too. Bad timing, I guess," she said and Dex could hear her forcing her voice to be light.

"I'm sorry," he repeated. "Look, why don't I make it up to you. Let's go out — I'll arrange everything and we'll meet in, say, an hour at Monte's?"

"Sure," Annabelle said. "I could use a break; I've been working nonstop on this Bish thing. I think you'll find it pretty interesting," she said, in the provocative voice she used when she had information on a case for Dex. It was one of his favourite things about her.

"Good," he said. "Monte's in an hour, then."

• • •

It took Dex only about a quarter of an hour to make the reservations and then he spent the rest of the time cleaning himself up and getting his apartment ready. He'd need water and food nearby, since he planned to spend the next several hours online in M City. He still found it unnerving to be experiencing almost real sensations of the virtual world — touch, taste, smell — and still move around in the physical world. He always did better if everything he'd need was close at hand.

He got to Monte's before Annabelle and grabbed their usual table. His avatar was dressed in its usual charcoal suit and felt fedora, but he'd added the bright crimson tie that he always wore for special occasions with Annabelle. When she materialized in the middle of the bar, he saw her smile at him, then get a puzzled look on her face.

"Do I need to change?" she asked, looking down at her tan trousers and garish tee shirt.

Dex shook his head. "I love you just the way you are," he said, grinning.

"You are such a Casanova," she said, rolling her eyes but smiling. "You know what I mean."

Dex nodded. "We have reservations at Lowell's," he said. "It's up to you."

"Lowell's?" Annabelle gasped. "Jesus." She winked out of the bar, then barely a second later reappeared. Now she wore a gauzy pale orange dress which danced around her body with its own sinuous movement. Her hair was long and gold and her eyes seemed somehow bluer than usual.

Dex whistled. "You clean up nice, kiddo," he said.

Annabelle thanked him for the compliment, then perched on the chair next to him. One of her usual cocktails appeared before her on the table and she lifted the glass. Before she took a sip, she asked, "So, what's the occasion?"

"It just seemed like we haven't gone anywhere nice in ages," Dex said, managing to ignore the pangs of guilt that were creeping around his gut. "Besides, I'm charging Stella Bish a mint for this case and your little consultant's fee doesn't come close to being fair. You've done all the work."

"I don't care about the money," Annabelle said.

Dex nodded. "I know, but I just want to do something nice for you. Is that good enough?"

Annabelle smiled. "Of course," she said.

They sipped their drinks for a few moments, then Dex said, "it's just about time to go. You ready?"

Annabelle knocked back the last of her drink, then stood. She looked radiant in the low light of the bar and Dex marvelled at his good fortune. "Let's go," she said and took Dex's hand.

• • •

Even with his upgraded sensation nodes, Dex found the concept of virtual restaurants surreal. Regardless, he had to admit that spending an evening and several hundred euros in Lowell's was a highly enjoyable experience. The virtual food was exquisite — it looked amazing and the tastes were unbelievable. Dex wondered if real food actually ever tasted that good. He guessed that it rarely did, but remembering the looks on René Biagini's face at a few meals, he figured it must sometimes.

Lowell's also had a great atmosphere. There was excellent avatar-watching to be had and you could always tell what the newest trend in the virtual street was by the bodies on display at the bar. A small stage between the bar and restaurant sections usually contained a group playing some kind of soft instrumental music, but once Dex had seen a full big band orchestra over there and the barroom had turned into an impromptu dance floor. Lowell's was a fun place.

Dex looked over his wine glass at Annabelle, as they picked at their appetizers. She speared a large prawn and held it impaled on her fork as she spoke.

"So, it's an internal credential error," she said, then raised the fork to her lips. Momentarily ignoring the virtual dripping morsel, she left the fork in place as she continued. "Well, not an error, exactly. I mean, it's an error because Bish's credential is fine and she should be able to log in. But the system was deliberately shutting her out. As if her credential was revoked." She finally popped the crustacean into her mouth and her eyes closed as she chewed.

"So, someone has spoofed the login system for everywherenet?" Dex asked, trying to get this straight. "And they're making it look like Bish isn't a legitimate user?"

Annabelle shook her head as she swallowed. "No," she said. "That's what I thought at first, too, but it's much simpler than that." She stabbed at another prawn and eyed it predatorily. "It really is the system locking her out. For a few hours, maybe longer, the system has decided that Stella Bish is not a real person."

"What?" Dex sputtered.

Annabelle smiled ruefully. "It doesn't appear to be a permanent issue," she explained. "I found a trace of timer code when I was poking around, so I'm guessing that any minute now she'd be able to log back in..."

"No," Dex said. "I mean, it's really the system? Someone in charge of everywherenet is picking on Bish specifically?"

Annabelle shrugged. "Certainly, whoever is behind this wants it to look that way."

Dex thought for a moment. "Could you do something like that?" he asked.

"In the next five minutes?" Annabelle considered. "No. But could someone like me do something like that with sufficient motivation and time? Yeah, probably."

"Huh," Dex grunted. "So, someone is personally out to make life very hard for one Stella Bish."

"It would appear that's the case," Annabelle said. "Except for one thing."

"Oh?" Dex queried.

"This looks very much like the same system software that's causing most of the fuck ups in M City — the graffiti, the broken storefronts, what have you."

Dex nearly dropped his fork, as he watched a wry smile form on Annabelle's lips. "So, it's not just Stella Bish they're after?" he said.

Annabelle shook her head. "From what I can tell," she said, "they're after everyone."

Sixteen

DEX BARELY NOTICED when the waiter cleared the appetizer plates and brought the main courses. His olfactory node, however, noticed perfectly well and soon his attention was drawn to the châteaubriand in currant glaze that sat exquisitely in front of him. Annabelle's poached fish shared its wafted aroma of dill and tarragon and Dex resolved to enjoy his night out.

They savoured the taste of their meals, while back at his apartment, Dex nibbled a food brick. The smell and taste of his meal at Lowell's had made his physical belly start to growl, so he was pleased that he'd planned ahead. They managed to avoid more shop talk until the coffee, tea and dessert, when Annabelle said, "So, there's a lot to think about here." Dex nodded, his mouth full of a forkful of banana mousse. "But there's one thing that I keep coming back to," Annabelle continued. "The differences between the Light of the Simulacrum Temple case and everything else."

Dex frowned and swallowed his dessert. "What do you mean?"

"Well," Annabelle said, "it looks like all the destruction was done deliberately and coded by a human or at least an agent attempting to render specific outcomes." Dex looked confused. Annabelle smiled and went on. "None of it is due to a bug or another error and nothing is part of a blanket change order either. It's all deliberate, it's all targeted."

"Okay," Dex said, scraping off another dollop of the mousse.

"But all the examples we've seen, from Stella Bish to the reports we got in Larsen's file, all those have been executed by root. The system, or someone spoofing admin access to the system, is allowing the code to run. Except for what happened to the Temple. That was a clever crack, well executed for certain, but it was done the hard way."

"So, what does it mean?" Dex asked.

Annabelle shrugged, making the fabric of her dress strain and billow in a most distracting manner. "I'm not entirely sure. I know you don't like coincidences, but I'm starting to think that they actually are entirely unrelated."

"Come on," Dex sputtered. "There's a rash of random destruction all over M City and at the same time, without knowing anything about it, someone decides that now's a great time to go and vandalize a church? What are the odds?"

"You don't want me to actually calculate them, do you?" Annabelle asked, her face innocent.

"No, I don't," Dex said, dropping his fork on to his plate. "It just seems awfully unlikely."

"You remember what Conan Doyle wrote about the impossible and the improbable, right?" Annabelle asked, her eyes twinkling.

"I'm more of a Dashiell Hammett man, myself," Dex countered and they both chuckled. "Fine," he continued, "I will admit that it is possible that it's just a coincidence." He practically spat out the last word.

"Good," Annabelle said, as she drained the last drop of tea in her cup. "That was a wonderful meal, Dex. Thank you. You really didn't have to."

"I know, dollface," he said, grinning. "But I wanna treat you right."

"Okay, gumshoe," she said playing along. "What now?"

"Now," Dex said, standing and retrieving his hat from the empty chair at the table, "now is when I take the lovely lady by the arm and whisk her off to a seedy motel for..." he leered at her, "protection."

Annabelle actually giggled. "Oh, Mister Detective," she said, in a faux innocent voice, "what would people say?"

"Sugar," Dex said, "if I don't like what folks are saying, I'll just have to introduce them to a bunch of fives." He campily waved a fist around and Annabelle cracked up.

"My hero," she said, batting her eyelashes as she took his arm and they linked out of the restaurant.

• • •

Annabelle was soaking in a giant tub filled with bubbly water, one ankle propped up on Dex's shoulder. She was trying to tickle his nose with her toe and he was trying to ignore her. "I think you've been had," she said as Dex squirmed away from the foot.

"How so?" he asked.

"This is no seedy motel," she said, looking around the enormous bathroom. The centrepiece was the marble tub in which the two of them were lounging, but the platinum and gold faucets, huge mirror and somewhat incongruous bookshelf added to the impressiveness of the room. And that was only the bathroom.

Dex laughed. "I told you that I thought you deserved something nice, kiddo," he said, seriously. "We can have a roll in the hay at the local hot sheet plaza anytime."

Annabelle laughed, then said, "Ooh, we can? Goody." Dex grabbed her foot and they wrestled in the tub until the floor was covered in sudsy water. "What a mess," Annabelle said.

"I'll clean it up," Dex said and sent the hotel room a message to dry up the bathroom floor. In a microsecond, it was as if they'd never spilled a drop from the tub.

"You get what you pay for," Annabelle said, easing herself from the tub. "This is fantastic."

"It sure is," Dex said, openly staring at her avatar's wet naked form. In his mind he was imagining the real Annabelle, how her soft skin would be covered by gooseflesh from the chill dampness. He smiled at her and she recognized the look. She turned away from Dex, grabbing a towel from the rack and wrapping it around her body.

She looked over her shoulder at him and said, her voice low in her throat, "So are you coming or what?" She walked out of the bathroom, as Dex scrambled to get out of the tub.

• • •

They lay in the big soft bed, Dex's head nestled in the crook of Annabelle's arm. He absently traced his finger on her skin, amazed at the realistic feeling his implants provided. He knew exactly what that skin really felt like and this was a shockingly good reproduction. Good enough that he could almost let himself forget that it was only that — a reproduction. But Annabelle was so much happier here, in the virtual world, than she was out there, that Dex would gladly bring her to expensive virtual screw palaces every week if it was what pleased her.

"I'm getting sleepy," Annabelle said.

"Me, too," Dex agreed, holding her closer for a moment. He felt her nestle into his body and almost ached for his physical reality to coincide with this simulation. He tried to put the feeling out of his mind and enjoy the pleasure he knew that he was giving Annabelle.

"Maybe five more minutes?" Annabelle suggested and Dex nodded. They lay together in silence for a while, then Annabelle said, "So how was the band?"

"What?" Dex asked, his mind elsewhere.

"Last night," Annabelle said, "the band you went to see. How were they?" Dex felt his entire body tense and for once was glad that his avatar betrayed none of it.

"Pretty good," he said. "Guitar, bass and drums — pretty old school stuff. Good entertainers, though. They put on a really fun show." He tried to force himself not to babble. He slowly rolled over from Annabelle and sat up on the side of the bed. "Not your favourite sound, though," he said as he stood. "I don't think you missed out on much."

"That's good," Annabelle said, sitting up. "I'd hate to think that you're out there gallivanting about town getting into all kinds of trouble while I'm stuck at home working." She smiled broadly and Dex knew that she didn't mean anything, but he couldn't help but hear an implicit accusation.

"Yeah," he said, gathering up his clothes. "So, why don't you log out and get some sleep and we'll talk more tomorrow, okay?"

Dex thought he saw Annabelle frown slightly but she didn't say anything about his abrupt change of pace. "Good idea," she said. "I'm really tired. I'll ping you tomorrow, okay?"

"Sounds great," Dex said and leaned over to kiss her. "See you tomorrow." He linked out of the hotel room and blinked his eyes a few times as he refocussed on his apartment.

His mouth was dry and he needed a shower, but most of all he needed to figure out why he wasn't telling Annabelle about Maks.

• • •

He was wearing his ugly but amazingly comfortable one-piece and sipping a large rum and water. It was late and he knew he ought to be getting to sleep, but his mind was racing and he just couldn't face the solitude of his bed. He took a large pull on his drink and sighed. It felt like coming home, like a long overdue ritual finally being performed. He couldn't figure out why he was having these feelings, but there they were. He took another slug from his tumbler and pulled up his video archive.

The light in the room was dim, but getting brighter as the sun rose. Dex could see himself and Maks in the main room of their old apartment, after a long night of music and talking. By this point in the recording, Maks appeared to be almost sleeping as he lay on the couch, except for the almost imperceptible nodding of his head in time to the music. Dex lay on the floor facing the wall and he remembered being so tired that he could barely move. In his apartment in Nice, the Dex of several decades later almost jumped when he heard his own younger voice say, "Do you want me to come with you? Do you need a hand on the train or anything?"

"Naw," Maks had said, "it's just the one crate. Besides, you'll need to pack up, too. You'll be out of here in a few days yourself." Maks sat up and rubbing his hands over his face, said, "Andy, we've had some good times here, haven't we?"

"Yeah," Dex had said, "we have, indeed." Dex watched as his younger self stood to get a glass of water, clearing his throat. He poured a glass, drank it and poured another which he gave to Maks, who downed it. Smiling, he gave Dex back the empty glass. "You should go soon," Dex said.

"Yeah," Maks said, standing up. He smoothed over his clothes, wrinkled from the night of lounging on the floor. He stood in the small kitchen area awkwardly, avoiding Dex's eyes. "It's not you, you know," he said, finally. "It's just that things change. I changed. I want a different life now, that's all."

"I know," Dex said, forcing himself not to swipe at the tears forming in his eyes.

Maks looked at his friend. "I wish everything would be the same for you once I'm gone, but it won't," Maks said. "It's a different world out there and I want to be a part of it now. I know it wasn't supposed to end this way, but I can't pretend that this is enough for me anymore."

"I know," Dex said. "I just wish it were."

Maks smiled and stepped closer to Dex. Dex looked up as Maks put his arms around him. They held the embrace for a long time. "You can't hold on to people forever," Maks said, his voice slightly muffled by the top of Dex's head. "We're all in motion, constantly. Sometimes, when we're lucky, we're moving in the same direction at the same time. But, if you try to hang on, all you do is grab on to thin air. It's no good." He pulled away and his eyes were shining. "You have to find your own way, same as I did. But you'll be fine — you've always been the strong one, anyway." He smiled and stepped out into the main room. He picked up his crate and turned back to Dex. "Take care, Andy."

"You too, Maks," Dex said, then Maks walked out of the apartment and closed the door behind him. After that the video ran on with only the sound of footsteps that got quieter until the file ended.

When it was over, Dex found that a hard lump had formed in his throat. He had this strange sensation that this was a night he'd relived a thousand times over, always ending with the same sense of loss. Now, though, he felt sad, but not for himself. Knowing how hard it had been for Maks to leave and how doubly hard it must have been to come back and find that Dex had already gone. And the hell of it all was that Maks had been right. Everything is constantly changing and you can't hang on to the present. The best you can hope for is to change with the people you love and hope that you end up in the same place.

He finished his drink and put the empty glass in the cleaner. He slipped into bed, thinking not about Maks but about Annabelle and how much they both had changed in order to be where they were now. Together. Dex fell asleep smiling.

SEVENTEEN

DEX'S HEAD WAS pounding when his system woke him the next morning. He couldn't remember the last time he'd felt so bad, but then again he couldn't remember the last time he'd stayed up so late and put such a dent in the rum bottle, either. He stumbled into the lav and rooted around in the small cabinet for the bottle of Flying Fish and took a small slurp. The stuff tasted like a cross between mud and high fructose corn syrup, but he'd gotten used to it long ago. When it hit his gut he immediately began to feel better and once the water was gone and the blower was drying him and the room, his headache had reduced to a dull throb.

He dressed in casual clothes, comfortable enough to spend the day in his chair while working online, but decent enough that if he had to go out he wouldn't have to change. Now that he worked from home, Dex was careful to avoid the temptation to just wear the one-piece or worse. He grabbed a food brick from the box in the cupboard and felt around to gauge how many were left. His hand brushed against the almost empty cardboard container, so he made a reminder on his system to get another box. He got a mug of coffee going in the zapper and stuffed half the gooey food bar in his mouth. Chewing, he pulled the steaming mug out of the zapper and sat at the small pull down table. He leaned back in his chair, sipping his coffee and propped his feet up on the end of the bed.

The Beauty of Our Weapons

He went online and materialized in his M City office in more or less the same position as he'd left his body back in Nice. No coffee and no food, but feet up and pensive. He looked at the leftmost corner of his desk and the small metal tray labelled *IN*. There were several notes and a small package bound in brown paper. He smiled to himself, enjoying Annabelle's detail work. He knew that if he logged in to his usual messenger client, he'd see a few pings and a file transfer waiting for him, but he liked the anachronistic feel of the paper mail that Annabelle's representation of his messages made when he was here in his office.

He scanned through the notes first. There was a reminder from Javier, the keyboardist and impromptu leader of Chemical Celeste, reminding him about the gig the following night. Annabelle had sent a brief thank you for dinner and a reminder about Dex's promise of stolen hours at a hot sheet motel. He grinned at the thought and moved on. The last note was from Reverend Martina Alford, ostensibly drawing his attention to the file she'd sent under separate cover, but he guessed that she was really prodding Dex for an update.

He had nothing to tell the reverend, so hoped that poking through the file she sent would make him feel like he was doing something to earn his fee. He pulled out the brown paper package from the in tray and tore open the thin covering. Inside was a sheaf of paper, with a covering note.

Mr. Dexter,

I'm sorry, but after a long discussion at a congregational meeting, it was decided that we are not willing to divulge the complete list of our congregation members. Privacy is central to our members and we cannot see that the release of this information would be valuable enough to justify its cost.

However, the leadership of the congregation has agreed to share their names and contact information with you. Please find

enclosed the complete list of the Board of Directors, Lay Service Leaders and Building Committee.

I trust that the discretion you promised will extend to these
names, and hope to hear from you soon.

Rev. M. Alford

Dex sighed.

He never understood why clients would go to the bother
of hiring an investigator, then refuse to provide the basic information needed to conduct a thorough investigation. How
did they think he could work without all the data? It was
maddening.

There were about fifty names all together, and Dex
doubted that any of them would be able to shed any light on
the investigation. But he couldn't just ignore the information,
so he brought up his system console and began to peck out a
script. He was no programmer, but anyone could put together
rudimentary search or reference scripts, even Dex. He didn't
know what he was looking for, so he decided to ask the script
to get biographical information on all the people on the list
and match it to anything on the case file. He was just about
ready to set the script loose, when he added another line asking for secondary matches to data in any of his case files. You
just never knew when things might be related after all, he
thought.

He knew that his query would take some time to run, so
sat back in the chair for a moment. He rubbed a hand over
his face and thought. After a moment, he lifted his feet off
the desk and lurched forward as the seat tilted back to its
proper position. He opened the lower right hand desk drawer
and pulled out his bottle of whisky. He eyed it suspiciously,
then poured a generous measure into one of the tumblers he
also kept in the drawer.

The Beauty of Our Weapons

He flicked open the menu listing possible neurostimulants which could be consumed as part of his drink. Dex wasn't a big user of stims; in fact he'd only ever tried them a few times. He'd never really enjoyed the effects, but his finger hovered over the menu choice for focus™. He knew it was a mild bit of pharma that helped rid one of distractions and think more clearly on a particular problem. Dex wondered if it would help. He'd never felt particularly in need of focus before, either with or without the trademark, but he felt stuck on this case.

His finger mashed the selector and he chose the smallest dose of the stim. He confirmed the selection and filed the receipt in the delete bucket. He looked at the whisky glass, trying to see if it looked any different. It didn't. He lifted the glass to his nose and sniffed. Peaty single malt, nothing unusual there. He took a tiny sip, more like wetting his lips with the stuff rather than taking a real drink and tasted nothing other than the simulated loamy liquor. He frowned and put the drink back down on the desk.

He pulled up a connection to the public boards — news, opinion, sports scores, all were available on some page or another. He ran a search for Light of the Simulacrum and sat back to read what the rest of the world thought about his client.

• • •

Dex wasn't surprised to find just about every possible view represented. He found a fair number of people boasting about how the Light of the Simulacrum had changed their lives, how they had finally a found a spiritual home in this complex multiversed existence. He skimmed over the glowing praise quickly — he'd gotten a better feel for the faith's beliefs from the reverend, without the saccharine and pious hyperbole.

At the other end of the spectrum were the haters. This group broke down into two main categories. One was comprised of the folks from rival religious denominations denouncing the Similes as blasphemers or infidels. The other was the adamantly anti-religious types who included the LoS along with all the other faiths that were ruining reason, undercutting science and destroying freedom of thought. Aside from them, there were the handful of posters who had specific complaints about the LoS — some took issue with its theology, others with its aesthetic and for some it was hard to pin down exactly what their objections were. Obviously, not everyone with access to a board and a typing or dictation tool was competent to use such things.

Dex glanced at the glass of whisky plus sitting on his desk. He didn't feel any different, but he'd hardly even had a taste of the neurostim. Even though he knew better, it still felt like cheating to use enhancers and he couldn't shake the feeling. He left the glass alone and tried to get a handle on things naturally.

He started methodically, first with the other religious people. He wasn't interested in their particular arguments; it seemed to him that they all fundamentally broke down to "you don't believe what I believe, therefore you are wrong and must be stopped." To Dex, the details were irrelevant and uninteresting. Instead, he paid attention to the vehemence in the tone and the few screeds which bordered on advocating violence or destruction. There was one poster who really stuck out — a Reformed Calvinist called Jae Beck.

Beck had numerous postings attacking the LoS and they were all full of vitriol. In the arguments, which Dex distilled down to basically being an issue with the Similes' acceptance of multis, the Calvinist attacked the congregation, their beliefs and even Reverend Alford personally. Dex focussed on one post specifically:

"These so-called people expect us to permit, nay, even accept their participation in the spiritual life of the community.

They are polluting the minds of unsuspecting innocents with their seductive talk of expanding one's mind in order to reach unity with the divine. They even have the gall to say that merely participating in one of their 'services' in that travesty of a building they call a 'temple' is a way to unite with the divine. We, the truly God-fearing people, should show these heathens what idolatry is. That abomination of a church should be taken down to the invisible bits of man-made code that it really is. Then maybe they will see that they have been worshipping a creation of the Beast, not an aspect of God."

The theology was beyond Dex, but his eye caught the statement about the building. Dex poked around, trying to find out more about Beck, particularly whether or not the posts were widely read or if it was more like the millions of publicly accessible but widely ignored online diaries. It turned out that Beck was a member in good standing at a Reformed Calvinist church in Europa, but was not part of said congregation's leadership.

Reading between the lines in his scan's of the church's newsletter, Dex guessed that Beck's strong opinions were barely tolerated among the church leaders and not widely followed within or without the congregation. Using one of the many extremely useful utilities Annabelle had given him, Dex checked the logs of Beck's posts and found that Dex himself was probably Beck's most loyal reader. Beck wouldn't be inciting anyone to do harm if no one was listening, he thought.

Beck's own bio made it clear that that the poster lacked the skills to be personally responsible for the attack. A self-professed abhorrer of M City, Beck worked as a clerk in a physical world store and even claimed never to have visited the online world. Probably not an elite cracker, Dex guessed and the tone of the writing made it seem like Beck was much more of a barker than a biter. Regardless, Dex used the *Contact Me* link on Beck's board and sent a vaguely worded request for an interview. He included the link to his office in M City, wondering if Beck really had never visited the virtual world.

After the message was sent, Dex continued on. The anti-religious posters were more reasoned in their arguments, but even there Dex found a possible suspect. Kaye Mattie Barton wrote several articles about the problems she perceived in the various newer religious movements. She was mainly focussed on critiques of the New Revelators, the Fortean Army and the Light of the Simulacrum. The main basis for all her arguments was the same — that religion was no more than a set of imagined stories which made people docile, stupid and malleable. She argued that the leaders of any religion always got some tangible benefit to the acquisition of followers, usually cash, and that the followers got little more than fairy tales which made their lives seem meaningful.

Her particular beef with the LoS was that their focus on the virtual world as an aspect of the divine appealed to modern people who would otherwise not have been tempted by religion. Dex thought that while that might very well be true, it wasn't in and of itself an argument against the group, but Barton banged on about how the Similes used their relationship with M City as an unfair recruiting device. Ultimately, she argued, if their "temple, a hip-looking virtual hang out space" was "no longer available", their numbers would drop and one more blight on the face of reason would be removed.

Dex saw that her posts were well followed and trolled through the comments to her screed against the Light of the Simulacrum. There were several comments which distilled down to "I agree," and the requisite number of "You're always wrong and look — here you are, being wrong again." He didn't find anyone who offered to go out and do the deed, but a glimpse at Barton's bio made it clear that she probably had the skills and the smarts to pull it off herself if she wanted to. Her writing style seemed to Dex more argumentative than threatening, but he didn't discount her. He flagged her name to his file, along with snips from her posts.

He was starting to wade through the other opponents of the Light of the Simulacrum, when his system pinged. It was an unknown caller, but Dex picked up the heavy black handset on his desk.

"Andersson Dexter Investigations," he said, professionally. He heard a deep laugh on the other end of the call.

"Andy," Maks's voice crooned. "You sound positively grown up. I'm impressed." Dex coughed out a laugh. "I was wondering if you were at home? Andrea's working again and I though I could stop over for a coffee. If you're not busy investigating, or something."

Dex thought for a second. "I could take a break, I guess," he said. "Give me a half hour. I'm on the eighteenth floor of the east tower."

"See you soon," Maks said and ended the call.

Eighteen

DEX HAD MANAGED to splash some water on his face and make sure his tiny apartment wasn't too funky by the time he heard the door chime. He had his system open the door and he saw Maks's long frame in the hallway, his face splitting into a wide grin.

"Come on in," Dex said. "Sorry —it's kind of cramped."

"No problem," Maks said, walking in and taking a seat on the edge of Dex's bed. "Andrea's is only a hair bigger and I've been living there with her for a week." He looked around the small apartment, then back at Dex. "To tell the truth, I think she's getting a little sick of me. It can't be much fun for her to have her old dad around all the time."

Dex grinned. "I know what you mean," he said. "You get used to living alone, then all of a sudden there's another body there. It gets pretty close pretty fast, I'd wager."

Maks grinned. "That experience talking?" he asked. "Is your Miss Annabelle sharing this closet with you?"

Dex laughed without thinking. "Not bloody likely," he said. He caught Maks looking at him appraisingly. "She's not the moving in type," he explained, then turned to the zapper. "Coffee?" he asked, changing the subject.

"Please," Maks said.

"Still with too much sugar and not enough milk?"

Maks laughed. "Yeah, I still take it the same way." Dex mixed the brews and put the two mugs into the zapper. When the machine was done, he handed Maks the steaming cup with the darker liquid and took a sip of his own coffee.

"So, I'll probably be heading back to Namerica soon," Maks said, after he'd had a taste of the dark brew.

"Oh," Dex said and he heard the disappointment in his voice. "How soon?" he asked, then added, "I, uh, have a gig coming up with this band I'm playing in."

"Really," Maks said, his voice enthusiastic. "You're still playing. That's fantastic."

"It's kind of a new thing," Dex said. "I started playing virtual mandolin, but now I play a real one here and pipe it in to the venue online."

"Cool," Maks said, grinning.

"Yeah," Dex said, "it is."

"So, when's the gig?"

"Tomorrow night," Dex said. "I can give you a link to the bar in M City, if you want."

"That would be great," Maks said. "Hey," he looked up at Dex, his eyes shining. "I'm not leaving that soon. Maybe I could hang out here while you play?" he asked. "It would be awesome to get the double experience, I bet."

Dex blanched. "I dunno," he said. "I haven't had anyone watch me play, not out here, in..." he counted the years. "A few decades, I guess. Would have been when I was playing with you and Jennie."

"Come on. It'll be fine," Maks said. "It's just me. It would sort of be like old times — I bet I could even scrounge up a guitar. We could jam together after." He sounded like an excited kid and Dex felt his old friend's excitement rub off on him.

"Okay," he said and heard his door chime sound again.

"Oh, that must be Andrea," Maks said. "I told her where I'd be in case she wanted something."

Dex opened the door and froze. It wasn't Andrea at the door. It was Annabelle.

· · ·

"So, this is the famous Annabelle Lewis," Maks said as Dex just stood there, his eyes darting wildly between the two of them. "I've heard so much about you," Maks continued, extending a hand to Annabelle. "I was afraid I might not get a chance to meet you before I left."

Annabelle was gracious enough and shook Maks's hand. "I'm afraid you have the advantage of me," she said, politely.

Maks shot Dex a look, but didn't say anything to him. To Annabelle, he merely introduced himself. "Maksym Voronin," he said.

"Maksym," Annabelle tried on the name for size.

"Maks," Dex said, finally engaging in the situation. "This is my old... roommate, Maks."

"Oh," Annabelle said, her eyes growing wide. She fought to control a frown and managed a well mannered smile at Maks. "I see," she said. "What a surprise."

"Tell me about it," Maks said, disarmingly. "I haven't seen Andy in, what is it, thirty years, right?" He looked toward Dex, who nodded robotically. "Then some asshole walks smack into me in a bar, spilling beer all over my new shirt and who is it, but this guy here." He put his arm around Dex and made no sign of noticing Annabelle's growing stiffness.

Dex noticed perfectly well, though, and slipped out from under Maks's arm.

"Andy?" Annabelle queried, looking at Dex with one eyebrow cocked.

"He's the only one who calls me that," Dex said simply.

"Old habits," Maks said, apologetically. "We've known each other since we were barely whelps and I'm not likely to change the way I think of him anytime soon."

"So," Annabelle said, looking at Dex but addressing Maks, "how long are you staying here?" She eyed the small apartment and Dex saw her gaze track across the room.

"He's not staying here," Dex said, hotly. "He's visiting his daughter. She lives in the complex."

"Daughter?" Annabelle blurted, before she remembered her manners and covered. "How unusual. How old is she?"

"She's a grown up woman of twenty-one who loves her old dad, but is getting a little tired of having him underfoot, I think," Maks said, grinning. "She's trying to work, so I stopped over here to get out of her way. Andy was just being a gracious host and letting me hang out and pester him." He looked between Dex and Annabelle, then said, "And it's about time that I stopped abusing that hospitality." He walked to the door and looked at Annabelle. "I'm so happy to meet you," he said. "I hope we can get together again — maybe at the gig tomorrow night?"

Annabelle shot Dex another glance, then said, "Maybe. That sounds nice."

"Great," Maks said. "I'll try to tear Andrea away from her ones and zeroes and get her to come over, too. It will be a great party!" He smiled at the two of them and with a nonchalant wave, disappeared into the hallway.

Neither Dex nor Annabelle said a word until they'd heard the clunk of a step on the downward spiral and even then they waited until it was certain that Maks was out of earshot. Dex closed the apartment door and turned to face Annabelle.

"So," she said, her face carefully neutral. "That's the competition."

• • •

"I see. That's what the fancy night out was all about," she said angrily, after they'd been around the subject a few times already. "A little present to make up for the cuckolding, is that it?"

"Damn it, Annabelle," Dex said. "I'm not fucking him."

"You're your own person, Dex," she said. "We never made any agreement about exclusivity; I have no claim on you."

"For Christ's sake, Annabelle," Dex said, exasperated. "I don't want anyone else. What you do..." his voice trailed off. "I can live with whatever you do. But regardless of whatever we did or didn't agree to, I love you and I want to be with you. Just you. Do you understand that?"

Annabelle was quiet, facing away from Dex and staring out the window. Dex wanted to go over there and touch her, put a hand on her shoulder or something, but he knew that it wasn't the right thing. Not for her. So he waited.

Finally she spoke. "Why didn't you tell me?" she asked, her voice small. "Wouldn't running into the person who was once the most important to you, someone you missed and ached for, wouldn't that be something you'd want to tell me? Wouldn't it be amazing news, the kind of thing you'd want to share?" She wasn't looking at Dex, but he was pretty sure she was crying.

"I don't know," Dex said, miserably. "I don't know why I didn't tell you," he said and sank down into the chair. He put his head in his hands and thought.

"It was so surreal," he said, talking into his hands. "Seeing him again, after all these years. And here of all places. I felt like, I don't know, like maybe it wasn't real, maybe it was just a dream. I know it wasn't, but it was so strange." He paused and looked up at Annabelle's turned back. "And I was afraid," he said.

"Of what?" her quiet voice asked.

"Of this," Dex said. "Afraid that you'd be jealous," he paused, weighing his words. "Afraid that you'd think I would leave you for him."

Annabelle was quiet and Dex could see slight shivers in her shoulders. Finally, she said, "What am I supposed to think? He's your long lost love and I'm just..." Her voice faltered there and she lowered her head.

Dex couldn't stop himself and stood. He walked up behind her and felt her flinch as he put his arms around her from behind. "You're my love now," he said. "You once told me that I'm not the same man I was back then, back when I was with Maks. And seeing him again makes me realize how true that is. The man I was then, sure, he might have dropped everything to run off with his old friend. But the man I am now," he put his head on Annabelle's shoulder, "isn't going anywhere."

Annabelle sniffled quietly, then shrugged her shoulders, subtly making Dex release his embrace. "I have to go," she said and looked at him quickly, then averted her gaze again. She managed to get to the door from the window without touching Dex and was opening the door before he could stop her.

"Annabelle, wait," he said plaintively as she walked into the hallway.

She paused a brief moment before grabbing the downward spiral. "Just give me a little time," she said, with a small smile. "I can't think out here. I'll call you." Then she grabbed the spiral's cable and disappeared past the floor of the lift.

• • •

Dex felt like a heel. He didn't really know why he hadn't told Annabelle when he'd run into Maks. Part of it was her jealousy — this wasn't the first instance of her assuming the worst. But part of it was that Maks really had been central to Dex's life once, so central that for a lot of years after Maks left he barely had a life at all. Dex was so used to thinking that things would be different if only Maks was here, that when he did appear, Dex worried that somehow that meant that everything had to change. Or maybe he really did still harbour some secret feelings for Maks.

He was angry with Annabelle, angry that she'd left before they could resolve this situation. But he knew that when she was upset the last thing she wanted was to be physically present. He'd probably just made things worse by trying to hug her. He put his head in his hands and felt the beginnings of a throbbing headache.

He was sitting there, feeling miserable, when a thought struck him. Annabelle really was not fond of the physical world and the only reason she ever went out was to please him. She'd gotten better at it over the last year, just like Dex had become more at ease in the virtual world with her. But she still was never going to be the kind of person to just drop in.

He was pondering this bit of extremely odd behaviour when his messenger chirped annoyingly and he paged over to see what was causing the ruckus. It was a reply from Jae Beck, the Reformed Calvinist and self-professed opponent of the Light of the Simulacrum. Dex opened the basic text file and read:

Dear Sir,

Thank you for the opportunity to discuss the Light of the Simulacrum; I look forward to discussing these godless impostors with you. However, as I do not participate in the so-called Marionette City interface, I am unable to meet with you using that technology. I propose a voice call at your convenience instead. Please send me a message with your preferred time and I would be pleased to talk with you.

Yours,
Jae Beck

Dex hadn't had such a formal message since he was in school and even then he suspected it was one of the teachers being pedantic on purpose. He sighed and took a chance on cold calling Beck. Unsurprisingly, the call was answered almost immediately.

"Mr. Dexter," a soft-spoken voice said. "How nice to hear from you so quickly."

"Thank you for taking the time to speak with me," Dex said.

"So, what is your interest in the Light of the Simulacrum?" Beck asked.

"I'm investigating the vandalism of their property," Dex said, not bothering to beat around the bush any longer.

"Property?" Beck asked, sounding confused.

"Their temple in M City was hacked," Dex explained and was not entirely surprised to hear Beck laugh loudly.

"Oh dear," Beck said. "How delightfully amusing. And of course, you've read my critiques of their philosophy and immediately jumped to the absurd conclusion that I had something to do with this little malfunction."

"I need to follow every lead," Dex said, trying not to get engaged in the banter.

"Of course you do," Beck said, voice still jovial. "Well, I confess that I am not overly distraught at this news. Might I ask, was the imaginary building destroyed? Or do those poor souls still have to upload themselves into that travesty of a church?"

"Uh..." Dex was not entirely sure how to deal with those questions. "The building still stands, but I understand that it's not usable for the time being."

"Oh, my," Beck said. "'The building still stands'? Have those misguided pagans gotten their clutches into you, too? I feel I must point out that there is no building, merely a collection of computer bits that render the image of a building. So it most certainly does not still stand, as of course, it never did." Dex heard Beck sigh, then carry on.

"To address your ultimate question, no, I was not responsible. I am no programmer, Mr. Dexter, so there is no way I could accomplish such a feat. I'd be happy to congratulate whoever did, however. He or she did those people a great service. I am sure that most of the people who claim to follow the Light of the Simulacrum are truly seeking a spiritual truth. And the sooner they can get away from the false prophets the sooner they can be turned to the one true light of God."

Dex could feel the conversation slipping into a dimension he did not wish to enter. "Can you think of anyone else I ought to speak with?" Dex asked. "Anyone who might have the skills to do this?"

"I'm afraid not," Beck said, a little sadly. "My views are considered too extreme by most of my fellowship and I have quite a bit of trouble finding like-minded individuals. It is only a matter of time, though, and God's will shall be done."

"Yes, well," Dex stammered, "thank you very much for your time."

"Feel free to call again, Mr. Dexter," Beck said. "It's always a pleasure to have someone with whom to discuss ideas."

"Indeed," Dex said and broke the call. What a nut, he thought, then promptly went back to feeling sorry for himself.

NINETEEN

DEX KNEW THAT it was up to Annabelle to make the next move. If he hounded her, he'd just be making the situation worse. But he hated the feeling of not being able to talk to her, of not knowing what she was thinking. He picked up his cooling cup of coffee and peered into the mug as if there was some answer hiding in the dregs of his drink. He dumped the contents into the recycler and took the bottle of rum down from the shelf. He poured a short drink into the coffee cup and took a sip.

He felt the warmth slide down his throat and settle in his belly. It didn't make him feel better exactly, more like it made him feel less. Which was good enough for now.

He sat back in the chair and linked in to his office. It was still a work day, so he might as well work. He sat at his desk and eyed the stim-laced glass of whisky still sitting where he'd left it. What was the point, he thought. There was no chemical on the planet like avoiding his real life to help get him lost in a case. He dumped the whisky into the wastebasket and watched as the liquid crystallized just before it hit the bottom. Dex marvelled at one of the nice things about virtual worlds — they clean up after themselves.

He shuffled through the files on his desk and found where he'd left off reading about the various reasons why the Light of the Simulacrum ought to be wiped from the face of the virtual Earth. There weren't that many people who had specific complaints about the organization, but there were some. And they were interesting.

Julio Cooke had been a member of the LoS, according to his many posts about them. He reminded Dex of one of those musicians who learn a new instrument, then think they can immediately not only speak knowledgeably about anything to do with the thing, but also tell everyone else what they are doing wrong.

Cooke came to the Light of the Simulacrum about six months before his posts started and he freely admitted that prior to his exposure to the congregation, he'd never thought seriously about the nature of the physical universe and how human-created universes might play into the nature of reality. However, once he'd been to a few services, he apparently had some kind of epiphany and began to decry the LoS as poseurs.

Dex couldn't be bothered to follow the man's thought processes, but he did pay close attention to the vehemence with which those ideas were expressed. Cooke particular liked to use words like "immature", "naïve" and "unsophisticated" to describe the congregation of the temple. That alone wouldn't have made Dex pay much attention, but Cooke spent one post describing what was wrong with the structure of the temple itself. He specifically pointed to the portal-style door, the decorations on the walls and the podium as "poor replicas of that which inspires a creature to seek the numinous." Dex didn't have a clue what that meant, but he knew exactly what Cooke's next phrase meant. "If the sad states in the Temple were given real opportunities to glimpse the rift between what is real and what appears to be real, then maybe they'd begin to truly understand enlightenment. Perhaps that is my calling."

At the other end of the scale, a poster called Hillary Kendrick had no complaints about the theology of the LoS. Dex wondered if she even knew that the group was a religious organization. Instead, she moaned about feeling alienated and unwelcome at meetings, charging the congregation with acting as a large clique designed to keep newcomers out. Unfortunately, her complaints were more petulant than reasoned and at one point she emotionally threatened to "tear the motherfucking place down, bit by bit."

There were a few more posters with complaints, each having varying degrees of a grasp on reality. Even among people who were talking about virtual existence being some kind of key to enlightenment, these folks were out there. From people talking about snubbed alien emissaries at one end to secret cabals of programmer-gods at another, they were the flakes and nuts which make online conversation lively. But Dex could find nothing particularly threatening among these posters and he moved on after amusing himself for an hour or two.

He set his system to run scans for any other information about Jae Beck, Kaye Mattie Barton, Julio Cooke and Hillary Kendrick. While he was building the query, he downloaded the results from his search on the list of LoS members that he'd set up earlier in the day. There were a handful of matches and Dex wanted to go through them carefully.

He recognized one name immediately. Tequila Kate was someone he'd met on an investigation years earlier into the death of his client's multiple identity. Kate was an activist for the cause of tolerance and rights for self created identities. Dex was a little surprised to see her involved in a religious group — she hadn't struck him as the spiritual type — however, he knew that the Light of the Simulacrum were very accepting of multis. He wondered if Kate was involved simply as a representative of the multi community, or if she really shared the ideas that the Similes believed.

The other names didn't ring any bells with Dex immediately. He scanned the list and saw that there were a couple of members of the congregation who were entrepreneurs in M City who had reported having their businesses targeted with vandalism themselves. He looked into the details of their cases and saw that one was the owner of a trendy café and bar while the other was a broker for custom neurostim treatments. Each had experienced a temporary but catastrophic failure of their online business presence. The café had been rendered impossible to enter for an hour and the neurostim broker had all her messages re-routed for over a day.

He knew that Annabelle thought that the destruction at the Light of the Simulacrum Temple was a solitary targeted act, unrelated to the other instances of vandalism in M City, but he wondered if it was all personal. Dex knew that most acts of violence aren't random and it struck him that two members of the congregation would experience the same problems that the temple had. He speculated that maybe it was these two individuals who were the targets, rather than the congregation itself. He made some notes, then continued down the list of names.

Nothing popped out at him and he sighed. He linked out of his office and peered into his now empty coffee cup. Another shot wouldn't help anything at this point, he knew, regardless of how tempting the idea might be. He needed something else. He needed something solid on this case.

He paged over to his messenger and put in a call to Reverend Alford.

"Mr. Dexter," the reverend's strong voice came on shortly after Dex completed the call request. "Do you have something for me?"

"No," Dex said, "rather the opposite. I was hoping you might have something for me. I've run through the list of names you provided, but I honestly don't think it's going to lead anywhere. Do you really think that one of the leaders of your congregation is responsible for the destruction of your temple?"

"No, of course not..."

"Well, then, maybe giving me the tools I need to do my job would be of more value," Dex said, trying to keep his voice level.

There was silence on the line and Dex wondered if he'd gone too far. "Very well," Reverend Alford said, finally. "I can provide you with a list of the members of the congregation who visited the temple the day it was... that last day it was intact."

"You can?" Dex asked. "And you've kept it to yourself all this time? With all due respect, reverend, are you trying to help this investigation or not?"

"I'm sorry, Mr. Dexter," Alford said and Dex thought she did sound genuinely apologetic, "the congregation is naturally concerned with privacy and I didn't want to invade anyone's more than necessary." She paused and Dex guessed there was more to it.

"What else?" he asked harshly.

"Well," the reverend said, "it's just that... it's not widely known within the congregation that this information is kept."

"You're spying on your own congregation?"

"No," she said, indignant. "It's just a real-time readout of activity in the temple, which I save. I don't even look at it, usually. It's just part of the system, you know, to help prevent..." Her voice broke off.

"You thought it might prevent something like what happened," Dex finished.

"That was part of the idea," the reverend said. "When we were designing the temple, the board thought we ought to incorporate some kind of security. The decision was made to keep the awareness of this feature to a leadership level."

Dex sighed. "In my experience, surveillance doesn't usually prevent anything," Dex said. "And, as you've seen, it doesn't even always tell you who's responsible if something does happen."

"Yes, well," Alford said. "It wasn't my decision to make. I'll forward you the list of names, but please be discreet."

"I will," Dex said. "But, I'm going to have to talk with these people, reverend."

"I know," she said.

"I'll make it clear to everyone I talk to that you and I have access to this list and no one else. I won't even mention any names, if I can help it, okay?"

"Yes," she said, "that will be very satisfactory. Mr. Dexter..."

"Dex, please."

"Dex, I'm sorry I didn't give you this information before. I can't imagine how useful it will be — the last recorded activity is well before the vandalism happened."

"Maybe we'll get lucky," Dex said. "Every little bit helps, reverend."

• • •

The list was short, just four names. He wasn't particularly surprised — the vandalism hadn't taken place on a day when services or any other activities were scheduled for the temple and Dex had to wonder why anyone would want to just hang out there otherwise. But Misty O'Hara, Desdemona Ashall, Roger Simmons and Krishna Oblesk had. The reverend had been good enough to supply contact information for each of them and Dex was about to link back in to his office to start cold calling when something stopped him.

Desdemona Ashall. He couldn't remember where he'd heard the name before, so he had his system run a search. Before long he saw that she was employed as a mid-level designer for one of the firms, working primarily with ease of use interfaces, whatever that was. Dex couldn't see how she would ping his memory, until he read down the file into other activities. Of course, she'd been the curator of the Looking Through Doors and Windows Gallery. A look at the image of her avatar jogged Dex's memory further and he remembered meeting the woman.

She was earnest and bright and was clearly a keen fan of the work. He hadn't realized when he spoke with her previously that she had ended her career as a curator. Perhaps the Looking Through Doors and Windows Gallery had been the victim of some attack as well.

Which would be awfully coincidental, for yet another member of the Light of the Simulacrum to be targeted. And Dex really did not like coincidences. He pulled up the contact information for Ashall and pinged her. He got put through to her "please leave a message" message. He did as the disembodied voice asked and requested that she contact him.

He shuffled the files on his desk again and thought. He had a hunch, and while his hunches didn't pay off most of the time, they did once in a while, so it was worth a shot. He fired up his messenger and typed up a request to Stella Bish. He forwarded her the names and IDs of the two M City entrepreneurs who were victims of attacks online as well as the four LoS members who had been in the temple the day it was destroyed. He asked Bish if she recognized any of them.

After he'd sent off the message, Dex realized that he had no idea if Bish's account was online yet. He wondered what

Annabelle had done to reconnect her to the online world and guessed that there would have to be some way for Bish to tap into her messages. It would be pretty tough to run a free-lancer clearinghouse without any access to communications. Dex closed his eyes and sighed. He wished he could just call Annabelle and ask, but it wasn't urgent and he knew she needed her space.

He looked over his messy office desk and realized that he'd just been sitting there staring at the manila folders for a half hour. He logged out and refocussed on his apartment. He stood, used the lav and went to the small cupboard. He pulled a food brick from the box and became uncharacteristically annoyed when the now empty container fell to the floor. He angrily wadded it up and stuffed it into the recycler, then slotted a cup of coffee into the zapper. He ate his last food bar while the coffee heated, then walked over to the small window with his cup.

He stood there looking at the courtyard, knowing that the crankiness he was feeling was because he wanted to talk to Annabelle, but couldn't. He often was amazed by the profound effect she managed to have on him. Usually it was a good thing but sometimes...

He gazed out the window at the usual suspects out in the courtyard, doing their exercises, or just hanging out. He thought he saw his neighbour Zeke talking with someone who looked a lot like Maks. Dex smiled without thinking, then frowned as he remembered how much of an idiot he'd been. He swallowed the rest of the coffee without tasting it, grabbed a light jacket from his cupboard and walked out of the apartment.

TWENTY

DEX WAS BACK in the apartment in under an hour, with a large box of Econoline food bars, a small bottle of gingapop and a plan. He shoved the box of food into the cupboard, popped the top of the gingapop and splashed a half glassful of it into his tumbler. He topped the glass off with rum and took an appreciative sip. He flopped into his chair and linked into his M City office. He fished a message out of his inbox — he'd seen something come in while he was on his errand, but he hadn't read it. It was from Stella Bish; she had gotten back to him uncharacteristically promptly. It seemed she was very pleased with the service Dex and his colleagues had provided.

She'd never heard of either Lynnette Foreman or Otis Gill, the two M City entrepreneurs Dex had asked after. However, she had some very interesting information about Desdemona Ashall.

Stella Bish was a classic middleman. Her detractors complained that she had no real skills of her own and it was unfair that she had somehow managed to make herself into the top businessperson operating in M City. What she had done, though, was start to organize the burgeoning online businesses back when M City was in its infancy. At that time, only a handful of people used the interface and most of them didn't recognize its potential for freelancers. Bish saw its potential clearly and soon became the go to person for anything that required specialization in M City.

She started with avatar builders, virtual architects and clothing designers. When the virtual space became more robust, she began adding programmers with other specialities to her team. Now, if you wanted to really live in M City and had the cash to pay for it, Stella Bish could find the people to make it happen. Short of uploading your mind to the system, she could give you a whole life online. Dex guessed that she'd be the first to know about the uploading business, too, if that ever panned out.

As a result, Bish knew everyone who was a star designer or programmer. And everyone wanted to get a recommendation from her. Thanks to Bish's contacts, there were more and more people like Maks's daughter who were earning a good living as a freelancer online and avoiding the firms. Bish was constantly being approached by people who thought their coding chops were good enough to earn them a spot on her roster and maybe eventually a ticket away from their day job.

It turned out that Desdemona Ashall was one of those people.

• • •

"Tell me everything you remember about Ms. Ashall," Dex asked, his virtual black handset tucked between his ear and his shoulder. Bish was much more amenable to taking his calls now, he noticed.

"We didn't have a great deal of interaction, Mr. Dexter," Bish's velvety voice sounded inside his ear. "We were introduced by one of her artist friends, some fellow who made absolutely exquisite floral instantiations for me. She wanted a job, of course."

"She wanted to be an art gallery curator for you?" Dex asked, confused. "I didn't think you went in for that kind of work."

"I don't," Bish said, a trace of a laugh in her voice. "She wasn't talking to me about art. She's a programmer in her day job — fancies herself a bit of a designer, I suppose. Her work is fine, don't get me wrong. She's excellent at what she does, the trouble is that so is every other commercial designer out there. She's good, but not exceptional. And I don't have room for anyone who isn't exceptional."

"She wanted to become one of your freelancers," Dex said, thinking out loud.

"Very good, Mr. Dexter," Bish said, laughing freely. "I see why they call you a detective."

Dex sighed, but otherwise ignored the barb. "Obviously, you turned her down."

"Indeed," Bish said. "I gave her some encouragement to strike out on her own first, you know, try to pick up the odd contract or make something to show off her skills. She did have potential — she has an excellent eye, of course. If she stretched herself a little, she might become exceptional one day. Just not yet."

"So it was the soft heave-ho," Dex said.

"It always is, Mr. Dexter," Bish replied. "I may be a shark, but there's no reason to be cruel."

"Fair enough," Dex said, pondering this new information. "So, what about your situation?" he went on. "Anyone been particularly threatening of late? Maybe someone who saw a little more shark than usual?"

"Hmm..." Bish made a little thinking noise that Dex didn't believe at all. "There isn't anything in particular I can point to," she said. "But one doesn't get to be the top of one's profession without making a few enemies along the way."

"Names, Ms. Bish."

"Now, now, Mr. Dexter," she said, her voice taking on that infuriating seductive tone. "There isn't anyone whom I'd care to name. No one has actually threatened me, ever. But, of course, any of my competitors would be happy to see me out of business. Still, I find it hard to believe that any of them would go to these lengths to accomplish such a thing. Particularly after all this time. Nothing new has happened, so why attack me now?" She paused for breath. "No, Mr. Dexter," she said, "I think you're looking in the wrong place."

"Perhaps, Ms. Bish," Dex said. "But I'll never find anything if I don't look."

She laughed, a silvery sound that tickled Dex's inner ears. "True enough, Mr. Dexter," she said. "True enough."

As she was speaking, Dex's messenger window appeared on his visual overlay and he saw that Annabelle was pinging him.

"I'm afraid I have to go, Ms. Bish," Dex said. "I'll be in touch." He broke the contact without waiting for her reply and answered Annabelle.

• • •

"I'm sorry," he said, before she could even say hello.

"I know," she said, "and I'm sorry, too."

"You don't need to apologize," Dex said, but then Annabelle broke in.

"No, I do," she said. "I know you didn't just forget to mention meeting Maks and you shouldn't have hidden it like you did. But I shouldn't have gotten all jealous and possessive, either. I had a right to be angry, but not because you may or may not have been sleeping with someone else. We've never made any claims on each other and I have no right to act as if we did."

Dex began to say something, but Annabelle cut him off again. "Maybe that's something we need to talk about, but it really isn't what's significant here. Why I really got upset is because you felt that you had to keep something from me, something that is obviously important to you. I know Maks meant a lot to you — that he still means a lot to you. Having him in your life again has to be a strange and wonderful experience. And I want to share those kinds of experiences with you. I want to be a part of your whole life, not just one part of your life. Do you understand what I mean?"

Dex was quiet for a moment, not wanting to answer glibly. Finally, he said, "Yes, I think I do understand." He paused again, searching for the right words to try to pin down the maelstrom of feelings. "I think I was just afraid," he said.

"Afraid of what?"

"Everything," Dex said. "Afraid that you'd be jealous, afraid that I would give you cause to be jealous. I didn't know how to react that night, I didn't really even know how I felt about the whole thing. I think, deep down, I was scared that I would want to leave this life I've made for myself, for the two of us, and just go back in time. I wanted that for so long that I was afraid that once the possibility appeared, I'd just revert back."

Annabelle was quiet. Eventually, she said, "And? Is that how you feel?"

"No," he said easily. "After our night out at Lowell's I thought about it a lot. Watched some of the old videos, had a good think. And it was so clear then. I'm not the man I used to be anymore. And the man I am now wants to be here, with you." His voice wavered a little and he paused again, getting himself together. "I'm sorry, Annabelle. I'll try to do better in the future, if you'll let me."

"It hasn't been easy for us," Annabelle said, after a long pause, "and we've both worked hard to make this relationship happen. I'm not willing to throw all that effort away now. But I want to be the one you call when things happen, whatever they may be. Good or bad, even if you think it's going to piss me off. I want you to want to tell me things. That's what friends do, that's what partners do. Okay?"

Dex grinned and although he knew Annabelle couldn't see it, he guessed that she could hear it in his voice. "Deal," he said.

"Good," she said.

"Okay," Dex said, after a happy pause, "now that we've got that sorted out, I have a question for you."

"Shoot."

"How come you came by my apartment? You never drop by."

"Oh, that," Annabelle said, her voice becoming wary. "Yeah. I'll tell you about that later. Maybe we can meet up at Le Rétro in a couple of hours? Talk a little shop?"

Dex frowned. Annabelle was never this reticent about information and her wanting a work meeting in person was unprecedented. Still, Dex could tell that she had her reasons, so he followed her lead.

"Sure," he said. "I'll see you there."

"Good," Annabelle said, her voice sounding relieved. "Invite Biagini, too."

She broke the connection and Dex wondered what the hell was going on. So far, Annabelle had managed to avoid René and the two had never actually met. Something very strange was going on.

• • •

Dex was sitting in his office chair, feet propped up on the desk and hat low over his forehead. He wasn't sleeping — that wasn't something that was particularly possible in M City, but he was letting his avatar be still and was just thinking. His reverie was disturbed by a knock on the glass door. The sound startled him and he nearly knocked his hat across the room before he got control of his virtual self.

"Come in," Dex said, triggering the link to allow whoever was in the hallway to enter his office space. A serious looking woman entered, her avatar a trendy, but conservative form. Dex stood, put his hat on the hatrack near the desk and extended his hand across the scarred wood surface.

"Kaye Barton," the woman introduced herself. "You wanted to see me about the attack on the Light of the Simulacrum Temple."

"Have a seat Ms. Barton," Dex said and she sat primly across from him. "You were aware of the vandalism before I contacted you, is that correct?"

She nodded sharply. "I follow news from all the religious organizations operating in M City. As I'm sure you know, I am a vocal critic of religion, particularly within our virtual communities."

Dex nodded. "Yes, that's why I wanted to speak with you."

Barton looked directly at Dex and said, "I'm sure you think I may have had something to do with the vandalism. I know that some of my articles can be a little, shall we say, over the top in tone. However, I did not attack the temple. I believe that action like that is counter-productive. No-one gets more sympathy than a congregation with a desecrated church. It make those of us who rightly criticize their ideas look like vultures. Any time a religious group has something destroyed or damaged they get public sympathy for a time immediately after. It's the opposite of useful to my cause, Mr. Dexter."

"I understand, Ms. Barton," Dex said. "However, are you certain that all the people who follow you and subscribe to your ideas share that view?"

She frowned. "Of course that's not possible," she said. "I can't be sure of what anyone else believes. Do I think that it's possible that someone read what I wrote and took it into their heads to vandalize the LoS Temple? Yes, it's possible. Do I think it's likely? Not in the slightest."

She crossed her legs and leaned in toward Dex. "I've been pointing out the obvious contradictions and flaws in the ideas of the Light of the Simulacrum for years. And I've been using the same rhetoric all along. It strikes me as unlikely that all of a sudden someone begins to read it as a call to destroy the building. However, if you like I can supply you with a list of the commenters to my board. It's a public board and everyone needs to supply identifying information."

"I'd appreciate that, Ms. Barton," Dex said and watched as she pulled a sheet of paper from her briefcase. "You came prepared," Dex commented.

Barton smiled without warmth. "I had a fairly good idea what you wanted, Mr. Dexter," she said. "I see no reason to make it difficult on either of us."

Dex took the file, which contained several hundred names. He'd look at it later, but he wondered strongly if he was barking up the wrong tree. Barton stood and Dex followed her lead. He opened his door and saw her out. "I appreciate your time," he said and smiled.

"I'm always willing to help," she said. "I don't approve of the LoS or any of the others, but they ought to have the same rights as the rest of us."

"What do you mean?"

"People and their property ought to be free from the threat of harm," Barton said, "in the physical world and in M City. That's the point of people like you, isn't it?"

"Indeed," Dex said, as he closed the door on her.

TWENTY-ONE

DEX WALKED INTO Le Rétro around three in the morning local time. The place was its usual calm oasis at that time of night and Dex walked past the other two tables of patrons as he made his way to where René Biagini was flirting with the staff. He slid into the moulded metal seat across from his friend and waited for the floor show to be over.

"Dex," Biagini said, extending his hands for a double-fisted shake. "It's good to see you again. You said that Miss Annabelle will be joining us also." He raised an eyebrow. "To what do I owe the unexpected pleasure?"

"I don't rightly know, René," Dex said. "Something's up. She dropped by my place earlier today, unannounced. And when I talked to her just now, she wouldn't tell me anything." He poked at the table's menu with a finger to order a drink and continued. "I think whatever it is she wants to talk about it in person."

"In person?" Biagini said. "How odd. What did she say when she dropped in?"

"Ah," Dex said and felt his face colour. "We didn't actually get to that..." His voice faded, as a roguish grin spread on Biagini's face.

"Well done, you old dog," Biagini said, eyebrows waggling.

Dex sighed. "Sadly, no," he said and briefly explained about Maks and Annabelle's visit.

"You are a fool," Biagini said mercilessly.

"I know," Dex said and smiled at his friend. "But somehow she's still putting up with me."

"You don't deserve her," Biagini said, harshly, then smiled to take the sting out of his words. "You're a lucky bastard, that's what you are."

As he was finishing the thought, Annabelle walked up to the table. Both Dex and Biagini stood, Dex giving her a short but very sincere kiss on the cheek. Annabelle turned to Biagini and extended her hand.

"It's good to finally meet you, René," she said, allowing him to pull her hand up to his lips.

"Likewise, Miss Lewis," Biagini said, only a hint of smarminess in his voice.

"Please," Annabelle said, extricating her hand from his grasp. "Call me Annabelle." She sat and the men followed her lead.

"So, what's going on?" Dex asked, getting down to business.

"This is going to sound kind of crazy," Annabelle said, looking between the two men, "but I think it's possible that our communications are being monitored."

"What?" both Biagini and Dex exclaimed.

"I know, I know," Annabelle said, her hands up in front of her defensively. "It sounds ridiculous and I can't be sure. I'm just trying to play it safe. Because that's not what I wanted to tell you." She paused for effect and both men leaned in toward her.

"Well," Biagini said, unable to wait. "What is it, already?"

"It's the firms," Annabelle said with an air of finality. Dex and Biagini looked back and forth at each other in confusion.

Eventually, Dex said, "What do you mean? What about the firms?"

"The vandalism in M City, the attacks on Stella Bish, all the problems we've been seeing online," Annabelle said. "It's the everywherenet consortium itself that's behind it all."

• • •

The server brought a tray of drinks and seemed a tad confused as she set them on the table and Biagini didn't even seem to notice. The waiter left the three alone in their stunned silence and only after she was back behind the bar did anyone speak.

"Are you sure?" Biagini asked Annabelle.

She nodded earnestly. "I'm sure. I was convinced it was some clever spoof and spent a couple of days looking for how they did it. Eventually I wondered if it was possible that the actual admins were making these things happen. Once I started working from that hypothesis, everything started to fall into place." She took a sip from her tea and put her cup back down in its saucer.

"They weren't even trying to hide it," she continued. "Maybe they didn't think anyone would be able to get that far into the code or maybe they just don't care. But it's definitely an admin and it seems to me like it's not just one person doing it. I've found enough heterogeneity to suggest multiple authors. But the admin timestamps are all there and when you look at the targets it all starts to make sense." She looked between Dex and Biagini expectantly.

"Well, maybe it makes sense to you," Dex said. "I'm not convinced that I even understood half of what you just said there. René?" He looked at his friend, who just shook his head in dismay.

Annabelle smiled and said, "Okay, I'll try it in English. I'm sure that the vandalism was caused by someone who is an administrator with the everywherenet consortium and I think it might not just be one rogue person. So that makes me think that what's going on is authorized by the consortium, so it must be the firms who make up the consortium who are behind it all. And when you notice that all the targets are freelancers, people who are making a living without adding anything to the firms' balance sheets, it starts to make sense."

"Shit, you might be on to something," Dex said, realization dawning on his face. "Remember what Stella Bish said? Something about... who was it again? Sunera? Anyway, some firm was trying to get a few of her people to come work for them? It's crazy but there is a kind of point to it."

"There is?" Biagini asked.

Dex nodded. "Sure," he said. "They're trying to get rid of the competition, on a grand scale."

• • •

They talked about Annabelle's revelation for an hour, until Biagini was nearly falling asleep in his soup. He took his leave and Dex and Annabelle were left alone at the table.

"So, what do we do now?" Dex asked.

"Follow René's lead, I guess," Annabelle said.

"Huh?"

"Go home," she said, grinning. "Let's go get some sleep." She stood and took Dex's hand. They walked to the train stop and in a half hour were falling into her large bed.

The next day, Dex woke first and padded around Annabelle's apartment quietly. He went online and saw that he'd gotten a message from Desdemona Ashall. He filed it under non-urgent. Annabelle had solved the case, even though he had no idea what to do about it. He was trying to think through what to say in the report he'd have to send to Reverend Alford, when he heard Annabelle stirring.

He slipped back into bed and snuggled up behind her as she woke. "Morning, beautiful," he said.

"Morning, yourself," she answered. "What were you up to over there?" she asked.

"Just trying to figure out what to tell the Light of the Simulacrum people."

"What do you mean?" Annabelle asked, waking up more clearly now.

"Well," Dex said, rolling over and looking up at her. "We know who's responsible for their troubles, now. We just don't know what to do about it."

Annabelle frowned. "No, we don't know who's behind it," she said. "The Simulacrum thing wasn't the same as the other instances. It wasn't the consortium who wrecked their building."

"It wasn't?"

"No," Annabelle said. "Remember, I told you it was different from all the others. This one is still a mystery." She got out of bed and walked into the lav.

Dex shook his head. He dove back into his messenger and resurrected the message from Desdemona Ashall. He flagged it as something to follow up on and walked into Annabelle's small kitchen. He'd gotten her pot of tea started by the time she was out of the lav.

"So, are there any leads on the Simulacrum thing?" she asked.

"Maybe," Dex said. "I just have to get back on that horse. I'll probably work in it a little bit today before the show at Fred's." He looked at Annabelle. "You still going to come?"

"Of course," she said. Dex looked away and then back at her.

"Maks wanted to come, too," he said, softly.

"That would be fine," Annabelle said. "No, that would be great. I really ought to get to know him better, don't you think?"

Dex nodded, then said, "I think he was planning on coming to my apartment for the show. Not to Fred's." He waited for Annabelle to answer. He saw her thinking, then she smiled.

"No reason he can't do both," she said.

Dex smiled at her. "No, I suppose not," he said. He stood and walked over to her. He waited for her silent signal that she was willing to have him touch her, then took her in his arms. "I love you very much," he said into her hair.

"I know," she said. "Now, you better get back to work. And I've got some ideas I want to noodle around myself." She disengaged from his embrace and looked into his eyes. "I'll see you at Fred's, okay?"

"Okay," Dex said.

• • •

He'd showered and eaten and was sitting in his comfortable chair within an hour, going through the reports on the critics of the Light of the Simulacrum. Jae Beck turned out to be telling the truth in their brief interview — the records showed that the religious nut really never had logged into M City and definitely couldn't have orchestrated a complex programming job like what was done to the temple. Similarly, Julio Cooke and Hillary Kendrick didn't have the necessary skills either, unless they were very shy about using them in public. It seemed unlikely.

Kaye Barton, on the other hand, seemed to be a bit of an amateur programmer. She might have been able to script up something to bother the temple. She seemed reasonable enough when they'd spoken, but one can never be sure. He flagged her as a possible. Dex sighed and rubbed his face. He seriously wondered about this line of investigation. There were no other leads, but honestly none of these wackos seemed likely. They all had the unmistakable aura of loud dogs — all bark and no bite.

Dex went back to the list of people who had been at the temple on the day it was vandalized. He pinged them all, actually reaching Krishna Oblesk, who had been in the temple from 18:01 to 18:49, M City time. He was the last one on the scene before the vandalism, which occurred sometime overnight.

"Yes, it's a terrible thing," Oblesk said, after Dex explained who he was and what he wanted. "Anything I can do to help, I'm happy to do."

"I expect the reverend has already asked if you happened to take a backup."

"Yes," Oblesk said. "I didn't — it's such a shame, knowing that I was the last one to see... But even if I'd known I couldn't have backed up the whole temple. I don't have the disk space for that sort of thing, I mean who does?"

Dex did and he wasn't the only one, but he didn't say that. "Did you notice anything unusual about the temple?" he asked instead.

"No," Oblesk answered. "It was beautiful, calm and serene as always."

"You didn't see anyone unusual hanging around outside, either before you entered or after you left?"

"No," Oblesk said, "I linked directly into the sanctuary. I didn't see anyone else."

"If I may," Dex said, trying for delicacy, "can I ask why you happened to be in the temple that evening?"

"Of course," the man answered. "A former colleague of mine opened a little place in Whiteacres, a shop. The interior was being instantiated that night and I was hoping to watch it."

"I don't understand," Dex said. "Why would you go to the temple to watch your friend's shop get built?"

"I didn't want to see the shop," Oblesk explained, "not the counter, the walls, the inventory. I wanted to see the creation of something new, the soul of the new property."

"I still don't follow," Dex said.

"We have a viewing wall," Oblesk said, as if that explained everything.

"A what?"

"It's a screen which shows a visual representation of all traffic in M City. Most of the time you can't tell what anything is specifically, it's just streaks of light in a random chaotic pattern, but something unusual and big, like an instantiation, shows up clearly. It's a beautiful sight, Mr. Dexter and I was so hoping to be able to see it."

"I see," Dex said, making a note to find out what most of that meant, "and did you see your friend's instantiation?"

"Sadly, no," Oblesk said. "It was scheduled for quarter after six, but I found out from my friend that all the new creations that afternoon got pushed back to the evening. Some kind of glitch in the system, I guess. I missed it by half an hour."

"So, why did you leave?"

"I had to go to work," Oblesk said. "And after my friend got the boot, I realize can't afford to be late. That's why this shop was so important — he'd decided to try to make a go of it as an independent. Good for him, I say; I don't have the guts for that. But with all the downsizing we've been taking thanks to Bellis moving in on our routes, I may have little choice."

"I see," Dex said and something niggled in the back of his brain. "Where do you work, Mr. Oblesk?"

"I'm a runner for Antover," he said. "We're the shippers in Asia. Well, we were, anyway. No one knows what's going to happen now that Bellis is muscling in on our territory." He paused, then said, "I don't see what my employment situation has to do with this."

"Neither do I," Dex said, "thank you for your time."

He ended the call and stood. He hadn't leaned anything that would help the LoS case, but he finally had an idea about why the firms would be bothered with a few shops and bars in M City. He logged on to his system and spent the next few hours on some ordinarily very boring boards.

TWENTY-TWO

DEX HAD CHANGED clothes about six times before he finally settled on his fanciest casual outfit — a pair of charcoal trousers with a loose fitting black shirt with a complex pattern of pleats. He stared at his reflection in the mirror and tried to stop caring about how he looked. After all, it wasn't a date, it was just Maks and his daughter coming over to watch him play mandolin. He probably wouldn't even notice them once he got going. It was one of the parts of playing music that Dex loved — he lost himself in the minutia of playing and when he was playing with others it was even more noticeable. Between his own fingering and keeping up with the other band members, it was like the rest of the universe melted away when he played.

He pinged Annabelle to remind her, even though he knew she'd never missed one of his gigs. She told him she was already on her way to Fred's, the M City bar where Chemical Celeste had played a few times before.

"I sent Maks the link," Dex said. "I don't know what he wants to do, but I think he might just watch the show from both locations," he explained, referring to his own apartment as well as the online bar.

"Good," Annabelle said. "I think I'll just stick to Fred's, if you don't mind." She was uncomfortable in Dex's small flat with just the two of them in the room and Dex was unsurprised that she would not want to be there with two other bodies. Regardless of who they were.

"I'll see you there, then," Dex said and they broke the connection.

Maks arrived at the apartment a half hour before the show was scheduled to begin, with a tall, brown-haired woman. Dex could see the resemblance in her eyes and he smiled at her. "You must be Andrea," he said, extending a hand. She took it lightly and let Dex squeeze it before he gave it back. "I hope you like music," he said, seeing her shyness and realizing that the daughter didn't necessarily share the same interests as the father. "This could be a pretty dull night if you don't."

She smiled slightly and Maks laughed. "Not to worry," he said, shouldering his way through the apartment door. "She's a crackerjack horn player and I made sure she brought her clari-synth." He gestured to a small box in her hand. He held up a large case and grinned. "And I managed to borrow a real wood guitar from one of the neighbours. Says you all had a little jam in the courtyard last week."

He laid the guitar case on the table and sat on the bed. "So, Andy, where's Annabelle?"

"She'll be meeting us at Fred's," Dex said. "It's a little cramped in here for her." He shot Maks a look and while the other man didn't acknowledge that he'd seen anything, he dropped the subject.

"Tell me, Andrea," Dex said, turning to Maks's daughter. "How long have you been here at Liberté?"

"About six months," she answered, her voice quiet but strong. "I was one of the first tenants."

"That's great," Dex said. "You work for Stella Bish, I take it." Andrea nodded, still not meeting his eyes.

"Most of us do," she said. "Do you?" Her eyes darted up to Dex, then veered off to the side to look out the window.

Dex laughed. "Not usually," he said. Andrea looked confused, so Dex explained briefly about his work for the Cubicle Men. His system pinged then, a reminder to make sure that he was set up to pipe the sound from his mandolin into his avatar in M City. He made a quick check of all the equipment, then sat in his chair, mandolin on his lap.

"There's rum in the cupboard," Dex said, "and a bit of gingapop. Help yourselves, just don't bump into me while I'm playing, okay?" He grinned at his two guests.

"I'm going to link into the bar," Andrea said and Maks nodded.

"I'll come too," he said, "but I probably won't really be paying attention there. You know how I am," he said to his daughter and she laughed.

"I do," she said. She looked at Dex and said, "See you on the other side. Have a good show."

"Thanks," Dex said and linked into M City himself.

• • •

Fred's was a small space, but it had capacity for hundreds of avatars to watch the show. Virtual spaces have some advantages over physical ones — everyone can have front row seats in a virtual club if they want, the system filling your view of the other tables with all the avatars who are really invisibly sharing your own table. It was a fine system, except that for the performers it made finding friends among the crowd a little challenging. Luckily, pinging an individual in the room would instantiate and highlight the avatar, which is what Dex did in order to find Annabelle. She materialized at the front and centre table, along with Maks and Andrea.

The Beauty of Our Weapons

"This should be a good night," Dex said, grinning at the table full of people. "You expecting Zizou?" he asked Annabelle.

She nodded. The captain rarely missed one of Chemical Celeste's performances. "I'm going to want to speak to her about that issue we were talking about earlier," she said, still not wanting to speak openly about what she'd discovered about the vandalism in M City.

Dex nodded, while Maks and Andrea shared a confused look. Dex turned to them and said apologetically, "Work. But that can wait. We're just about to go on, so I better get ready." He walked up to the small stage and greeted Javier, the keyboardist and unofficial band leader.

"Suzi and Arvind are just getting set up," Javier said. "We're just waiting on Kandace..." As he said this, a tiny whirlwind of a woman appeared in the middle of the stage.

"Sorry I'm late," Kandace said, opening her small case and setting it on the mixer stand. "I'm ready to go, though."

"Good," Javier said. "I think they're ready, too," he gestured to the assembled crowd of avatars sharing tables and standing room space in the bar. After a few more moments for the five of them to get ready, Arvind clicked his drumsticks together four times and they launched into the opening bars of their first song.

• • •

Partway through the first set, Dex noticed Zahara Zhang join Annabelle and the others. He quickly lost focus on his friends, though, and spent the rest of the time engrossed in the music. After the show was over, he chatted with his bandmates for a moment, then made his way over to the table.

"Not bad for an old gumshoe," Zizou said, a wide grin on her face. "You all are just getting better and better every time I see you."

"Thanks," Dex said, shyly.

"You're piping the sound in from a physical instrument, aren't you?" she asked and Dex nodded. "It sounds great," she said. "And now, introduce me to your new friends here," she said, indicating Maks and Andrea.

"This is Maksym Voronin," Dex said. "Maks is actually my oldest friend — we just reconnected recently."

"Nice to meet you," Maks said, shaking the captain's hand. "You're Andy's boss, is that right?"

"I guess you could call me that, couldn't you, Andy?" Zhang emphasized the unfamiliar name and raised an eyebrow while looking pointedly at Dex.

He shrugged and grinned. "You know how it is," he said, "you can't teach old friends new tricks." The captain nodded and turned back to Maks.

"And the lady?"

"This is my daughter," Maks said proudly and Dex noticed that the captain kept any look of surprise off her face. "Andrea Voronin."

Andrea shook hands with the captain and said, "It's nice to meet you. Mr. Dexter is the first independent investigator I've ever met and now I'm getting to meet a captain. It must be very interesting work."

"It is," Zhang said, without elaborating. "It certainly is." She stood and turned to take in everyone at the table. "And it never ends, either. So, I must be going. Dex, Annabelle, I'll see you both at the squad meeting. Mr. and Ms. Voronin, it was lovely to meet you both. I'm always happy to see that my people have more to their lives than the work." She turned to Dex, "However, work is always there in the background, looming its ugly head. We will have to talk more about what Lewis told me. I'll be in touch." Dex nodded as Zhang stood, walked to the door of the bar and disappeared from view.

"What a lovely woman," Andrea commented.

"She can be damn tough when she wants to be," Dex said.

"Indeed," Annabelle agreed and while Dex noted a sour trace in her words the others seemed oblivious.

"So, Annabelle," Maks said, turning to her. "Are you going to be joining us out there for a little more music and merriment?" He grinned disarmingly.

"Not tonight," Annabelle said, equally genially. "I still have some work to do on a little project." She looked at Dex significantly and he nodded. "It was a lovely evening," she said to Maks and Andrea. "I'm sure we'll meet again soon." She stood and kissed Dex quickly. "I'll talk to you later," she said.

"Is everything okay?" he asked.

She shook her head almost imperceptibly, but said, "Fine. Nothing that can't wait. Go have fun and I'll contact you." She put her hand on his shoulder, squeezed quickly then winked out of the bar.

Dex turned to Maks and Andrea with a somewhat silly grin on his face. "Shall we?" he asked and vanished from the bar.

• • •

Back at the apartment, Dex stretched, used the lav and drank a glass of water. The two hours he'd been playing had fled past with him barely noticing, but his body betrayed the time he spent in the chair. After he was feeling more ambulatory, he poured a glass of rum and water, then sat back down.

He took up his mandolin and began to pick out a tune. Soon, Maks started to smile and he pulled the guitar up on his lap. After a moment, he started following along with Dex's lead. Andrea let the two men play for a while before bringing her clari-synth up to her lips and finding the melody with the electronically tuned horn.

They played without speaking for several hours, each of them alternately taking up the mantle of leader. Every once in a while, one would drop out for a moment to use the lav, get another drink or just sit and listen. The sun was high in the sky by the time they finally played the last song and Maks and Andrea rose to leave.

"That was a really good time," Andrea said, still having a hard time meeting Dex's eyes. "I haven't played with anyone since I got here," she admitted.

"You know there's a bunch of musicians in the complex," Dex said. "Sometimes we get together in the courtyard. Usually whenever there's a party — check the boards."

"I will," Andrea said, smiling shyly. "Yes, I think I will." She glanced at her father, then made some excuse to head back to her apartment without him. Dex watched Maks smiling after her as she spiralled down to the lobby.

When she had gone, Maks turned to Dex. "I'm so glad we ran into each other again," he said. "Not just for me, but for Andrea. I think she's been having a hard time adjusting to independent life."

Dex frowned. "Why would that be?" he asked. "I mean, she grew up independent, didn't she?"

"Sure," Maks said. "But like father like daughter. She wanted to see what real life was like." He drew air quotes around the words 'real life' and rolled his eyes for emphasis. "Unsurprisingly, it didn't suit, but living on her own hasn't been easy either. She always had me around before and I guess I was enough to keep her amused." He looked serious. "She's never been very good at making friends. I was always bringing people by or involved in some scheme or another. I never realized how much she relied on that until she moved out here."

Dex nodded. "I thought there was something familiar about her," he said and Maks looked confused. "I saw a lot of myself in her," Dex explained and Maks smiled.

"You seem to be doing just fine," Maks said.

"That's a relatively new phenomenon," Dex said. "If you'd seen me a few years back you wouldn't think things were going so well. I'd have made Andrea look like the life of the party."

Maks shook his head. "Well, I don't think that's ever what she will be," he said, a trace of sadness in his voice, "she didn't get that from me, anyway. But I think knowing a few people here will help her out. Especially Annabelle."

"Annabelle?" Dex asked.

"Sure," Maks said. "They're in the same industry and I don't know if you've noticed but my Andrea is a lot happier online than she is out here."

Dex gawped at Maks. "How did you know that Annabelle..." His voice trailed off.

Maks smiled. "Some things are pretty obvious," he said. "Your lady makes her preferences pretty clear."

Dex shook his head. "You are something, Maks," he said and his friend grinned.

"You know it, boyo," he said, then leaned in to give Dex a close embrace. "I'll see you again before I leave," he said into Dex's shoulder. "Take care, old man."

"You too, Maks," Dex said, pulling away from his friend's arms. He watched Maks walk down the hall and only closed the door long after he'd seen his old friend disappear down the spiral.

TWENTY-THREE

DEX SLEPT LATE the next day and had already pinged Annabelle before he realized that she was back on her work week. He puttered around the apartment waiting for her to get back to him, but finally he couldn't stand the waiting any longer.

He linked into his office and opened up the file on the M City anomalies and saw that entries had continued to be added to it over the past few days. There were now hundreds of reports of issues and Dex quickly scanned the summaries. All the reports were from people who had some kind of on-line business, almost all with a storefront in M City. One stim bar had been entirely demolished for a day and when it did reinstantiate, it was half the size. It still hadn't been restored and its owner was looking for a new location to simply rebuild the whole thing. An entire shopping mall of clothing and ava-tar extension boutiques had been blockaded, with no means to access any of the individual businesses inside. Even direct links didn't work.

Dex read over dozens of reports and thought about the similarities. With Annabelle's information, it all seemed rather obvious. It was an old-fashioned intimidation racket, but not the amateur operation that Mack Larsen thought was going on. This was as organized as crime could get.

He'd wondered why the consortium didn't just shut down the independents if that was the point of the attacks, but after the research he'd done, he realized that it wasn't the whole consortium. But who was it, exactly? After searching the news boards dedicated to the firms' business, Dex had learned that several of the major firms were making plays outside their traditional areas and he guessed that M City was one of the target zones.

It seemed likely that the attacks in M City were coming from just those members of the consortium that were part of the expansion. Dex wondered if they intended to make the attacks look like regular vandalism or some kind of bug in the system, or if the people responsible even cared whether or not someone figured out who was behind it.

Knowing that the full weight of all the firms was not behind the attacks made Dex feel a little better, but only a little. Even knowing that it was a rogue group within the consortium didn't help in trying to stop it. The consortium answered only to the Boards of Directors of the member firms, and there wasn't anything anyone other than those Boards could do to stop even part of the consortium from doing whatever it wanted to with the system.

He sighed and closed the case file. He didn't like the idea that there was nothing that could be done about the campaign against independent businesses, but he couldn't see any way around it. The feeling of impotence was maddening and Dex wasn't sure what to do about it. He linked out of M City and threw on some clothes. He left the apartment and started walking.

· · ·

Dex was sitting on a bench, staring out over the ocean at the thousands of satellites lighting up the night sky when his system pinged. It was Annabelle, done with her workday and wanting to meet. Dex had somehow lost the entire day between reading through the case files and wandering the city. He agreed to go over to Annabelle's apartment and stopped off at a shop to get a bottle of a synth-wine that she liked.

When he arrived, she was just stowing the wrapper from a food brick and Dex realized that he was starving. "You have another one of those?" he asked and Annabelle handed him one of the foil-wrapped bars. He traded her the bottle for the bar and she arched an eyebrow.

"What's the occasion?" she asked.

"It's been a while since we had a nice night in," Dex said, between bites of the meal bar.

"True," Annabelle said. "I was planning on talking shop, though," she admitted.

"Of course you were," Dex said, laughing. "That doesn't mean that it has to be a chore." He opened the cupboard door and found a couple of wine glasses. Annabelle popped the top on the bottle and Dex watched as the chiller engaged and condensation appeared on the bottle. Annabelle poured two large measures and they clicked their glasses.

"Mmm," Annabelle said, after taking a sip. "Not bad."

Dex sat at the table and set his glass down. He spent a few minutes explaining his theory about who was responsible for the attacks.

"So you think that this is just collateral damage from some firms getting too big for their britches?" Annabelle asked.

"Yes and no," Dex said. "I think they really are attacking us, attacking the independents. But it's not personal; it's because they need to expand their power base if they're going to take on the other firms. Get some fingers in the M City pie."

"Jesus," Annabelle said, putting her wine glass on the table. "That fits. And there's no doubt that weird things are going on at my job. We've never taken on someone else's territory before, not that I can remember."

"No one has," Dex said. "A few business analysts are talking about it on the financial boards, but it's still early days."

"This is bad news."

"I know," Dex said. "So, fill me in on your end of things," he said. "I get the impression that you've been a busy little bee in the past day."

"Not as busy as I'd like to be," she said, her voice losing its lilt and her face creasing with a frown.

"What do you mean?"

"Picture's worth a thousand words, right?" she asked. Dex nodded, confused at the turn the conversation had taken. "Well, vid's gotta be worth more still. Here, watch this."

Dex felt his system ping and a small video file began to transfer from Annabelle. "It's the conversation I had with the captain at Fred's the other night," she explained. "We met on an encrypted private channel. It was the best I could do without a transatlantic flight."

"You recorded it?" Dex asked.

"It wasn't on purpose," she said, "I just left the vid rolling when we went over to the private channel."

"I don't follow," Dex said.

"I always record your gigs," Annabelle said, smiling. "Could be worth something someday."

Dex grinned. "You mercenary, you."

Annabelle didn't laugh, though, so Dex just fired up his viewer and started watching the recording.

• • •

The file started in the middle of one of the longer songs Chemical Celeste played and Dex saw the head up display Annabelle used scrolling information on the lower right corner of the image. He saw her send a coded message to

Captain Zhang, asking for a private conversation. He heard the captain's voice, as if in his own ears and saw her avatar appear in the recording as if she were sitting in front of him.

"Where's the fire, Lewis?" the captain said, smiling to take the sting out of the question. "This is a decent song we're talking over."

"Sorry, sir," Annabelle said. "But this is urgent. I think I've discovered what's going on in M City and it's bad. Really bad."

"Go on."

"I've looked at code from over a thousand instances of all three types of anomalies," Annabelle said, "and it's evident when you take them all together that the issues are being instigated by someone with administrator access. In fact, more than one person — I've isolated four separate coding styles, but there could be more."

"What are you saying?"

"It's the everywherenet consortium," Annabelle said, whispering even though that wouldn't make any difference. "This is a dedicated attack on M City and it's originating from the firms."

The captain scowled, but said nothing for a moment.

"Can you prove it?" she asked. "Prove it definitively enough that we could take it to the consortium?"

"We can't go to the consortium," Annabelle said, her voice rising, "they're the ones responsible. The firms must be aware, they must be behind..."

The captain cut her off. "Just answer the question. Do you have undeniable proof?"

"No," Annabelle said, miserably. "It's all circumstantial, but with all the examples put together, it's the only logical conclusion..."

"I'm not saying you're wrong, Lewis," the captain said, softening her voice. "I believe that you believe that it really is an attack by the firms. Hell, I'd give twenty to one odds that you're right. But that's not enough. What you're talking about is... hell, I don't even know what you'd call it. Enough to start a revolution. We need more than your say so to do anything about it. Because if you're right," she gazed off and Dex saw what he was sure was a flash of fear cross the captain's face. "If you're right then it cannot be allowed to stand."

"Sir?" Annabelle said, questions weighing down the word.

"I don't know how it happened," the captain went on as if Annabelle hadn't said anything, "but somewhere along the line we gave up most of our freedoms in exchange for job security and we didn't even notice. How many people today even question the idea that their employer owns their home, owns the clothes on their back, that without a job with one of a handful of companies, they'd be on the streets with nothing? The stockholders off in their enclaves, the executives in their towers, they own us in so many ways already. M City has let some people get out of that cycle and given the rest of us a place to get away from the stinking world out there. And we're not going to stand for anyone trying to take that away."

Captain Zhang faced Annabelle, her face stony. "And that's why we have to be sure. One hundred percent with no other option. Because if you're right, we have to fight. And it's going to be long and it's going to be tough and there's no way to know how it will turn out."

The captain was quiet for a long moment, her eyes boring deep into Annabelle's. Finally Annabelle said, her voice hoarse and quiet, "I'll get the proof, sir."

"Good," the captain said, "and I'll start working on a plan."

• • •

"So what are you going to do?" Dex asked Annabelle when he'd closed the vid file and refocussed on the apartment.

"I don't know," Annabelle said and Dex thought he could detect an unusual note of defeat in her voice.

"Do you want me to talk to the captain?"

"I don't think telling the captain your theory will help my case much," Annabelle said. "She needs proof, not more theories. But I don't know how to make that happen. It's not like I'm going to break into the consortium's system on spec — hell, I'm not even sure that I could. And there isn't any reason to believe that they'd leave some file called *Master Plan to Fuck With M City* sitting on their servers for me to find. Especially if it's only a few of the admins who are in on it." She looked up at Dex. "We have to prepare ourselves for the possibility that there may not be any proof that's good enough for the captain."

Dex sighed. "There has to be something," he said. "You traced the code back to some specific administrators' logins, right?"

"Not exactly," Annabelle explained. "It's the pattern. There's no stamp saying Jane Smith, Admin on anything, but you can see evidence of root access from several different nodes — that means different people."

"Couldn't it be someone else," Dex asked, "someone who was just imitating an administrator?"

Annabelle shook her head. "No. If it were some cracker who'd somehow gotten root, it wouldn't look like this. The nodes the code originated from are all known root access zones. We're talking physical locations here."

"Sounds pretty conclusive," Dex said. "So what's the captain's beef?"

"It's complicated," Annabelle said. "I mean, do you really understand what I've just told you?"

Dex shook his head. "But I know you know what you're talking about..." He broke off and felt his stomach flip.

"Exactly," Annabelle said. "It's just my word, mine and probably a few other people's who could see the pattern, too. And just going on our say so isn't enough, not for what we'd need to do."

"Shit."

"Yeah," Annabelle said, refilling her wine glass. "Shit."

• • •

After a half hour it became evident that Annabelle wanted to be left alone, so Dex walked back to his apartment. He had that annoying itchy feeling he always got when he was stuck on a case, so he linked into his office. He didn't know what he could do to help Annabelle, but if he could at least make some headway on his own case, it might distract him for a while.

His messages were full of the usual reminders to look at case files and return calls and as he scanned the list of incoming messages, Desdemona Ashall's name popped out at him. She'd returned his call earlier that day and he still hadn't gotten back to her.

Dex felt like a dog chasing its tail, but it was either plod away at the investigation or fret about the captain's ultimatum to Annabelle. He knew he couldn't do anything about the latter, so he figured he should go for the option that at least looked productive, even if he didn't think it would get him anywhere. He couldn't imagine what light talking to Ashall again would shed on the case, but it was something to do.

TWENTY-FOUR

"FINALLY WE'VE MANAGED to connect, Mr. Dexter," Ashall said. "What can I do for you today?"

"As you know, I'm investigating a series of vandalism attacks on online businesses based in M City," he said, not technically lying. "I understand that the Looking Through Doors and Windows Gallery has closed down. I was wondering if something like that had happened to the gallery."

"How odd that you should ask," Ashall said. "No, we never had any problems like that. I simply tired of the work — the art world can be very cruel, Mr. Dexter. I was putting in a lot of work into the gallery and I just wasn't seeing the reward I wanted to."

"What a shame," Dex said. "You had some excellent shows there."

"Thank you," Ashall said. "But as I said in our last conversation, I am certain that none of the artists I've represented are responsible for the vandalism you're referring to. I fear that I am at a loss as to why exactly you want to talk to me again."

Dex ignored the question and continued on with his own enquiries. "So, the gallery was never the victim of vandals, Ms. Ashall?"

"No," she answered again.

"I see," Dex said, making notes and quickly scanning the file. "You're a member of the Light of the Simulacrum, aren't you?" he said.

"That is none of your business," she answered hotly. "What makes you say that?"

"Reverend Alford hired me to look into the vandalism at the temple, Ms. Ashall," Dex answered calmly, "and she supplied me with a list of the people who'd been to the space shortly before she found the temple in its current state. Your name is on that list."

"Is it?" Ashall said, "I'm going to have to talk to Martina about expectations of privacy."

"She's quite aware of the members' expectations," Dex said, "and I've guaranteed discretion. I'm hoping that the people who were at the temple that day might remember something that could lead us to whoever did this. I'm sure you can appreciate that."

"Of course," Ashall said, somewhat sourly.

"Could you describe how the temple looked when you were there? Anything you remember would be helpful."

"I suppose," Ashall said. "Well, when I got there, Misty — another congregant — was in the sanctuary. We spoke briefly, then I sat and read for a while."

"That's all?" Dex asked.

"No," Ashall said, "Before I left I went to the viewing wall. I find watching the swirling pattern of all the incoming and outgoing traffic in M City quite soothing. I stood at the wall for, I don't know, maybe ten minutes."

"Anything interesting in the pattern?"

"Oh, the usual," Ashall said, "the green lines of incoming traffic intersecting with the red lines of the outgoing. And, as it happens, I was lucky enough to catch the bright light of a new instantiation. It is a beautiful sight, almost like lightning across the board, as a new creation comes into existence. A truly awesome experience, Mr. Dexter."

"Indeed," Dex said, something in the back of his mind setting off alarm bells. He rapidly paged over to his notes from his conversations with the other congregants. "Ms. Ashall," he continued, as he scanned his notes, "what time do you estimate you were at the temple?"

"Early afternoon, M City time," she said. "That's my usual."

"If I told you that the temple's logs show you entering at 13:04 and leaving thirty eight minutes later, would that seem correct?"

"Yes," Ashall said, a note of confusion coming into her voice. "Is the time that important?"

"I'm afraid it is," Dex said. "According to M City records, there were no instantiations after noon until 19:21 that day. If you saw an instantiation, you must have returned to the temple after your afternoon visit. And there is no record of such a visit, which must mean that the temple code was already damaged by the time you were at the viewing wall. Ms. Ashall, do you have something you want to tell me?"

"No," she said, but Dex could hear the panic in her voice. "You must be mistaken. I... maybe it was another day I saw the instantiation. I go to the temple often enough."

"I don't think so, Ms. Ashall," Dex said. "I'm sure you would remember exactly what you saw at the temple on the day someone flailed around in the code and wrecked the place."

"Come on, now," she said. "It wasn't a hatchet job. You should know that modifying the temple would not be easy to accomplish, Mr. Dexter," she said. "It was a great design feat, one which anyone with an eye for talent would recognize."

"I understand you are looking to make a career change," he asked, changing tacks rapidly.

"What makes you think that?" Ashall asked, her voice wary.

"You did approach Stella Bish about becoming a freelance designer, did you not?"

"How do you know about that?" Ashall asked, angrily.

"It is true, isn't it?" Dex asked.

"Yes," Ashall admitted, quietly. "I'd hoped that I'd be able to turn the gallery into a full time business, but even online there isn't much money in art. So, I thought I could go independent, maybe make it work that way. But I didn't have enough experience, I had nothing to show to prove that I could do more than just make boring corporate interfaces better." She ran out of steam.

"Ms. Ashall, you vandalized the temple, didn't you?"

"I don't know what you're talking about," she said, bluster not even coming close to covering the panic in her voice.

"Did you really think that a bunch of virtual wallpaper was going to impress Stella Bish?" Dex asked, hoping for a reaction.

He got one. "You wouldn't know art if it bit your philistine ass," she said, "the temple is easily my best work. Ms. Bish would change her tune if she got a look at that piece."

"Perhaps," Dex said, incredulous. "But why the Light of the Simulacrum Temple?"

"Regardless of what a troglodyte like you may think, I am not a destructive person by nature. I had no wish to deprive anyone of anything they might need, so the temple seemed the obvious choice. And, I assumed that they would appreciate the work," Ashall said drily.

"Appreciate it?"

"Yes," she said. "Followers of the Light of the Simulacrum believe that fully exploring virtuality will help us to recognize the inherent illusory nature of all life. Once we can truly see and experience the illusion, we can transcend it and become more than human." She stopped talking as if that would explain everything.

Dex said, "I have a basic grasp of the LoS philosophy," he said, "but I can't see anywhere in it where the members would be happy to see their worship space destroyed. Especially after they spent so long raising the funds necessary to instantiate it."

"Pah!" Ashall spat. "The building was just an illusion, the money we spent to build it was just as much an illusion. By changing the appearance of the space I was just making the mutable nature of reality more obvious." She laughed harshly. "They ought to thank me. Dealing with the broken temple — facing our attachment to the design rather than its purpose — has been a more useful spiritual activity than any of the services in that temple ever were."

Dex shook his head. "Did you think you were going to get away with it?" he asked.

"Of course not," Ashall said, derisively. "How could I possibly use it as an example of my work unless I claimed credit for it?"

"Then why have you been silent all this time?" Dex asked. "You're a member of the Light of the Simulacrum, you know how desperate they are to fix it."

"Yes," Ashall said, the defiant pride leaving her voice. "Well. I wasn't quite expecting people to be so upset. These are my friends and colleagues, after all. I never intended to cause anyone any..." she seemed to be searching for the words. "Any discomfort or anxiety. It was a purely intellectual, purely aesthetic endeavour. Truly, it was."

Dex didn't know what else to say, since she really didn't seem to understand what she had done, so he simply told Ashall that he was going to have to forward a copy of the conversation to the leadership of the Light of the Simulacrum Temple. "It will take me about an hour to send the report," he said. "I expect the space to be reverted back within a day. I trust, for your own sake, that you took a backup of the code before you destroyed it."

"Of course," Ashall said. "But only a day..." Dex could hear the pout in her voice. "I still haven't been able to get thorough to Stella Bish to show her the work."

Dex sighed. "You've probably got time to take some video of the site," he said.

"Oh," Ashall said. "Yes, I suppose that would be better than nothing. What a shame they just didn't understand..." She broke the connection and Dex wondered about her mental state. He also wondered how Reverend Alford and the rest of the congregation would take to the vandalism coming from one of their own members. On the other hand, the way Ashall described it, he wondered if it was just a matter of time before something like this happened. If everything is an illusion, what difference does it make if you destroy something?

• • •

Dex wrote up his report for the Light of the Simulacrum congregation and updated the case file. It took him at least an hour and when he was done he pinged Reverend Alford. He asked her to meet him in his M City office and she agreed to be there right away. Dex linked in quickly and managed to tidy up his desk before he saw the shadow cross the glass of his door.

He opened the door for the reverend and gestured for her to sit. "Do you have news for me, Mr. Dexter?"

"I do," he said and sat across from her. He didn't mince words or waste time. "The person who vandalized the temple is a member of your congregation. Desdemona Ashall. I have an audio log of her confession here."

"Des Ashall?" Marina Alford seemed surprised. "But, Des is an active member of the congregation. If I remember rightly, she gave generously to the new building campaign. She's a regular attendee of services and runs some of the lay workshops. I'm afraid I have a hard time believing that she would do anything to hurt our congregation."

"I don't think she perceived of the act as a truly destructive one," Dex explained. "But ultimately she did it for material gain, or at least the hope of material gain. I think you'll find the log of our conversation quite revealing." Dex sent Reverend Alford a copy of the audio file, along with his report. "I'm sure she'll restore the building," he continued. "She doesn't seem to really understand the gravity of what she's done, but she did appear to take my suggestion that she fix it as more of a threat than it really was."

Alford's avatar had frozen while Dex was talking and he guessed that she was scanning through the audio conversation. He let her finish and when her face reanimated, he thought he saw a trace of amusement among the sadness.

"Des always did have a strong personal theology," Alford said with a small smile. "In some ways, I think she may even be correct. However, it just goes to show how strong the illusion of reality is, when we all felt so strongly a sense of loss when the temple was altered." She thought for a moment. "Maybe Des did do us a favour after all, Mr. Dexter."

Dex just raised an eyebrow.

"I appreciate all your help, Mr. Dexter," Alford said, standing. "We can take it from here." He shook the reverend's hand and saw her to the door. He didn't understand these people and their beliefs, but as long as they weren't trying to force their strange ideas on him, he didn't mind them either. He wondered, though, if Desdemona Ashall's belief that fundamentally nothing she did mattered was common among the Similes. And if it was, what did that mean for them as a community? And what did it mean for everyone else?

TWENTY-FIVE

THE NEXT DAY, Dex linked into his M City office and tidied up the files on the Light of the Simulacrum case. He saw a brief note from Reverend Alford thanking him for his work and letting him know that Desdemona Ashall had restored the temple to its former glory. There was no indication about what the congregation was going to do to the person who had caused them such difficulty, but it wasn't really any of his business. His work there was over, so he just saved the data and filed it.

Once that was done, he sat at his desk, staring out the window. After he glanced at the clock and saw that over an hour had passed, he decided something had to be done. He hated being between cases — having no problems to solve made him crazy. Though, as he thought about it, he did have a problem still to solve. A big problem.

He flipped through the Rolodex of contacts on his desk and stopped at the Ls. He was loathe to ask the man for help, but Dex was out of ideas. From what he could tell, there was no-where else to turn. He'd just have to swallow his pride and make nice. He pulled the card from the holder and squinted at it.

Mack Larsen, Lieutenant
mcity://squad.kanzai

So Larsen kept an office, too. Well, good for him. This was the kind of thing you wanted to do face to face, or at least avatar to avatar. Kanzai was a long way from the Maynard Arms, but he could hoof it over there in about an hour. Maybe the walk would do him some good.

• • •

The Kanzai district was all glass and chrome towering office blocks and postage stamp gardens; the opposite of the neighbourhoods Dex preferred. He found the squad's building and took the outdoor elevator up thirty-six floors to the penthouse. They obviously weren't trying to stay under the radar here.

He approached the reception desk and after watching the sharp-dressed fellow taking names, decided that it wasn't a bot. What a crappy job that must be, Dex thought. "Hi," he said to the young man when he reached the front of the queue. "I'd like to see Mack Larsen, if he's in."

"I'm sorry, sir," the receptionist said, "do you have an appointment?"

"Give him this," Dex said, passing his card over to the man, who took it like it was a particularly malodorous piece of street trash.

"I'm afraid the Lieutenant is a busy man..."

Dex leaned over the shiny reception counter and lowered his voice. "Look, sonny. I don't know if you can get busted any lower than impersonating a secretary-bot, but if you don't pass that contact to Larsen in the next thirty seconds, I'm going to find somewhere so shitty to stick you that you'll be dreaming about rising back up to the lofty heights of reception. Now hop to it, before I start to get mad."

Dex wasn't sure if he succeeded in scaring the guy, but he did put Dex's card in a communications slot and push an intercom button. He tried to keep his voice low, but Dex heard him say, "Brute... card... Dexter... yes, sir."

Dex felt the smile cover his face when the receptionist said through gritted teeth, "Go ahead, sir. Fourth door on the left."

"That wasn't so hard, now, was it?" Dex asked as he took his hat and walked down the hall.

• • •

He didn't need to pay too close attention to the receptionist's directions, because when he turned down the hall, he saw a door open and big Mack Larsen stick his head out. "Dex," the man bellowed, "how nice to see you. Come in, come in."

Dex stuck his hand out for a shake and took a deep breath. "How are you doing, Mack?" he asked as the lieutenant showed him into a large shiny office with a window that dwarfed the one back in Dex's office. The view was crappier, though, Dex noted happily.

"Never better," Larsen said and indicated a pair of plush chairs near a low table along the window. "Have a seat. I saw the result on the Light of the Simulacrum case. Good work."

"Thanks," Dex said.

"Now," Larsen said, leaning back in his chair, "what brings you all the way down here?"

"Mack, I need your help."

"I'm listening."

"The word on the street is that your people have more inside poop on the powers that run this joint than anyone, is that right?"

"We keep our ears to the ground," Larsen said, a smug smile creeping over his face.

"This is no time for false modesty," Dex said, trying to keep the annoyance out of his voice. "Annabelle Lewis thinks she's figured out what's going on here, but all the evidence is circumstantial. We need proof and we need it now."

Larsen frowned. "There's no report from Lewis on the file."

"I know," Dex said. "It's... sensitive information." He looked around the office. "Do you have an encrypted voice channel we could talk on? One to one only?"

Larsen's face registered surprise, but he merely said, "Of course. I'll ping you."

• • •

Dex explained Annabelle's theory as best as he could and waited while Larsen sent a request to one of his technical staff to analyze the anomalies in the same manner as Annabelle had done. He was careful not to mention anything specific to the tech, but gave the instruction that it should be done immediately.

"Grimes should have the results back sometime today," Larsen said on the encrypted channel. "So, you really think that conversations are being monitored?"

"Who knows?" Dex said. "But it's possible and if we're going to fight this, they certainly will be. We have to start being more careful."

"I agree," Larsen said. "But it all seems highly improbable to me. Why would the firms care about some shopkeeper down in Whiteacres?"

"We think they're making a play for the virtual markets," Dex guessed, "but I think it's a bit more complex than just that. You know how out there the firms generally have their areas and they stay out of each other's way?"

"Sure, each company controls its own zones. Nothing new there."

"Right," Dex said, "well, I've been hearing lately that a bunch of markets out there are branching into the competitor's territory. Omnitrack, Bellis and Sunera for sure and there may be others."

Larsen pondered for a moment. "You think the firms are going to start duking it out with each other?"

"It's a possibility," Dex said.

"Shit," Larsen said. "There hasn't been outright hostilities between the firms in, what, a couple hundred years?"

"Something like that," Dex said. "But the signs are all there. And this could all just be part of it. M City is becoming a valuable market, a worthwhile asset to control in the event that they will be duking it out for real. And you know who the casualties are going to be."

Larsen nodded. "If you're right, this is going to be the biggest threat to most people in a couple of generations."

"I know," Dex said. "That's why we need to be one hundred percent sure."

"Okay," Larsen said, standing. "We'll do what we can. I'll get back to you when we have something."

Dex stood and shook the big man's hand. "I appreciate it, Mack."

"No problem," he said. "You know, I used to think you didn't like me much. Glad to see I was wrong."

Dex forced a smile. "Keep in touch."

• • •

"I thought she needed proof," Dex said.

"She does," Annabelle said, "she's just a little more confident in my ability to get it than I am."

Dex was sitting on a chair in Annabelle's apartment, while she flattened herself on the opposite wall. They had been spending much more time than usual in close quarters and the strain was starting to show.

"So Zizou has already started planning how to deal with the consortium's attacks on M City, even though she's not sure they're really doing it."

"I'm think she's fairly sure," Annabelle said. "Anyway, she wants the three of us to meet on a private channel in an hour."

"Is it secure?"

"Not entirely," Annabelle said. "But it's the best we've got without her flying over here to meet. And that's not going to happen. Besides, paranoid as I am, there's no evidence that the consortium really is spying on us, not yet anyway. It's just that they could and I don't want to take the chance."

"Okay," Dex said and stood. He saw Annabelle visibly control her urge to flinch and he made sure he didn't move any closer. "Look, I can hit the meet from my place as well as from here. Why don't I head home and give you a little space for a bit." He smiled and Annabelle's face relaxed.

"I'm a lot better," she said, a sad smile forming on her lips.

"You're fantastic, kiddo," Dex said. "And don't you forget it. I'll see you — well, hear you anyway, in an hour."

• • •

Dex sat in his chair and pondered the irony — it felt absolutely bizarre to be meeting with the captain and Annabelle by voice only, rather than in some squad room or backroom bar in M City. He sipped his coffee and smiled to himself. Maybe old dogs can learn new tricks after all.

His system pinged and he saw that both Annabelle and Zahara Zhang were on the call. He joined the conversation as Annabelle was saying, "...honestly no real leads on where to get the evidence we need. I'm sorry, sir, but that's the situation as of today."

"Hi, folks," Dex broke in. "I think this might be my cue."

"Go ahead, Dex," the captain said.

"I had an idea and took a little trip into the Kanzai district to see Mack Larsen."

"I don't believe this," Annabelle blurted, but Dex ignored her.

"He's agreed to put the bloodhounds on it for us and if that gang can't find anything, we're really done for," Dex said.

"True enough," the captain said. "Larsen's people are... well, how they do it isn't important, but he does get some good inside information. That was good work, Dex. I'm glad to see you recognizing the skills of your colleagues."

"Well," Dex said, "this was an emergency."

"All right," the captain went on, "let's work on the assumption that Larsen, or someone else, turns up some corroborating evidence. We're going to need to be prepared to pass that information through the M City community, but we need to do it in such a way as we hide our hand as much as possible from the consortium."

"You've got a plan, cap?" Dex asked.

"Yes," Zhang said. "Lewis, you know of anyone who can gin up some kind of private crypto that we can pass around, something that will let people talk to each other, share files and conduct business without letting the consortium get their fingers inside?"

"Sure," Annabelle said and Dex could hear the wheels in her head turning. "If we keep the code on a person's individual system, rather than the everywherenet, we can control the encryption and keep it out of their control. But how can we share it if it's all individual?"

"Don't worry about that for now," the captain said. "Just get started on the code and I'll see about finding some upgrade rods in Europa for you to use."

"Are you talking about making an upgrade package signed by some no name group and just hoping people will shoot the load?"

Dex asked, incredulous. "Come on. This is the software that runs inside our heads. You shoot something nasty and you're whole system could get fucked. Who's going to risk that?"

"No one," the captain said. "Which is why we need a trusted distribution network. I'm working on that, but you'll need to recruit. Talk to Biagini and get his contacts involved. And Lewis, find a way to make your package as trustworthy as possible. I don't know how you can do that, but try, okay? Given the other option, we need this to be something that people will want to take. The more distribution we get, the safer we all will be. But if we don't get critical mass," she paused ominously, "it won't matter how many of us can happily talk to each other in private if we lose M City."

• • •

Dex was sipping a spiked cocoa when Annabelle walked into Le Rétro. He stood, but waited for her cue to give her a hug and kiss.

"How's it going?" he asked. "You look kind of tired."

"You old charmer, you," Annabelle said, but smiled. "I am tired. I've been working straight on this code and it's slow going. But I'm getting there. I don't know if there's any point, though."

"What do you mean?" Dex asked. "You don't think Larsen is going to come through?"

"I'm surprised you do," she said with some heat. "You think I don't know why you dislike the man so much?"

"He just rubs me the wrong way is all," Dex said.

"That's not it and you know it," Annabelle said. "It's that he's M City squad. A squad you don't even think should exist. You think he runs a little empire built on smoke and mirrors and that he and his crew should leave the policing to real people."

"Jesus, Annabelle," Dex said. "I've never said anything like that."

"You don't have to," she said. "I know you, I know how you think. The truth is that Mack Larsen is a fine lieutenant and he'd probably make a great detective. And after some of the cases you've run, it's no surprise that he'd want to get you on his team. The Reuben Cobalt thing, particularly — that whole case lived and breathed in M City. But it's not a real place to you, Dex, and you still have such a problem with those of us... with people for whom it is real."

"Annabelle..."

"No," she said and deflated slightly as she sat. She rubbed her tired face with her hands and sighed. "I'm sorry. This isn't about us. It really isn't. Obviously you are trying, trying hard. You even went to Larsen, which completely surprised me. I'm just tired and I'm taking it out on you. I shouldn't have said anything." She leaned across the table and put her hand over Dex's. "Come on, why don't I let you take me home. You can watch me snore or something."

"Now who's the sweet talker?" Dex said with a smile on his face, but in his mind he turned over Annabelle's words. He didn't like the way they made him feel and that wasn't her fault. He downed the last of his cocoa and tamped the feeling down. "Let's get you into bed, shall we?"

"Dirty old man," Annabelle said, grinning. "Just one more thing I love about you."

TWENTY-SIX

NEARLY A WEEK had gone by with no news, before the mid-afternoon knock on Dex's apartment door.

"Yeah," he said into the intercom, not expecting anyone. "Who is it?"

"Mack Larsen," a familiar voice said and Dex nearly didn't recognize the name. Out of context, he briefly wondered if it was a new neighbour.

Recovering quickly, Dex opened the door to find a small, nondescript man in the hallway. A centimetre or two taller than Dex, but several kilos lighter, the guy who stood there in expensive but conservative casual clothes looked more like a banker or a manager than the bruiser who sat in Mack Larsen's chair in Kanzai. But the voice was right, so Dex let him in.

"Surprised to see me out here?" Larsen asked, when Dex had shown him to the chair in his small apartment.

"Of course," Dex answered. "You live in Nice?"

Larsen shook his head. "Milan. I took the early train." Dex nodded, still unsure how to proceed.

"Look," Larsen said, "I know this is pretty unusual. But it turns out that you and Lewis were right. I got what you wanted — I sent her a message letting her know, but we both agreed that the details are too hot to trust to electronic communication." He reached into a slim briefcase and pulled out a sheaf of papers, a large data key and several smaller ones.

"First, I've got to tell you something," Larsen said. "Something that isn't widely known and I've got to ask for your discretion."

"I can't make any guarantees without knowing what it is," Dex said.

"I know," Larsen said, "Just... I want you to know that this is real," he gestured at the documents and data, "and I trust that you'll do only what you have to with the information."

"Okay," Dex said. "You've certainly got my curiosity up, anyway."

"A lot of us on the M City squad," he began, "not everyone, but the core group, we all work for the consortium on the outside."

Dex felt his eyes go wide. Adrenaline started ramping up in his body and he could feel his muscles tense as he tried to figure out what this meant. Larsen could see the effects his words were having and held his hands up, palms out, in a calming gesture.

"That's why we're on this squad, not a regular city team," he said, then spread his hands in a conciliatory gesture. "None of us are high up. We're not admins, we don't have root. I know admin sounds like a grunt job," he explained, "but those guys are exec level. No one I know has ever even seen them. None of my people have system access of any kind. Susana Bells, my number two, she's a Security Level One, Hitori Sommerdale is an aide to the caterer and Peter Klausman is the mechanic for the janitor for Christ's sake."

"What about you?" Dex asked, his voice level.

"Records clerk," Larsen said. "Filing and reconciling, that's what I spend my days on. But," he handed Dex the paper documents, "a lot of bits pass under my fingers."

Dex took the papers and flipped though them. It looked a lot like the snippets of code Annabelle had been analyzing, along with some annotations he didn't really understand. He looked up at Larsen.

"That's just a hard copy of what's on this key," Larsen said, holding up the large data key. "In case the systems really do get boned."

"What does it mean?"

Larsen pointed at one set of gibberish. "This is one of the instances, a storefront being vandalized. Over here," he pointed at some numbers, "you can see the physical node where this new code originated. And over here," he indicated another set of numbers, "is the consortium analyst's login that goes with that node."

"Annabelle said that there was no identifying information in the code," Dex said.

"There wasn't," Larsen said, "not exactly. I added these logins, from a list of who was using which nodes at the times of these incidents."

Realization swept over Dex's mind like a tsunami. "You matched the nodes with the admins," he said. "Using internal records at the consortium, you got the names of the people who actually did this."

Larsen nodded. "I'll be canned if this information gets back to the consortium," he said. "Maybe worse. I'm hoping we can keep a lot of the details out of what goes public. This key," he handed Dex the large key, "has everything — all the evidence. These keys," he opened his hand to reveal the smaller data chips, "have just enough to prove it, along with Annabelle's analysis. I hope these will convince most people. That," he nodded at the large key, "is for Captain Zhang. I haven't quite figured out how to get it to her, though."

"That's one area," Dex said, "where I might just be able to help."

• • •

Dex had seldom visited the south tower of Liberté and he found the backward layout confusing. After a few false starts, he located apartment 1146 and pushed on the chime. He knew he wasn't expected, but hoped that someone would be home. After a minute of waiting, he was about to turn back to the lift, when the door pinged his system asking for identification. He passed his credentials with a swipe of his hand and almost immediately the door shushed open.

Andrea stood in the doorway, looking up at Dex through lowered eyelids. "Sorry about that," she said. "I'm not used to unannounced visitors."

Dex smiled. "It seems to be going around," he said. "I probably should have called first, but I'm trying to stay offline." Andrea looked confused, but invited Dex in.

"Dad's just in the lav," she said. "Do you want anything while you wait?"

"Actually," Dex said, "I'm here to see you as much as Maks." Andrea looked up quickly, surprise in her face. "I think I need your help," Dex said.

• • •

The three of them were seated on Andrea's small settee and Dex started to explain.

"You know how the everywherenet works?" he began.

"Not really," Maks said, "as long as I can remember, it's been there."

"Technically, it's pretty much the same as a corporate network," Andrea said, "just on a global scale."

"Right," Dex said. "It was created by the firms way back when. Before there were a whole bunch of individually managed communications networks and one global network. But access to it was spotty and finally the firms all got together to manage the one, huge network we all could use."

"So, you're saying they actually cooperated," Maks said. "Seems unbelievable."

"Compared to the way business once was," Dex said, "the firms nowadays cooperate a lot. But I'm getting to that. Creating everywherenet was the beginning of the way things run now. At the time everywherenet was created, it was of value to all the firms to consolidate communications. They could all reduce their costs and increase coverage if they worked together. As the firms became in control of more aspects of daily life, like housing and transport, they needed a reliable network over long distances and working together was the only cost-effective way of making it happen. So, the everywherenet consortium was created."

"That's the group of lackeys who control the 'nets," Andrea said.

"It's technically a 'semi-independent body' made up of representatives of the major firms. It has its own staff, but it's controlled by a committee made up of top-level executives of the firms," Dex said.

"Okay," Maks said. "So this is interesting and everything, but what exactly is this history lesson in aid of?"

"Annabelle has figured out the rash of troubles in M City have to have originated from one or more everywherenet admins," Dex explained. He gave the two a moment to let it sink in, then said, "and I'm guessing that the orders came straight from some members of the committee."

"What?" Maks asked, incredulous.

"I think some of the firms are getting tired of being stuck operating only in their designated market areas," Dex said. "There's a lot of rumblings of branching out and it's starting to look like outright competition is going to start."

"What do you mean?" Maks asked. "There's plenty of competition out there."

"Sure," Dex said, "for consumer stuff. But there's really no difference between any of the products and they can't even be bothered to undercut each other's prices. It's more like they agree to share markets rather than really vie with each other. And the big ticket industries — transport, food, stims — they've all carved out geographic markets so we don't even have a choice." He looked between the two of them. "Looks like that's all changing now."

"Okay," Andrea said, "but what does this have to do with what's going on in M City?"

"They're making a play for the virtual world," Dex said, "to increase their leverage. It's collateral damage in their overall strategy, but it's a full out attack from our perspective."

Dex watched as looks of horror passed between father and daughter. He expected them to second guess his analysis, but they both just began with practical considerations.

"Who can we appeal to?" Andrea asked. "There must be some manager or supervisor or something we can complain to."

Dex shook his head. "The only higher authority than the consortium's steering committee is the boards of directors of the individual firms which appoint members to the committee. And even then, a majority of the boards would have to agree in order to effect change on the committee." He looked at Maks and Andrea in turn. "I'm guessing that the ultimate direction for these attacks came from some of those very boards of directors, so there isn't much chance of getting them to change the orders."

"No, probably not," Maks said, sourly.

"Besides," Andrea added, "there's no way for people like us — or even Captain Zhang — to influence the boards of the firms."

"She's right," Dex said. "The shareholders are the only ones who hold that kind of power and they wouldn't be interested in anything that didn't increase the profit margin. I don't know anyone who's a corporate shareholder, do either of you?"

They both laughed — the notion was ridiculous. "Do you even really know where the shareholders live?" Maks asked. "There's a rumour of a private enclave in Asia."

"I heard they live on an orbital," Andrea said. "But where they live doesn't matter; they aren't going to help us fix this."

"No, they aren't," Dex said. "And because this is part of a risky strategy that has to have more than a handful of the firms behind it, it's going to be hard to stop. And, since they control all modes of communication, they are probably monitoring them as well."

"If they aren't now," Maks said, "they sure as hell will be once we start to fight back."

Dex nodded. "So far everything they've done has been fairly innocuous, at least in the long term. But they have the ability to destroy any virtual object, cut off communications, even prevent login access."

Maks whistled low. "That's a lot of control," he said.

Andrea nodded, her brow furrowed in thought. "Yeah," she said. "It's always been that way, we just never really noticed it. But they control the network, which means they control everything that operates on the network. Communications, M City, everything." She shook her head. "I can't believe we've been so naïve to think that they wouldn't interfere."

"Well, Captain Zhang thinks she's got a way to get some of that control back," Dex said, grinning. "But it's going to take a lot of people working together to make it happen. And it's going to have to start with us."

The door chime sounded again and Andrea frowned. "It's probably Annabelle," Dex said. "She had to get some parts together, but she can tell you more about the plan." Andrea checked the ID from the door and keyed the lock. The door opened and Annabelle stepped in to the apartment, clutching a small bag.

"Hi," she said. "Nice to see you all again." She stayed close to the door, as Maks and Dex both stood. Her eyes widened slightly as Maks came toward her, but Dex put his hand on his friend's arm lightly and Maks stopped short.

Dex reached forward and took the bag from Annabelle and put it on the low table by the settee. "I've given them the nickel tour," he said, sitting back down again. "But I think they need you to fill in the details."

Annabelle pulled a chair from the table over to a spot a metre away from the rest of them and sat. "So, I've written up a package that folks can install on their onboard systems. It's mostly anonymization code that should block the admins from anything that originates from your own system."

Maks frowned. "So, it's sort of a personal security script?"

"Sort of," Annabelle said. "All your individual activities in M City would be covered, including anything that's instantiated from your system. I'm also working on a way to automatically clone login credentials so users can just hot load a kind of multi account in case they get blocked from their accounts."

"That hasn't actually happened?" Andrea asked, her eyes wide.

"I'm afraid so," Dex said. Andrea shook her head in disbelief.

"I'm hoping to be able to get copies to the major independent disk providers," Annabelle continued, "so that anything hosted from them is protected too. The trouble with all of this, of course, is that you need to install it on a physical system."

"Hang on," Maks said. "How are we going to distribute something physically all around the world?"

"That's the tricky part," Dex said. "I'm hoping that you'll take this data key with the evidence, plus copies of the code back to Namerica with you and meet up with Captain Zhang. She has contacts throughout the western continent and over time we should be able to get saturation there. I've got contacts here to spread it through Europa."

"What about everyone else?" Maks asked. "And how long is this going to take?"

"It is going to take a long time," Andrea said, understanding showing on her face. "Annabelle, is there a decent point to point encrypted communications tool in the package?"

Annabelle frowned. "No," she said. "I didn't think of that."

"Think of what?" Dex asked.

"If we include a specialized communications program in this script, then two people who both have it installed will be able to communicate with each other without having to worry about eavesdropping," Andrea explained.

"We've got that already, don't we," Dex asked. "A private channel does that, right?"

"Sort of," Annabelle admitted. "It's better than nothing, but what Andrea's talking about can't be cracked, even by an admin on the system. And it includes sharing data digitally, so we could pass files safely as well."

"So once there are a few people with the new script running, we could share upgrades and other code without having to physically pass it on," Maks said.

"Exactly," Andrea said. Turning to Annabelle, she said, "I can probably give you something to add to your package. I've been working on encrypted voice and data lines for an online game. It would work just as well outside the game world and be a hell of a lot more useful."

"Great," Annabelle said. "Once you've got it ready for the public 'net, put your program on an upgrade patch. I'll add it to my package." She pulled a bubble-wrapped blank patch from the small bag on the table and handed it to Andrea.

"I can have this ready by tomorrow morning," she said, fingering the tiny metal rod which attached to the electronic connections people wore to interface with their onboard systems.

"Let's meet again this time tomorrow," Annabelle said. "Is it okay if we meet here?"

"Sure," Andrea said. "Dad's leaving late tomorrow, so it makes sense that we do it here."

Maks turned to Dex. "You'll make the necessary introductions?" he asked.

Dex nodded. "You met Zahara Zhang at Fred's already," he said, "and I'll send her a message asking her to meet you in person. She knows to expect you."

"Okay, then," Maks said.

"Annabelle," Andrea said, "can I talk to you about your package? I'll need some of the details of how you've built it so that I can optimize my program to fit."

"Sure," Annabelle said, then looked around the crowded room uneasily.

"Well," Dex said, standing, "I know when I'm unnecessary."

"Me, too," Maks said. "Want to go grab one last drink, Andy?"

Dex looked sideways at Annabelle questioningly, who smiled broadly at him. "Go," she said. "The two of us need to have a little girl talk and you'll both be in the way." She touched Dex's arm and said quietly, "Have a good time. These moments don't come by every day; make the most of it."

"I will," he said and leaned over for a brief kiss. "See you two tomorrow," he said to the two women, as he and Maks walked out of the apartment.

TWENTY-SEVEN

THE TWO MEN walked into Le Rétro and found a table near the back. Dex ordered a pitcher of the local real ale and Maks lifted his eyebrows.

"Pricey stuff," he said and Dex grinned.

"Sure," he agreed, "but it's an occasion. Why not splurge a little, right?"

The server arrived with the dark brew and a couple of frosty glasses. Dex poured and they were both silent for a moment as they enjoyed the first taste. "Strong stuff," Maks said. "I haven't had anything like this in a long time. I try to stick to the cheap booze these days," he said with a disarming grin.

"Why change the habit of lifetime?" Dex asked.

"Why, indeed," Maks said, his face growing thoughtful. "So, do you think the ladies will be able to make the upgrade in time?"

"If I know Annabelle," Dex said, "she'll find a way to make it work come hell or high water. And Andrea seems to be cut from the same cloth." Maks nodded his agreement with Dex's assessment of his daughter. "If anyone can pull it off," Dex continued, "I think it's the two of them."

"We sure did manage to hook up with some impressive women," Maks said. "I sometimes wonder why Andrea still puts up with me. I haven't been necessary for years and I can tell I'm more trouble than I'm worth a lot of the time."

"She loves you," Dex said. "You're her dad. I doubt she thinks of you as a burden."

"One lives in hope," Maks said, laughing, as he raised his glass to Dex in a silent salute. He was grinning and Dex could see the shadow of Maks's young self in his friend's lined face. He found himself smiling back, when he saw a familiar figure over Maks's shoulder. Maks frowned as he noticed Dex's face change.

"What?" Maks asked. "Is something wrong?"

"No," Dex said, lifting an arm to draw attention to himself, "nothing's wrong. In fact, the timing couldn't be better."

• • •

René Biagini introduced himself to Maks and Dex had to laugh as his old friend was treated to Biagini's incorrigible flirtation. True to form, though, Maks took Biagini's trifling with aplomb and managed to give nearly as good as he got.

"Where did you find this young man?" Biagini asked Dex campily, his eyebrows arched almost as much as his voice. "And what are your plans for him?"

Dex chuckled. "René, not everyone is a hound dog like you are."

"More's the pity," Maks said, smirking at Biagini, who made a mock-outraged face.

"Maks is my oldest friend, René," Dex explained. "He's heading back across the pond tomorrow and we're trying to have a little send off."

"Of course," René said. "Well, then, I'll leave you to it," he smiled good-naturedly at them both, then made to stand up.

"No, wait," Dex said. "I've got something to talk to you about."

"Can't it wait?" René said, glancing at Maks. "I mean, don't you have better things to do than talk shop with me?"

"René is Captain Zhang's counterpart here," Dex explained to Maks.

"I see," Maks said to Dex then turned to Biagini. "Actually, René, it really can't wait. Why don't you get a drink." He pulled up the table menu and rotated it to face Biagini. René looked between Dex and Maks, then shrugged flamboyantly and poked at the menu with a studied movement.

"So, gentlemen," Biagini said, settling back into his chair. "Where's the fire?"

• • •

Dex and Maks spent the next hour filling Biagini in on the cause of the M City vandalism and what they planned to do about it. "I'm going to meet with Zahara Zhang when I get back home," Maks said. "We're hoping that she can coordinate with the other captains in Namerica." He looked at Biagini pointedly.

"And you were hoping I'd do the same over here," he guessed, a smile spreading on his face.

"I know you've been looking for an excuse to get a little continental travel in," Dex said, grinning. "This is the perfect thing."

Biagini nodded. "It is, isn't it," he said. "When can you get me copies of the upgrade?"

"Tomorrow," Dex said. "It needs to be ready for Maks to take back with him and his flight leaves tomorrow night."

"We only have a handful of upgrade rods," Maks said, "so you'll probably have to collect them once they've been used and pass them around again."

"Or if you happen to see any lying around," Dex added, "you could copy the package."

Biagini frowned. "Distribution is going to be difficult, I think."

Dex nodded. "It's going to be a slow process."

"Nothing we can do about that," Maks said. "And better that it's slow rather than not at all."

Biagini nodded, all the lightheartedness gone from his manner. He seemed to sip his third synth-wine almost without tasting it, as he pondered the ramifications of the scheme he was becoming a part of. "You are correct," he said, nodding earnestly. "And I will see what I can do about finding some more upgrade rods."

"We want the single package, write once type," Dex said. "It's going to be tough enough to convince people that this package is legit — the last thing we need is someone adding their own little goodies somewhere along the way."

"Hmmm," Maks made a little thoughtful noise and the two other men looked his way. "How are we going to convince people to shoot up with our no name upgrade package?" he asked. "I've done some nutty things in my time, but I don't think that even at my worst I'd have upgraded with a generic rod some dude handed me in a back alley."

"That's why we need people like René and Zizou," Dex said. "It's not just for distribution, but for credibility. The organization operates just barely off the radar of the firms, but everyone knows about us. I'm hoping that through the street teams we'll be able to pass on the package with enough credibility to get it installed and in the hands of other people with equally good reputations among their communities."

"Yeesh," Maks said. "That's a tall fucking order."

Dex shook his head once and smiled. "No one said it would be easy."

• • •

After René left, Maks ordered another pitcher of the ale and a couple of food bars. As he unwrapped one, he waved it in Dex's direction. "Need to keep our strength up," he said, grinning.

"I don't know how you're going to fly tomorrow..." Dex checked the time on his display. "Make that in a few hours."

Maks grinned. "That's for future me to worry about," he said. "As for now, I'm just happy to be here." He looked at Dex and held the other man's eyes for a long time.

Dex sighed. "Oh, Maks," he said. "This has all been so strange..."

"For me, too," Maks said, softly. "It's been weird enough being here with Andrea. She has her own life now and I don't really fit in anymore. I knew all that in my head, of course, but it's another thing entirely to see it right in front of your face every day for two weeks. And then to see you — god, I wasn't prepared for that." He ran his hands though his hair, messing it up even more than it already had been.

"You seem to be handling everything just fine," Dex said. "You always did. It's like nothing ever gets to you."

Maks laughed, a short clipped sound that contained little mirth. "Oh, Andy," he said, "you really have no idea. When I left the apartment that night, the last night I saw you..." His voice trailed off and Dex nodded for him to continue.

"I think I knew it even then that I was making a terrible mistake. But I was so sure that I needed to grow up, to move on. I thought I could just make it work. But all night, the whole time we were hanging out, drinking, listening to music, all I wanted to do was grab hold of you, hang on and never let go." Dex felt his throat constricting and a burning sensation in his sinuses. He blinked his eyes a few times and let their wetness blur his vision.

"Then when I came back," Maks continued, looking down at his half empty beer glass, "and you were gone... fuck, I nearly lost it. I had this image of you, as sort of an anchor that would always be there, like you were a symbol of my life. And when I couldn't find you — man, I was so lost. That's how I ended up with Elena. She was there, she was solid, she was something to hang on to, you know. She was just a replacement for you, really, and the terrible part is I think she knew it."

"Maks," Dex began, his voice hoarse.

"No," Maks said, looking up at him and smiling. "You don't have to say anything. After the way it all turned out, I couldn't ask for things to have been different. I loved Elena in my way and Andrea is the best thing I've ever been a part of. None of that ever would have happened if I'd stayed with you and so I can't be sorry for the choices I've made."

He took a sip of his beer and looked at Dex. "I guess I'm just saying..." He broke off and looked away. "I just wanted you to know that I missed you." He looked up at Dex. "All these years, I've missed you. You're my best friend, Andy, you always were and you always will be. Those missing decades don't change it. I'm just glad that I didn't fuck up your life as badly as I tried to fuck up mine." He smiled sadly at Dex, who wasn't bothering to hold back the tears anymore.

"Oh, Maks," he said, wondering if he should tell him abut the years he'd spent brooding over their lost friendship. Wondering if he should tell him about the feeling that followed him for years that a part of him was missing. Wondering if it would make things worse for Maks to know that even now Dex periodically lost himself in memories of their life together. Finally he just said, "I've missed you, too. More than you can imagine." He smiled and wiped the wetness from his cheeks. He picked up his beer glass. "Here's to happy coincidences," he said and the two men clicked their glasses.

"Here's to old friendships found again," Maks said. "Let's try not to let thirty years pass us by this time, okay?"

"Hey, I know where your kid lives," Dex said, grinning. "You can't get away from me that easily anymore."

They grinned foolishly at each other and drank, talked and laughed until long after the sun came up.

TWENTY-EIGHT

DEX HAD HIS feet up on the seat across from him and stared out the window at the countryside rushing past. The train had already passed through a dozen villages, all with their short buildings and single intercity train stops. He couldn't imagine living in a town as small as these little hamlets. He still found Nice, with its vibrant street life and almost complete lack of broken down neighbourhoods, to be unbelievable after living in a Namerican city for sixty-odd years. But these small towns seemed to be throwbacks to a previous era.

He knew that each village had one or two firms operating there and that nearly everyone worked for those companies. He knew that the sense of choice that a city offered was more an illusion than a reality, but he still couldn't imagine the life of someone in one of these small towns. He noticed, though, that each village was more like the neighbourhoods in Nice than smaller versions of his hometown. There were people out in the street in each little community, talking to each other, sipping coffee at al fresco eateries.

He'd never thought about the difference an ocean of space and time could make, and wondered how different things were for people in Afrika or Oceania. Realizing how much he'd taken for granted, how much he didn't know about the world, made his head hurt. Dex closed his eyes and put those thoughts out of his mind. This was his second straight week of travelling and he was tired of it. Tired of the cramped and unfamiliar guest rooms, tired of meeting contacts in back rooms of stuffy and rundown taverns. Tired of explaining why he was there, what was going on in M City, why the upgrade rods were needed.

He had dozed off in his seat when his system woke him with a ping. His eyes popped open and he had a moment of panic until he remembered that he was on another train. At least this time he was heading west, getting closer to home. The sound in his inner ears didn't exactly get louder, just more insistent, and Dex paged over to the program which activated the encrypted communications package Annabelle and Andrea had created. He entered his token and answered the call.

"Andy," Maks's voice boomed from across the encrypted distance. "Where are you today, my friend?"

"Fucked if I know," Dex answered sourly, then checked himself. "I left Petersburg this morning. That was three stops and..." he let his eyes stray to the lower right corner of his overlay and checked the time, "five hours ago. So I must be getting close to Frankfurt by now. This is the slow train, I guess."

"Well, you get what you pay for," Maks said and Dex chuckled without mirth.

"I'm lucky I could afford even this," Dex said. "All this travelling costs a fortune and it's not like I have a paying client to expense it to."

"Well then, you're going to be happy to hear this," Maks said. "I've been talking to the folks in the neighbourhood, the bar owners and other businesses, and they've been pretty interested in this project. Some of the people don't care, of course, since there are plenty of them who don't bother with M City at all. But the ones who do have been really positive."

"That's great, Maks," Dex said wearily, "but how does their zest to participate translate into paying my way for jaunting across Europa with a bag of upgrade rods?"

"Oh, you always were low on faith," Maks said, laughing. "One of my neighbours runs a dance hall in the Zubers block in M City and she suggested we take up a collection from everyone we pass the upgrade on to. Not a fee, more like a suggested donation."

"Interesting," Dex said. "I mean, I don't think we can charge for this — the more people and places that have access to the encryption and communication software, the better and more stable we make all of the everywherenet."

"I know," Maks said, "that's why it's not a fee. It's just an option for people to drop a euro or two into this account we set up. The soft sell, you know? Anyway, it's been paying off already."

"Really," Dex said. "You got a hundred or two from the neighbourhood?"

"Not quite," Maks admitted. "More like a thousand."

Dex could hear his friend grinning. "You've got to be shitting me," Dex said, the ennui finally draining from his body. "That's unbelievable."

"Enough people think it's worth it to help fund The Mission."

"The Mission?"

"Yeah, that's what they're calling it on the street, what we're doing," Maks said. "A bunch of the bars and shops down here are advertising that they're agents of The Mission. Someone even did up a logo. It looks like an ad for a band or something, if you don't know what it is. But the word is getting out and we're still shooting up more people every day than we did the day before."

"That's amazing," Dex said.

"I've put together a file of the posters and a link to the secure account," Maks said. "I'll send it to you and you can pass it on to the contacts you've already upgraded in Europa."

"Great idea," Dex said. "If we get even half the rate of return in donations that you have, I'll be able to pay for this whole trip easily. Maybe even hit some of the smaller centres I've had to skip this time."

"And we can reimburse René for his trip, too," Maks said. "Between the two of you we got all the major cities, right."

"Yeah," Dex said. "It's been tough, though."

"I'm sure," Maks said. "When do you think you'll get back to Nice?"

"A few days still," Dex said, "and it's not a moment too soon. It drives me crazy paying for an apartment I'm not using, not to mention I miss my bed."

Maks laughed. "I'm sure that's not all you miss, eh?"

Dex flushed, but ignored the embarrassment. "No, that's not all," he admitted. "But it's at times like these I realize how much I need everywherenet and M City to still be there, still be free. I don't think I could have managed this trip without getting to see Annabelle every other day."

"She's one in a million, man," Maks said. "You're lucky."

"Don't I know it," Dex said, smiling. "Don't I know it."

• • •

The train glided to a soundless stop on the main platform in Frankfurt just after noon local time. Dex stepped off with his small bag and took a breath of the sour city air. It reminded him of his old neighbourhood back in Namerica and he was surprised not to feel even a pang of nostalgia. He hoofed it to the nearest intracity trainstop for the Star district. His contact, a woman he knew as Magda, was expecting him at a small restaurant there. He had only a half hour to get there or she would leave.

The train arrived quickly enough and Dex managed to jam into the car with about a million other tired, sweaty passengers. He kept most of his focus on his physical surroundings, with only a map on his overlay to try and get his bearings. He squeezed out at his stop with ten minutes to spare and tried to cool off on the short walk to the bistro.

A physical bell dinged as he opened the door and he waited while his eyes adjusted to the gloom. He saw a row of several tables along the wall and walked toward the back of the restaurant. There were no other customers except a woman staring off into the distance as if she were online. She caught Dex's eye, however and he slipped into a chair at her table.

"I've heard the synth-wine is terrible here," he said, uttering the code phrase they'd previously agreed on and feeling ridiculous.

"It is," the woman agreed, "and the glasses are too small." Dex nodded and reached into his bag. He pulled out a small sack with about two dozen upgrade rods.

"You know how to use these?" he asked. Magda nodded and hefted the bag in one hand. "These are the read only, write once types, so they can't be modified. Try to get people to pass them on or at least return them. We're running low on supplies."

"Understood," Magda said, pocketing the bag of rods. "You want a bite to eat or something to drink?" she asked. "The pies are very good and the beer is better than the wine." She smiled and Dex couldn't help but laugh.

"I'm a food brick man," Dex said, "but a small beer would be nice."

Magda slipped out of her chair and went through a door recessed into the back wall. She came back with two glasses full of foamy amber liquid. She handed one to Dex then clicked her glass with his. "This is thirsty work," she said and took a sip. "I appreciate what you and your friends are doing here. I'll get these rods passed around."

"Thanks," Dex said. "It's no magic bullet, though. Don't forget that the firms own everywherenet and if they want to fuck with it, they will. There's nothing in here that can stop them vandalizing someone's rez. Let your contacts know they have to try to backup as much as they can as often as they can."

Magda nodded sharply and Dex felt a weight in his head. He unfocussed briefly to see Maks's download appear in his inbox. "When you get yourself fixed up, ping me," he said. "I've got some materials which might help with distribution."

"I will," Magda said. "So, where are you headed to next?"

"It's better if I don't say," Dex said apologetically. "At the moment, we don't know what's compromised and what's safe, so we're playing all our cards close to our chest."

Magda nodded. "Understood," she said. "I do have one question I'd really like an answer to, though."

"Sure," Dex said, only a little nervously.

"How did you find me?"

"Ah," Dex said. "That's easy to answer at least. You work for Stella Bish." Magda's eyes opened wide. "Don't worry," Dex said, "I don't know your real name. No one does, except for, I assume, Ms. Bish. I understand that she operates a secure communication network with some of her people who do more... delicate work. Her contacts in Europa have been working together to try to get me a meeting with as many of her freelancers as possible."

"Why didn't Bish just contact me directly?" Magda asked. "Why all the cloak and dagger with the anonymous paper message left at the bar?"

Dex laughed. "I wondered how they were contacting you all. I assume the message included the information we have proving that a group within the everywherenet consortium is targeting M City businesses?"

"Of course," Magda said. "I wouldn't be here otherwise."

"Well, the paper messages are to make sure that the work we're doing here is both untraceable and offline."

"Well," Magda said, "it worked and I'm glad of it. Losing the 'net, losing M City — that would kill much of my work."

"Many of us share that concern," Dex said. "It's more than just business, though."

"Yes," Magda agreed, "for us, it is, anyway."

"Indeed," Dex said and finished his beer. "I need to get back to the station," he said.

"Good luck," Magda said and stuck out her hand. They shook and the woman held his grip a little longer than necessary. "I'll be in touch."

"I look forward to it," Dex said, smiling. "Good luck to you, too."

• • •

Four stops, six secret codes and eighteen trains later, Dex was curled up against the window on the overnight back to Nice. He'd offloaded all the upgrade rods he'd brought with him and eaten the last food brick in his pack. Tired of the flashing scenery, he'd dimmed the window by his seat and balled up his jacket to use as a pillow. His eyes closed, he pinged Annabelle, knowing she'd be home from work by now.

"How's the delivery business?" she asked and Dex could hear her grinning.

"Tiring," he answered. "I'll tell you all about it tomorrow, after I've slept for a day in my own bed. You know, train seats really were not well designed for sleeping in, kiddo."

"I'll take it up with management," she said and they both laughed. "It feels like you've been gone forever," she said, the mirth gone.

"Hard to believe it wasn't so long ago that I lived halfway around the world," Dex said.

"It's amazing what a little time can do," Annabelle said and Dex knew she was talking about herself.

"You're what's amazing," he said. "Time is just the medium that shows it off."

"You're babbling," she said, a false laugh hiding her modesty.

"Sure," Dex said. "A babbling fool. That's what I am, kiddo. I'm a fool for you."

"You need some sleep," she said.

"I sure do," he agreed. "And I need to get home."

"Home is where your bed is," she said.

"No," Dex said. "Home is where you are. And I'll be there soon enough. I love you Annabelle."

"Aw, Dex," she said.

"See you tomorrow, kiddo," he said and broke the connection. He managed to drift off to sleep, head mashed against the window, a smile on his face.

TWENTY-NINE

TWO DAYS AFTER he got back to Nice, Dex finally felt normal. His timing was still a little off, though, so he ended up walking in to the squad meeting early. Usually there would be several other people in the virtual space, chatting and mingling. Now the room was empty but for his avatar. He knew it would stay empty except for Annabelle's, their only contact with the rest of the squad an often scratchy audio feed. The squad had been meeting in person for the past month, only piping the audio from the meeting over a secure, encrypted channel to Dex and Annabelle. Everyone was hoping that this would be the last time such complicated arrangements would be necessary.

Annabelle linked in about five minutes after Dex and settled in beside him. Dex heard the captain call the meeting to order and ask for a report from Jay Shiraishi, the street team lieutenant. He gave the usual run down on the odd fight or dispute that his people had dealt with over the past week. Then he began his report on the distribution of Annabelle's special upgrade packages.

"As we all know," he began, "this is slow going. Statistically, we've hardly made a dent. There are new cases of vandalism, broken instantiations and even people being locked out of their accounts every day. On the face of it, we're not accomplishing a whole lot."

Dex could hear unhappy grumblings and could picture Shiraishi's grim face. The lieutenant went on. "But, it's still early days and there are small victories happening all the time. We're continuing to gain access to more groups each day," Shiraishi said. "Word is beginning to spread among the different communities and the flyers we've put up in the cafés, bars and playspaces are bringing more people in. There are a half dozen M City meeting places that are 100% covered and even more importantly, the word is getting around. People are talking and we've started even getting requests. The main problem at the moment is getting the upgrade rods back — we've got barely a fifty percent return rate. So we're going to run out of delivery systems pretty soon and there just isn't budget to restock."

"Are people passing on the rods to their friends," Ginger Ayala asked, "or hanging on to them for whatever reason?"

"It's about half and half," Shiraishi said. "They tell me that we can tell by the saturation of the new code how many people are using it, and it's spreading faster than our own distribution numbers can account for. Even so, we need to get those rods back if we're going to continue to distribute it all."

"I think I have an idea," Melissa Vonruden, one of Shiraishi's goon squad members, said. "My boss at the stim bar where I work really wants to help. I think I can get him to offer a drop off coupon or something. Ten percent off for any rods brought in, something like that."

"That kind of thing wouldn't hurt," Shiraishi said. "We should all use our contacts in the business community, online and off, to see if we can get others on board with some kind of offer. It won't get all the rods back, but every little bit helps. I've also got some good news to report from a different arena." The lieutenant cleared his throat.

"I've been working with a contact I've got M City," he began, "and I've managed to get copies of the upgrade to one of the leaders of the multi community." Some surprised noises emerged over the feed and Dex shot Annabelle a knowing look. "Of course, as people who meet and truly exist only on-line, they are a difficult community to access with a physical upgrade. Tequila Kate — that's our contact — she is working with members of the community to try and make the upgrade available anonymously. As I said, these people are very private and we have to be careful about openly talking about the up-grade online."

"So, how are you able to communicate with them about this, then?" John Ochoa asked.

"Luckily," Shiraishi explained, "since they are concerned about being discovered, the community has some unusual crypto for its meetings. As it turns out, passing the informa-tion has been easier with them than for a lot of other groups. I'm even able to provide the upgrade package online and many of them have agreed to load it onto rods and pass it on in the physical world under their first identities."

"The rumour is that it's a pretty diverse group of people who have multis, isn't it?" someone called from the back of the room.

"So it seems," Shiraishi said and Dex smiled to himself. As far as he knew, Dex was the only one in the squad who knew that Shiraishi himself maintained a multiple identity. "I think that using this group we will be able to make pretty good headway into other communities we'd previously thought that we'd have trouble accessing."

"Excellent," the captain said. "Is that all, Mr. Shiraishi?" The leader of the street team must have nodded his agree-ment, because the captain then went on. "Now, can I get a report from Annabelle Lewis about our squad room. I'm getting a little tired of meeting in random apartments."

"Good news on that front," Annabelle said. "The encryption is all set up and I've expanded the point to point communications network in the packages to be able to function on a multi-party private channel. Mack Larsen's squad have been using the new code for a few days and they've ironed out most of the bugs. I'm just waiting on an upgrade to the instantiation of the meeting hall, which should be done this week. I'm confident that we can go back to meeting online for the next meeting."

Dex and Annabelle could hear a few muffled cheers on the audio feed and Dex smiled at Annabelle.

"Will we be able to pass files back and forth?" the captain asked. "Are we any closer to being able to securely share the upgrade package remotely?"

Annabelle frowned. "These are two separate questions," she explained. "Our case file and messaging system is already good to go — it was probably secure enough from inception and we just beefed up the walls, so to speak, so we can communicate and share information no problem there. However," she continued, "the upgrade package is a different story.

"Its code has to run on a personal onboard system and it has to be installed physically, while the person is offline. While it is theoretically possible to download the software online, expand it on to a rod, then use that to update a system, there's a lot of room for error there. Other than for people running multis, where there's no other way to get them the package, I really don't think downloads are the way to go. I don't know about you, but I don't have any interest in putting potentially broken code in my head. We're a lot safer using the locked rods and passing them on physically."

"Okay," Captain Zhang said. "I'm just trying to find some way of getting this upgrade out a little faster."

"Understood, captain," Annabelle said. "But slow and steady wins the race here, I think. Already about ten percent of the M City businesses are running the new code and the vast majority of independent freelancers. Vandalism is up a little but there have been very few reports of login failures. On the face of it, things haven't changed much but I expect to see improvement as we get better saturation. We're making a dent, captain. And it's only going to get better."

"Very good," the captain said, then moved on to other cases. The meeting went on for only a few more minutes and then the captain dismissed the squad. "Dex, Annabelle," her voice came over the encrypted channel. "I need to talk to you both."

"Sure, Cap," Dex said. "What's up?"

"Can we meet?"

"There aren't that many safe spaces up and running, sir," Annabelle said. "You have somewhere in mind?"

"We could grab a table at Monte's?" Dex suggested. In the days after Annabelle had created the upgrade package they had discovered that a friend of René Biagini's knew the group who owned and ran the bar. After passing copies of the upgrade through their various connections, Monte's had been one of the first places upgraded with the new secure private channels. At the doorway, on the bar and in their advertisements they now displayed the subtle red flower symbol that indicated to those in the know that the place was secure.

"I've booked us a room at the M City squad's building in Kanzai," the captain said. "Here's the link. I'll see you both there in ten minutes." It wasn't a suggestion — it was an order. Dex and Annabelle shared a confused glance at each other.

"Sir," Dex said and broke the connection.

"What do you think that's all about?" Annabelle asked.

"It feels eerily like we're about to get chewed out for something," Dex said, "but I don't think we've fucked anything up recently."

"Maybe there's something wrong with the package," Annabelle said. "Shit, I haven't felt this nervous since... well, since everything that happened across the pond." Dex felt her stiffen and then forcibly relax her body.

"Look," Dex said, "we can work ourselves into knots wondering what's going down or we can just go over to that modernist architect's disaster and face the music."

"You're right," Annabelle said. "Let's go."

• • •

The link the captain had given them took them directly into a small conference room high in the squad building. There was no one else there when they linked in and Dex walked to the ceiling high window to look out at the Kanzai district laid out below them. It was bright and shiny and avatars walked, drove and flew around the place as if there was nothing to worry about in this created world where they played. He could feel his heart rate increasing as he wondered what was going on and fought to keep calm. He jumped when he heard the door open and he turned to see Captain Zhang walk into the room.

"Dex, Annabelle," she smiled at the two of them. "Have a seat."

"Captain?" Annabelle asked as she sat and Zhang turned to her.

"I'm sorry for all the cloak and dagger," she said, pulling a thin folder from a case she placed on the table. Dex slipped into a chair across from Annabelle and caught her eye. "This is just the kind of thing I prefer to do face to face, but it couldn't wait until our own squad room was up and running. Besides," the captain looked at each of them in turn, "this is kind of appropriate." She gestured with her hands to indicate the room they were sitting in.

"So, first of all," she said, leaning back in the softly padded chair. "Ever since this trouble started, the M City squad has been getting swamped with cases. This is their beat, after all, and it's become clear to the folks at central that the little street team we have in here now just isn't cutting the mustard. So, some changes are coming down, and they're coming down soon.

"First, the M City squad is going to become a proper city team. Goons, detectives, techies, the whole bit. Larsen's been promoted, of course. It's his crew and the man deserves it." Zhang looked directly at Dex as she said this and he nodded.

"I don't like the guy," Dex said, "but he's done good work."

"Right," Zhang continued, opening her folder. "And that brings me to the next thing. I know neither of you is going to like it, but it's done and you're just going to have to accept it."

Annabelle and Dex looked at each other, both their eyes wide. "As of today, you've both been transferred to the M City squad."

"What?" Dex blurted.

"Captain," Annabelle said. "I don't understand. I thought we..." She faltered a moment, then took a breath. "I thought we had a relationship." She gestured at the captain and herself. "You know, beyond the work."

"We do," Zhang said. "That's why I'm not thrilled about this either, but the truth of the matter is this: with this war we're caught in the middle of, Larsen's squad needs bodies and they need the best. They need the best cracker we've got, they need the people who broke this thing wide open and they need a detective who can handle cases that don't just involve banging down doors out there. Which means it's got to be you two." She leaned over the table, looking down for a moment, then sat up to face the two of them again.

"You aren't the only ones — all in all about a dozen people are moving over and there will probably be more down the line. You heard Shiraishi today, we're barely making an impact in here right now. This thing is going to get worse before it gets better... if it gets better at all. We need the best people we have working on this and it's got to be coordinated. It's obvious that the M City squad is where this fight has to originate, and so it's obvious that's where you two have to be."

She paused and looked from Dex to Annabelle. "I don't want to lose you two," Zhang said, a trace of real emotion in her voice. "But it's right for the organization. Hell, it's right for everyone who uploads into this damn place. So I need you two to accept it and give Captain Larsen the same respect you'd give any captain." She looked at Dex, her dark eyes boring into him. "As a favour to me, okay?"

Dex took a breath. "Yes, sir," he said. Then he smiled. "We'll still see you at the gigs, right?"

Zhang's face broke into a smile. "Wouldn't miss them for the world," she said. "Now, get out of here. You'll be spending enough time in this glass and chrome monstrosity, I'd wager."

"Sir," Annabelle said, sticking her hand out. The captain took it and they shook. "It's been a pleasure," Annabelle said.

"Likewise, Lewis," the captain said. "I'll see you." She vanished from the room, leaving Dex and Annabelle alone with a void that felt more substantial than either could articulate.

After a moment to let it sink in, Annabelle turned to Dex. "I don't know about you," she said, "but I need a drink.

THIRTY

DEX AND ANNABELLE walked over to their favourite booth and sat. Drinks materialized in front of each of them and Dex pulled a cigarette from the red pack next to his glass. He lit it and stuck the butt in the corner of his mouth.

"Fucking Mack Larsen," Dex growled around the cigarette.

"It's not Larsen's fault," Annabelle said, taking a long swallow of her drink. "The captain's right. It's where we belong."

"Fuck that," Dex said. "I belong out there, cracking heads and solving puzzles. Not in some godforsaken office with conference rooms for Christ's sake. It's... it's unnatural."

Annabelle looked at Dex then laughed. "I'm pretty sure they won't make you work from their office building," she said. "Most of the time you won't even be able to tell the difference."

"What about you?" Dex said, his eyebrows condensing into a glower. "Captain Zhang knows you, the folks on our squad have been through a lot with you, with us. These guys don't know you from Adam. What's it going to be like working with strangers?"

Annabelle shrugged. "It's going to be weird. But we have bigger concerns that where we have our squad meetings and who gets our reports. Everything is weird right now, in case you hadn't noticed."

Dex nodded and they sat silently drinking for a few moments. Eventually he ground out his cigarette and lit another. "You're right," he said, sighing. "I just on't like it." He looked around the room, at the tables full of his team mates — former team mates — talking and laughing, unwinding after a long day's work. "It's going to be a long time before things are back to normal, isn't it?" he said.

"Depends on what you mean by normal," Annabelle said.

Talking around the smoke, he said, "What do you mean? You don't think we'll ever be able to go back to the days of treating this..." he arced his arm around to take in the bar, "the same as we do out there?"

"I don't know," Annabelle said. "In the short term, if we can get most people set up with the new code, things should go back to the routine. But it's going to take a long time, a really long time to get decent saturation. It's just so hard to pass things around the physical world — not that many people travel and even then some people just don't care about this sort of thing. We'll never get everyone upgraded, but at least we can know where is safe and where isn't."

Dex nodded, when he caught sight of a familiar silhouette instantiate near the table. He smiled with some warmth at the interloper and stood to greet her.

"Mister Dexter," she said, her voice low, leaning in to air-kiss his cheek. Dex saw Annabelle out of the corner of eye bristling, but she said nothing.

"Stella, please, call me Dex already." He indicated a seat at the table and invisibly set his private voice channel with Annabelle to include the new addition to the table.

"And the inimitable Ms. Lewis," Bish said, turning her charms toward Annabelle. "It's so nice to see you again."

"Likewise," Annabelle said, briefly shaking Bish's hand.

"I can't thank you enough for everything you've done," she continued to gush in Annabelle's direction. "Not just for me but for all of us. You are a true hero."

Dex grinned, but Annabelle flushed. "I was just in the right place at the right time," she said, modestly.

"If you ever want to leave the workaday world," Bish said, "you know that someone with your considerable talents would never want for work in here."

"Thank you for the offer," Annabelle said, "but I'm happy where I am for now."

"If you ever change your mind," Bish said, "please do call me first. I'd hate to lose you to some other upstart." She smiled her predatory grin and turned back to Dex.

"Now, Mister... that is, Dex," she said, "I'm pleased to report that I've managed to get the upgrade distributed to everyone in my buildings, almost all of the OC groups and all of my freelancers. I've spent more time on long range trains and airflights that I could ever have imagined, but I'm confident that my people are covered."

Dex nodded. "We appreciate the effort you've been making," he said. "I know the cost hasn't been insubstantial."

"No," Bish said, "it has not, but as you know, I do well enough. I can afford it. The cost of letting my business and my own online identity be threatened, on the other hand, isn't something I could ever pay."

"It's nice to see the red flower on more and more establishments," Annabelle said.

"And contractor's business cards," Bish added. "You really have done something remarkable here," she said and stood. "Please remember my offer, if you ever tire of working for the enemy," she said to Annabelle and lingered over the handshake. "I'll see you around, Dex," she said and turned to walk out the door of the bar.

She'd long since dematerialized when Annabelle said, "That's really what it is now, isn't it?"

"What?" Dex asked.

"Sides have been drawn," Annabelle said. "They're attacking us and we're defending ourselves. That means there's an us and there's a them and we're working against one another." She drained her glass and a refill automatically appeared before her. "We've started a war, Dex, and we aren't going to know how it plays out until it does."

"We didn't start anything," Dex said. "The firms didn't have to expand and the consortium didn't have to interfere with what people were doing in their off hours. That was the first salvo. All we did was defend ourselves."

"Sure," Annabelle said. "But we've responded now. Do you really think they're going to just let us install our upgrade, run our crypto and carry on like nothing's happened? Look at the trouble and expense Stella Bish was willing to go through for her business. You really think the firms aren't just as committed to theirs?"

Dex dropped his cigarette butt to the floor and watched as it vanished. He lit another and blew out a plume of not quite random smoke. "No," he said, finally. "No, I don't think that this is going to be the end from them, but I don't think that it's the end for us either. Who knows, this might be the beginning of something more than just taking back the 'nets. Maybe it's the beginning of challenging the firms' right to control everything else — maybe people will demand more freely available housing, more career choices. Or maybe people will just move lock stock and consciousness into a free M City. I don't know."

"Or maybe they'll just find a way to lock us out altogether," Annabelle said, bitterly.

"Maybe they will," Dex said. "But for now we're managing to do something good. Something that's bringing people together."

"But for what?" Annabelle asked. "To get fired from their jobs, cut off from the everywherenet entirely? It could come to that, you know."

"I know," Dex said. "And don't think that it doesn't bother me; it does. But the way things are now isn't really that much better, if the firms are trying to take away the tiny bit of freedom we have in this world."

"And if we get booted from their 'net we'll just make our own," Annabelle said ironically.

"Maybe we will," Dex said. "We've started something, kiddo, a common purpose among hundreds of thousands of people. A force like that can accomplish a lot. Who knows, it might not last, but nothing ever really does. So we might as well enjoy the beauty of what we've created, this common purpose, because even if everything goes to shit in the long run, at least we've got that."

She laughed and took his hand. "I never knew you were a revolutionary."

"I'm not," Dex said. "This isn't a revolution. It's evolution."

ACKNOWLEDGMENTS

My heartfelt thanks go to the following people who contributed to funding the release of this novel through my IndieGoGo campaign.

@forschungstorte
Robert Biegler
Donovan Crone
Francis Hamit
Mary Lareau
Pamela & John Marchant
Andrew O.
Ann Smith
Mark Stanley
Evo Terra

SteveBickle
Jim Brittain
Andrew Faulkner
Jörn Huxhorn
Josh Macleod
Leonard Nichols
Nobilis Reed
Steve Southwood
Karen Taylor
Sytse van der Leest

Thanks also to JT Lindroos and, always, Steven Ensslen.

ABOUT THE AUTHOR

M. Darusha Wehm is a two-time Parsec Award finalist and author of the SF novels **Beautiful Red**, **Self Made**, **Act of Will** and **The Beauty of Our Weapons**.

Her short fiction has appeared in *Thaumatrope Magazine*, Podioracket's *Glimpses* anthology and *Luna Station Quarterly*.

In the physical world, she was a civil servant with the Government of Canada and is now engaged more or less full-time in writing.

She is based in Victoria, BC, Canada and is currently living in New Zealand after sailing down the west coast of the Americas and across the Pacific Ocean with her partner, Steven, on their sailboat, Scream.

For more information about her writing and her travels, visit Darusha on the web at http://darusha.ca.